EBUR

THE HIDD

Akshat Gupta belongs to a family of hoteliers and is now an established Bollywood screenwriter, poet and lyricist. He is a bilingual author and has been working on The Hidden Hindu trilogy for years. He was born in Chhattisgarh, grew up in Madhya Pradesh and now lives in Mumbai. You can connect with him on Instagram, @authorakshatgupta, or send him an email on akshat.gupta0204@gmail.com.

THE
HIDDEN
HINDU

BOOK 3 OF THE TRILOGY

AKSHAT GUPTA

EBURY
PRESS

An imprint of Penguin Random House

EBURY PRESS

USA I Canada I UK I Ireland I Australia
New Zealand I India I South Africa I China

Ebury Press is part of the Penguin Random House group of companies
whose addresses can be found at global.penguinrandomhouse.com

Published by Penguin Random House India Pvt. Ltd
4th Floor, Capital Tower 1, MG Road,
Gurugram 122 002, Haryana, India

First published in Ebury Press by Penguin Random House India 2023

ISBN 9780143456551

Typeset in Bembo Std by Manipal Technologies Limited, Manipal
Printed at Thomson Press India Ltd, New Delhi

www.penguin.co.in

Contents

Chapter 1

Who Am I

The tale of Dr Batra's lonely death, unheeded struggles and how mercilessly he was thrown out of the submarine into the unforgiving sea without a proper funeral broke Mrs Batra to the core. The last thread of hope of seeing her husband again was all she had been clinging on to, but now, even that had snapped. Utterly devastated by the realization, Mrs Batra walked to the door, opened it and asked Prithvi to leave. Prithvi could feel her pain and knew that he could in no way soothe her acute agony. He started to make his way out.

'Don't you want to know what happened to those people who killed your beloved husband and why he was killed?' Prithvi asked before stepping outside.

Mrs Batra stood there for a silent moment, looking at Prithvi. She shut the door and Prithvi walked back to take his seat. She knew what her heart longed for, so she took her spot on the couch to hear how it all ended. Sensing that she was yearning to know more about Dr Batra's assassins, Prithvi began narrating the tale from where he had left off.

In the month of Jyeshth (May), when the whole world had come to a standstill due to Covid-19 and the death count was spiking, stories of losses were painted all over social media, in newspapers and on news channels. Optimism seemed to be dissipating as dark clouds of uncertainty fogged people's lives. While the death toll from Covid-19 was crossing all estimations, headlines of other catastrophes began to make the rounds: the glorious and tranquil Mansarovar being overpowered by Rakshastal; the destruction of Roopkund— the lake of skeletons; the Taj Mahal, one of the seven wonders of the world, suddenly turning black; and the overnight siege of the ghost village of Kuldhara. This series of unbelievable events started seeding many conspiracy theories as the news read, *'Mysterious phenomena plaguing India adding to the miseries of Corona. Are these signs of doomsday closing in?'*

A worried Ashwatthama sat in Gyanganj on Mount Kailash with his wounds still healing. He looked at Parashurama and Kripacharya's motionless bodies as they remained trapped in Om's subconscious mind. Next to them was Om, lying unconscious after the battle of Kuldhara. When Ashwatthama asked Ved Vyasa about Vrishkapi, he received another painful answer.

'Vrishkapi is on his deathbed. It's just a matter of a few hours before he gives up the fight for survival and leaves his body.'

'I don't know what to do. I don't know if we have lost as Vrishkapi is dying and Milarepa is long gone or we won as Nagendra is dead too. I don't know what I should be feeling right now,' said Ashwatthama, consumed by his thoughts.

Ved Vyasa was about to say something but to their surprise, Kripacharya and Parashurama returned to their bodies from their astral state and stood up, as normal as ever. Ashwatthama stood up from his place to greet them.

'You're back! How did you open that door?'

'We didn't have to. Something suddenly changed within Om and after that, there was no retaliation, no more tussle to trap us, and there wasn't a door holding us back anymore,' Parashurama replied, still wondering about the whys and hows.

A confused Ashwatthama thought out loud, 'But how could that be? Where's the door gone?'

'I destroyed it,' came a voice from behind them. Ashwatthama turned in wonder, though he already knew who it was. It was Om, who had also sat up, with a distant gaze. 'The door is gone because there's no barrier, no bridge, no door between me and my hidden past. Not anymore. Now I know who I am,' said Om, glancing at all four of them.

'Who are you?' Kripacharya asked.

Everybody's intrigued stare was glued on Om.

Om closed his eyes and took a deep breath, 'I am Devdhwaja.'

'But that can't be! We checked and you don't have the birthmark! How's that even possible?' Kripacharya said, trying to piece everything together around the new revelation.

'Hold on! I am confused. The birthmark of Devdhwaja
that the immortals saw in Om's memories was there on
Nagendra's foot, and Om is claiming to be Devdhwaja
himself. So, who out of the two is the real Devdhwaja?'
asked a confused Mrs Batra of Prithvi.

Prithvi replied, 'Both of them.'

'You mean they're twins?' asked Mrs Batra.

'No, they are not twins. They are the same person.'

'Split personality?'

'Not even that.'

'You are not making any sense, Prithvi. How can two
men be one person? This is beyond my understanding.' Mrs
Batra raised her hands in disbelief.

'Does it have something to do with the immortals in
Kailash Parbat?' Ashwatthama asked. 'What do you mean
that the birthmark is on Nagendra's foot, but you are
Devdhwaja and not him? We have all seen in your memories
that Devdhwaja had the birthmark. Now, if Nagendra
has it, as you are claiming, then that means Nagendra is
Devdhwaja and not you.'

'We were born as one child and were named Devdhwaja,
son of Vishnuyasha and Lakshmi, in a faraway land where
the three seas meet. Born on a very unusual night between
the darkest hour and the first hour of *Brahma Muhurta*[1], my
mother delivered us with the help of a man who appeared
from nowhere at the right time and vanished before the
villagers gathered to help. We were told about this incident
several times in my childhood,' said Om **while** looking

---

[1] The divine hour

at Kripacharya, whose order he had overruled a few days ago in their astral form when he had helped the pregnant woman who was struggling alone. 'It always felt like a story my mother had made up or something she had hallucinated in pain while delivering. No one ever knew all of this then, but now I know that the man that helped my mother deliver was no one else but me. Maybe Kripacharya was right to suggest that we were not there to make changes but just to observe. Maybe that child was not meant to enter earth. I don't know now if it was even supposed to happen because Nagendra was delivered by me.'

'Maybe we were supposed to end your existence before taking you into your past because now the threat to earth is you,' Kripacharya snapped angrily and walked away. Parashurama and Ashwatthama followed Kripacharya, leaving Om with Ved Vyasa.

'I have questions, Om,' said Ved Vyasa gently.

'Seer! You will get all your answers, but Vrishkapi's life is still in danger. Let me help him first,' Om said calmly and left the room.

Om visited Vrishkapi and found him still unconscious. Om approached him and asked the sages to turn him upside down. They did as requested. Vrishkapi's wound was neatly dressed. Om took a closer look at his wounded shoulder. The skin surrounding the gash was black and rotten. Even the veins underneath were visible and turning black.

'It's spreading rapidly. We have done everything we knew, but there is no antidote to this venom,' said a sage, disappointment evident on his face.

Om looked at the sage and said, 'This venom can only be taken out by the one who bit him. Only then will the body be free of it.'

'But Nagendra is dead, killed by Ashwatthama. Does that mean Vrishkapi's death is inevitable?' asked a sage, looking at Vrishkapi sympathetically.

Om unwrapped Vrishkapi's dressing gently and placed his palms on the wound. He began to experience pain so immense that it was painted all over his face.

Slowly, Vrishkapi's bite mark started healing, but at the same time, the sages noticed a growing spot of blood on Om's shoulder, exactly where Vrishkapi was injured. Within moments, Om's back was soaked in red and weakness engulfed him, forcing him to sit down. The sages removed the cloth draping Vrishkapi and were perplexed. While Vrishkapi's wound had healed completely, it had miraculously been transferred to Om. They knew that Om had taken it upon himself to save Vrishkapi.

They hurriedly started to dress his wound and while doing so, one of the sages asked, 'Why did you do that?'

'Because I am responsible for his condition, so his pain and injury should also be on me.'

The sages did not understand what he meant but before they could inquire further, Om said, 'Vrishkapi is out of danger now. He will be fine.'

'How did you do that?' asked a sage.

'It's an old, lost practice.'

'Older than us?'

'Older than all these immortals, even older than me.'

'Can you please teach us?'

'It cannot be taught or transferred. I am sorry.'

Just then, Ved Vyasa entered the hut. Om tried to stand up out of respect and walk towards him, but the poison had already started its effect on him. When he tried to get up and take a few steps, he had to hold on to the wall to remain upright.

'Are you okay?' asked a concerned Ved Vyasa, keeping him from falling.

Om slumped back to the ground with Ved Vyasa's help and smiled. 'Yes, seer! I will be fine.'

As Om leaned against the wall, Ved Vyasa asked, 'How did you suddenly recollect all your memories?'

'Back in the ghost village of Kuldhara, Nagendra's face was bleeding after a fierce fight with me. He was on my back to acquire the last element needed for the completion of the process of Mrit Sanjeevani: my blood. When he bit me on my shoulder, I screamed in pain. But just before he could suck my blood, Ashwatthama blew his head off and he never swallowed my blood. However, as I screamed in pain due to his bite, a drop of his blood fell on my tongue. His blood . . . that actually is mine. That's what brought back all my memories and left Nagendra dejected.'

'If the two of you have the same blood, why did he need yours?'

'That's because the blood in my body that he was after is Dhanvantari's, and it had all the qualities and powers that would make him an immortal. When I was brought to Dhanvantari, I was dead and my blood had almost drained out of my body. What little remained within had frozen in the Himalayan trail before reaching Dhanvantari. After he performed the process of Mrit Sanjeevani, he transfused his blood into my body and Sushrut helped him with that. No one except Dhanvantari and Sushrut knew this truth. Later, though Nagendra had Dhanvantari captive, he could never get a hold of the books of Mrit Sanjeevani. He lost Dhanvantari before he could possess the books, thanks to Milarepa. I wish I could have forgiven him for killing Dhanvantari. Unfortunately, I can't.'

'But the Mrit Sanjeevani books are still missing, and we need to get them back to Kailash, where they belong. I am glad that this is over with Nagendra's death. Now that he's dead, the earth is safe,' Ved Vyasa sighed in relief.

'I need some time to absorb and disinfect the poison I consumed from Vrishkapi. Please allow me to meditate, to recollect all that had happened before my death.' So Ved Vyasa blessed Om and left. Om slowly closed his eyes, sat still, leaning against the wall, and meditated.

While Ved Vyasa walked back to his shelter, he heard two disembodied voices that caught his attention.

It was Parimal's voice that echoed, 'How did Shukracharya and Nagendra meet?'

LSD answered, 'I don't know how long they have been connected, but I know that Nagendra is one of Shukracharya's best protégés.'

Shukracharya's name itself was enough to raise tension in Ved Vyasa's mind and make him apprehensive.

'But what is with Shukracharya? Who is he, and why was a powerful man like Nagendra serving him? And why did hearing his name matter to an immortal like Ved Vyasa?' asked Mrs Batra.

'Maintaining order in the world requires a balance between both the good and the evil in this universe. The fear of the devil makes humans worship many gods, if not all. Guru Shukracharya is the grandson of the creator of this universe, Lord Brahma himself. Shukracharya, the mysterious guru, chose asuras[2] as his disciples to counter Guru Brihaspati, the guru of the devas.[3] On the one hand were the immortal devas, while on the other were the asuras, who were bound to die. Shukracharya played a vital role in maintaining the balance between good and evil by resurrecting the asuras with the help of his Sanjeevani Vidya to keep them fighting the devas.

'As adolescents, Shukra and Brihaspati studied under Brihaspati's father named Sage Angirasa. Shukra was wiser than Brihaspati and had all the qualities of a sage, making him Angirasa's best protégé. But Angirasa's bias towards his son Brihaspati never brought him the deserved recognition. Legends state that Lord Indra also favoured Brihaspati and even forged an alliance with him. Shukracharya did everything and learnt all the *vidyas* necessary to become the greatest sage of all, but the alliance between Indra and Brihaspati became a roadblock for him. Indra insisted

---

[2] Demons
[3] Demigods

that Lord Vishnu choose Brihaspati over Shukracharya. The hatred that seeped into Shukracharya against Vishnu compelled him to become the guru of the asuras. That's how Shukracharya, despite being Lord Brahma's grandson, became the foremost priest of the asuras.

'However, before Shukracharya's alliance with them, it was believed that the asuras were easily defeated by the devas. Many asuras would be massacred in battle and the devas would walk away triumphantly. But after becoming the highest-ranked priest of the asuras, Shukracharya went in search of a weapon that could defeat the devas and serve as the supreme protector of the asuras. He started performing penance to obtain Sanjeevani Stotram, a rare science that he wanted to acquire from the conqueror of death, Lord Shiva himself. The Sanjeevani Stotram is a powerful stotram that can heal and rejuvenate and has extremely strong supernatural powers of granting immortality—a stotram that would make even the asuras invincible and immortal.

'Meanwhile, Shukracharya asked the demons to take refuge in the abode of his father, Sage Bhrigu, while he was away. Sage Bhrigu is believed to be one of the sons of Lord Brahma. The devas realized that it might not be possible to defeat the asuras ever again if Shukracharya managed to acquire the mantra of invulnerability. They decided that the most favourable time to attack the asuras was in the absence of Shukracharya, at Sage Bhrigu's premises. The devas sought help from Lord Vishnu, who agreed and led the army for the planned attack.

'When Sage Bhrigu wasn't home, the ambush began. The demigods charged at the demons as Vishnu chased some of the asuras with his most powerful astra, the Sudarshan Chakra. Feeling helpless and unprepared, the asuras ran to Shukracharya's mother, Kavyamata. They went to her asking for shelter as her guests, thus making her obliged to protect them. So Kavyamata abided by her duty and saved the asuras with her yogic powers, eventually defeating Lord Indra. When Lord Vishnu's Sudarshan Chakra approached the house, Kavyamata's powers didn't allow it to enter the house and kill the asuras. With no choice left, Vishnu then beheaded Kavyamata with his Sudarshan Chakra. When Sage Bhrigu returned and saw the severed head of his wife, he cursed Vishnu to be born on earth several times and suffer the vicious cycle of death and worldly life. Hence Vishnu's reincarnations on earth, like Rama and Krishna. He lost his loved ones through these avatars and was subjected to experiencing emotions as painful as Sage Bhrigu felt when he lost his beloved wife.

'When Shukracharya returned with the boon of the Sanjeevani Stotram and learnt what the devas had done in his absence, and how Lord Vishnu had beheaded Shukracharya's mother, it was the last straw. At that very moment, Shukracharya made Lord Vishnu his greatest enemy and decided to defeat the gods. He soon began to gain popularity for his ability to resurrect the dead by using the Sanjeevani Stotram, thus triggering a never-ending war between the asuras and the devas. He tried to win over the gods many times with the army of his disciple demons and the boon of the Sanjeevani mantra that could revive the dead, yet, he couldn't create an immortal. Every time the demons were killed by the demigods, Shukracharya brought them back to life, thus stretching the war to the present.

'Shukracharya was born on a Friday, and Friday is known as Shukravaar in many Indian languages. That's where Shukracharya's name is derived from,' said Prithvi, ending the background on Shukracharya and returning to the series of events that had unravelled in 2021.

At Gyanganj, Vrishkapi was almost healed, showing signs of life and movement. Om was as silent as a stagnant lake, now that he carried the wound. His veins were turning black as the poison spread deeper inside him with every passing minute. It reached a point where Om could barely breathe, which became a matter of concern and worried the sages—everyone except Ashwatthama.

'I have seen his heart being pierced and him then recovering in a few days. He will overcome this too. We just have to give him time,' said Ashwatthama, his confidence reassuring everyone.

'Respected sages, please inform me immediately when you see Om recovering,' Ashwatthama requested before leaving the hut. It was disappointing to know that Om needed more time to heal, but on the bright side, Vrishkapi had opened his eyes. He had finally recovered. He was shocked to find Om's body in such a dreadful state.

'What happened?' he asked.

'You were almost dead but Om took your wound upon himself to save your life.'

'How did I get here? The last I remember is flying as high as I could, detaching myself from the skeletons that attacked me at Roopkund and then seeing a Yeti coming forward and carrying me on his shoulder.'

'Milarepa saved your life with the help of the Yeti. He was the one who brought you back.'

'Was?'

'He died fighting Nagendra in Agra.'

'Where are the others and where is Nagendra? Did we stop him?'

'Yes, we did. Nagendra is dead. Ashwatthama killed him.'

While Vrishkapi was relieved to hear of Nagendra's death at the hands of Ashwatthama, deep down in the forbidden chamber, Nagendra's body was stirring again. Now immortal and invincible, he was gradually coming back to life. His frail, creased body was transforming before Shukracharya's eyes. His spine had straightened and the wrinkles had vanished from his face as Nagendra smirked with vengeful eyes dripping with fury.

'Welcome back!' Shukracharya announced with pride. The black birthmark on the heel of Nagendra's left foot was now prominent.

His eyes met Shukracharya's and he bowed before him touching his feet to get his blessings. Even as the immortals felt assured of Nagendra's death and the earth's safety, Nagendra stood up, emerging more powerful and eager than ever before.

'Now that Nagendra is finally an immortal, how have you imagined our mortal lives with each other to be after being free from him forever?' asked Parimal, smiling.

LSD opened her mouth to answer but was interrupted by the muffled sound of Nagendra's footsteps. Within seconds, Parimal could also sense Nagendra coming closer. Nagendra opened the door and saw them together. Parimal was awestruck by the bewitching man in front of him. The perfect figure looked so charming that Parimal couldn't avert his gaze. Nagendra's eyes shimmered like the brightest star and his skin glowed like the ambrosial moon. But LSD looked at Nagendra with the same old blunt expression. Nagendra's eyes were glued on LSD as he walked towards her. Before any of them could anticipate a move, Nagendra's arms snaked around LSD's waist and he pulled her into a passionate kiss, right in front of Parimal, as if he weren't even there.

Everything happening in that chamber was unbelievable and unacceptable to Parimal. He felt jealous and back-bitten for the first time as he was absolutely unaware of the background of what he was witnessing. While Nagendra continued deepening the kiss, the air in the room filled with questions, revelations and a noiseless fight for possession. A moment of unuttered claim felt like years of betrayal. LSD glanced at Parimal, who was already looking at her. She felt ashamed about what was happening and lowered her eyes while Nagendra continued his act shamelessly.

How have you imagined our mortal lives to be after being free forever? Parimal now had his answer. He wondered why this question had even occurred to him. He just wished to erase the gross sight he had seen. In a hopeless effort to absorb what he was witnessing, Parimal silently started walking towards the chamber door, feeling agonized and subdued.

'Parimal!' Nagendra called out, and Parimal turned around to look at him.

Nagendra knelt in front of LSD and caressed her belly before saying, 'I told you not to fall in love with her. She carries your child and you have mated with her, but you must know that I am her soulmate. Let's all celebrate this twisted family equation and our reunion. Take us to Goa.'

Chapter 2

The Drowned Dwarka

Nagendra walked towards Parimal and pointed at some numbers while handing him a note.

'We will go to this location after Goa.' The order was issued with a poker face.

Still caught in the freshly brewing emotional turmoil, registering the fact that Nagendra had addressed himself as LSD's soulmate, Parimal could do nothing but bow like a slave and follow the commands issued. Nagendra turned around, took LSD's hand and began walking out of the room.

'C'mon, honey, till then we shall spend some quality time in my room.' Parimal wished to see her in person and ask her about many things before they could leave the room. Alas. Keeping his gaze averted, he hung his head while LSD's stare remained locked on him.

Nagendra had died but was now resurrected. The legendary priest, Shukracharya, was in the submarine. LSD's real name was not Lisa Samuel D'Costa but Latika. All the predecessor's pets whom he thought were mere animals, were incarnations of his wife. And now, as if everything else was not enough to boggle his mind, watching Nagendra get closer to his wife and calling her his soulmate baffled Parimal to the extent that he could barely separate truth from illusion.

Restless and handcuffed by his obligations, Parimal acknowledged the moment of defeat as he accepted that there was no end to either his slavery or to the relays of heartbreaking surprises. He gathered himself and diverted his attention towards the note Nagendra had handed to him. Planning for the next stop after Goa had begun.

What he held in his hands were some coordinates. *Latitude 22° 13' 48.00" N, Longitude 68° 58' 12.00" E.* Parimal wondered where these could be on the map. It turned out that it was not too far from their submarine's current location. *Why does Nagendra want to go as far as Goa and then return to the coast of Gujarat?* he thought. He decided to dig deeper and find out where they might proceed after Goa and why. As he entered the coordinates in the system, it displayed the submerged Dwarka, the lost kingdom of Lord Krishna. He felt it imperative to know everything significant about Dwarka, and so his research began. He scrolled through numerous sources while the submarine sailed stealthily under the sea from Gujarat's Mandvi Beach towards the coast of Goa which was 653 nautical miles away, estimating their arrival in sixty-five hours at a speed of 10 knots.

Back at Gyanganj, Parashurama and Ashwatthama had learnt that Kripacharya was about to go back. As the threat named Nagendra was neutralized according to the Gyanganj residents, they knew Om's presence wasn't settling well with him.

'What is it about Om that is bothering you, Kripacharya?' asked Parashurama.

Suppressing his anger, Kripacharya replied, 'When he overruled me behind the door, I spared him thinking he was a nobleman, simply being kind to someone in need. But now I realize that nothing about him is as simple as it seemed. He had planned everything and we were tricked. We shouldn't have helped him, and now, after learning about his past, I think we should not let him go out of Kailash. He should be either killed or held captive forever.'

'He is an immortal like us. He cannot be killed,' replied Parashurama.

'Yes, but he can be imprisoned, right?' What Kripacharya said sounded more like an order than a suggestion.

Parashurama pondered over it, silently moving his gaze between Ashwatthama and Kripacharya.

Kripacharya looked at Parashurama and added, 'I think he is unworthy of immortality and not fit to be left free. He now remembers his past, but we still don't know who he is! Although we're not aware of that past, we know that whoever he is, he is powerful. Even before recollecting his roots, he was strong enough to trap both of us in his past. Nagendra has been neutralized and the door between him and his past is now destroyed. There is no need for me to stay here any longer. I must leave now. The rest I leave to your instincts and Ashwatthama's understanding.'

Ashwatthama bowed to Kripacharya and said, 'I respectfully disagree.'

An unhappy Kripacharya paid no further heed, bid Parashurama farewell and left.

Parashurama asked Ashwatthama, 'You have been the closest to Om since we brought him here, Ashwatthama. What are your thoughts on keeping Om captive?'

'I don't think Om is a threat to any of us, though it is a fact that we don't know anything about his past and he knows everything about us now. Om indeed helped a pregnant woman in delivering a child, disregarding Kripacharya's instructions, but I believe he was only trying to help. He was oblivious to the fact that he was helping her give birth to Nagendra, or, as he says now, to himself. This is a paradox in destiny. No one can tell if Om went to his past and brought Devdhwaja to life or if Devdhwaja helped Om reach us to help himself in his birth.

'Was it destined for Om to be present there through the doors of the past? Otherwise, how could he be present at the exact moment his mother was about to deliver? Was the stranger who helped his mother deliver Devdhwaja, and whom she always talked about, Om himself?' It was a contorted riddle locked by mystery, perhaps the key to which was Om.

'He came to Kuldhara against my orders, but he did that to help me. In the same way, he overruled Kripacharya's orders in his memory, but he did that to help the pregnant woman, without even knowing that she was his mother.

Whatever the truth may be, helping a mother and child in such circumstances is proof itself that Om is a good soul. I don't see a threat in Om, but if you order me to hold him captive, I will do it without question.'

'No! You don't have to do that. At least, not now,' said Parashurama. 'He says he is Devdhwaja, which means he is claiming to be Nagendra. What made him say that? Is there a hidden motive? Have we missed any clue? Talk to Om and find out everything about his past. We cannot ignore the truth that he is an immortal and immensely powerful, making him one of us, irrespective of whatever past he had. So continue his training and make sure that he does not leave Gyanganj again without my orders.' Parashurama got up and said, 'I am going to see Ved Vyasa. The Mrit Sanjeevani books are still missing. Nagendra may have been eliminated, but the threat still looms large. The books are somewhere out there in the world, and we need to get hold of them before it's too late.'

In Vrishkapi's room, Om began to show signs of recovery when he took his first breath after many hours. His veins were regaining their normal colour, indicating that the poison's effect was wearing off. Om was overcoming death again, but he still remained in a deeply meditative state.

As Kripacharya stepped out of Gyanganj, he called out, 'Ballhaar!' and stood there patiently. An enormous Yeti covered in a dense coat of thick, white fur emerged from the camouflaging snow and stood in front of Kripacharya.

They exchanged curt greetings and without wasting another second, Kripacharya commanded, 'Stay around.

Keep an eye on him and if you see him leaving Kailash alone, tear him to pieces and eat him.'

Ballhaar nodded in agreement as his nostrils made a wisp of cloud when he exhaled sharply. Kripacharya walked away in the direction Ballhaar had appeared from and soon vanished in the snowscape, leaving Ballhaar to guard the invisible entrance to Gyanganj.

'Time to wake up, Om,' Ashwatthama said.

Om opened his eyes, looked at Ashwatthama and said, 'I have to go to Roopkund immediately.'

Ashwatthama wasn't ready to hear that. 'What made you want to do that suddenly?'

'While I was meditating, I brushed up on all my faded memories and other details before I was killed and my dead body taken to Dhanvantari. I realized that someone is waiting for my return at Roopkund,' replied Om.

Ashwatthama argued, 'Om, this is Kali yuga! The memories you've retrieved are from thousands of years ago, from Satya yuga. A mortal being would not still be alive. Besides, as soon as Nagendra extracted the word, Roopkund was destroyed forever.'

'Your questions and my explanations can wait, but Nibhisha can't wait further for she has waited too long for me. I will tell you everything once I return,' said Om as he hurriedly got up to leave.

'I cannot allow you to leave Gyanganj till Parashurama says so, Om. Stay here till I return,' Ashwatthama said sternly and left.

Om was unaware of the discussion between Parashurama, Kripacharya and Ashwatthama about him being held captive in Gyanganj. So he silently agreed to wait for permission. He did not want to overrule any more orders. While Om sat there, Vrishkapi came closer to him with a wide smile and thanked him for saving his life.

'He who puts a life in danger must be the one to save it. I simply did what I was supposed to,' replied Om.

'I don't understand what you mean. You did not try to kill me, Nagendra did. Then why are you . . .'

Before Vrishkapi could finish his question, Ved Vyasa entered the room. 'Vrishkapi, I need to talk to Om. You should go and meet all the animals on the other side. They have been missing you for many days.' Vrishkapi understood that it was not just a suggestion but a subtle command. He respectfully took everyone's leave and walked off.

Om knew what Ved Vyasa had on his mind, yet he wanted to hear him address it aloud. 'Tell me everything you remember from your beginning till your end.'

Underwater, the submarine was smoothly cutting its way through the currents, heading towards Goa. Parimal was still engrossed in his research. So far, he had learnt that Dwarka was one of the holiest cities in Hinduism and one of the four main abodes,[4] along with Badrinath, Puri and Rameswaram. The city is extremely significant to Vaishnavas. Above all, the legendary city of Dwarka was once the dwelling place of Lord Krishna.

Dwarka has been mentioned in several religious texts, including the Mahabharata, the *Shrimad Bhagavad Gita*, the *Harivamsha*, the *Skanda Purana* and the *Vishnu Purana*. The

---

[4] Dhams or the home of the gods.

dedicated and rigorous efforts of marine archaeologists, scientists and technicians from the Marine Archaeology Centre of the National Institute of Oceanography discovered Dwarka, which was allegedly founded by Shri Krishna. Dwarka was an important landmark in the validation of the historical relevance of the Mahabharata. Its existence dissolves the doubts raised by historians regarding the historicity of the Mahabharata and even of the submerged city. This has significantly narrowed the widening gaps in Indian history by establishing the grounds for continuity of the Indian civilization from the Vedic age to the present day.

On the same day that Krishna departed from the earth, the doomed, dark-bodied Kali yuga commenced. As a result, the oceans rose and swallowed Dwarka entirely. The ancient texts say that approximately thirty-six years after the war of Kurukshetra, in 3138 BC, when Krishna left the earth for Vaikuntha and major Yadava leaders thoughtlessly wiped out their clan, Arjuna went to Dwarka to bring Krishna's grandsons and the Yadava wives to safety to Hastinapur. After Arjuna left Dwarka, it was submerged in the sea, and this is the account of what he had witnessed as mentioned in the Mahabharata.

'The sea rushed into the city and coursed through the streets and buildings. The sea covered up everything in the city. I saw the beautiful buildings being submerged one by one. In a matter of a few moments, it was all over. The sea had now become as placid as a lake. There was no trace of the city. Dwarka was just a name, just a memory,' said Arjuna after returning.

The first archaeological excavations at Dwarka were conducted by the Deccan College, Pune, and the Department of Archaeology, Government of Gujarat, in 1963 under the direction of H.D. Sankalia. They revealed artefacts that were millennia-old. Between 1983 and 1990, S.R. Rao's team unveiled flabbergasting discoveries that cemented the presence of the submerged city.

'Until recently, the very existence of the city of Dwarka was a matter of legend. Now that the remains have been discovered underwater and many clues strongly reinforce the place as the legendary Dwarka, where Lord Krishna once dwelled, could it be that Lord Krishna and his heroics were more than just a myth?' asked Mrs Batra.

'After all that I have seen, heard and done since my birth in the last twenty-one years, I have absolutely no doubt that what the world simply labels "Hindu mythology" is actually a rich and magical history which has become so ancient that people today have lost faith in it and instead speak of it in the jargon of myth and mythology. And to answer your question, yes! Lord Krishna did exist. Lies don't have legs and thus they die crawling, but the names of Krishna and Ram still prevail after not only decades or centuries but epochs. This is enough to prove that their stories stretch far beyond mere myths.

'Marine archaeology has proved that the existence of Dwarka and its submergence in the second millennium BC, referred to in the Mahabharata, *Harivamsha*, *Matsya* and *Vayu Puranas* is a fact and not fiction. The implication of accepting the archaeologists' findings as proof that the sunken city is indeed the legendary Dwarka is a huge step towards understanding what the Mahabharata is. It would no longer be a compilation of myths and legends, but a genuine account of past events, at least to some extent,' explained Prithvi.

Parimal continued reading the correlation between the excavated structures and artefacts that carried scriptures of Dwarka in the *Harivamsha Purana*. It was mind-boggling how the carbon dating of artefacts traced them back to around 3500 BC, the same period when the Great War had occurred and Dwarka was taken by the sea, as concluded by many astronomers.

Before the discovery of the legendary city, some scholars believed that the Mahabharata was no more than a myth, making it a futile objective to hunt for the remains of the ancient city and that too, under the sea. A few other scholars were of the opinion that the Mahabharata was just a family feud that was later exaggerated into a war. However, excavations carried out by Dr S.R. Rao at Dwarka strongly established that the descriptions found in the texts were not to be discarded as fancy stories, but must be regarded as based on evidence and science.

Thus, results have proven that the paragraphs written in the Mahabharata describing the majestic and wonderful capital city of Dwarka were not hollow figments of imagination but credible testimonies of what stands even today. Parimal also found out that all antiquities that were excavated were currently housed in NIO, Goa. That's when Parimal knew he had arrived at his answer.

By now, he was so immersed in the mission, while contemplating the intention behind going to Dwarka, that he did not sense Nagendra and LSD's presence right behind him. Before Parimal could react, he heard, 'You have been brilliant since childhood and I hope you have researched everything about Dwarka for us to be well-prepared with the tools we would need at the location,' announced Nagendra, smirking and tightly squeezing his shoulders.

Nagendra continued, saying, 'Presently, Dwarka is still one of the best-studied underwater sites in India, but the work on further excavations has met a formidable roadblock in the form of academic indifference and governmental apathy. The lack of progress on the project for almost a decade now has made it obvious that the Central government isn't as interested in unearthing more of Dwarka. A proposal drafted by Dr S.R. Rao was submitted to the government, but it has simply been accumulating dust for all these years. And that is because of me!

'The necessary support and funds needed to finish what they started cannot be given to them because I have not allowed it. We have more people than you know, sitting in every city, town, village and street of this so-called God's land,' finished Nagendra, dropping his hands from Parimal's shoulders.

Parimal stood up from his seat and had to stop his jaw from dropping at the sight in front of him. Nagendra had undergone a complete makeover. He was dressed in white baggy pants, a half-sleeved, bright, floral green shirt and a hat to complete his outfit. He looked like a flamboyant and charming young adult who was on the verge of transforming into a party animal and getting drunk even before stepping into Goa. Nagendra sensed that Parimal was a little taken aback by his fresh appearance.

'Who said immortals can't party?' Parimal stood there perplexed as Nagendra continued, 'I am an immortal and I have all the rights to celebrate my life as I want, just like the mortals who will die one day. Other immortals can join the party too, but sadly none of them will be able to do that. Do you know why? Because I don't want them to know my party venue.'

Parimal's face remained blank while Nagendra's expressions were bursting with various hues, adding truth to what his words meant.

'We will be back in a day,' Nagendra cooed, holding LSD's hand tightly. Caressing her hair, he said, 'Let me treat you to a day's holiday, Malti! LSD! Oops, Latika!'

LSD silently walked with Nagendra, who suddenly halted, dropped her hand and turned around, now walking towards Parimal. Bringing his lips close to Parimal's ears, he whispered, 'I never told you an important thing about yourself.'

Parimal cautiously eyed LSD, expecting some revelation as she stood afar, and his ears perked up to catch what Nagendra was about to say. Nagendra only closed the gap between his lips and Parimal's cheek, laying a quick, warm peck to divert his attention. 'You are a handsome young man. Take care of my ship till we return.' Nagendra then entwined his hand with LSD and walked off.

Vrishkapi had reached the place where many pairs of eyes were desperate for his return. As he looked around, he saw quaggas, a subspecies of zebra that grew 8 feet long and 4 feet tall, grazing on the vegetation; the elephant birds that weighed almost 1000 pounds; the blue buck, a long-haired species of antelope, which had a curved tusk, as heavy as 12 tons and as tall as 13 feet or more. These gigantic mammoths, which were last spotted around ten millennia ago, were now gathered here, looking at Vrishkapi stepping closer to them. From being oblivious about when he would return, to now seeing him hale and hearty, the creatures expressed their happiness in their own peculiar ways, letting Vrishkapi know how happy they were to see him there. Although he couldn't share every detail about what had happened, he still told them about the man who saved his life and how.

The month of Jyestha (May) had seen some disturbing incidents. From cross-border clashes between Indian and Chinese soldiers at the Nathu La crossing to Cyclone Amphan hitting the coast of east India, to a sudden gas leakage at a chemical plant in Visakhapatnam, Andhra Pradesh, which was also a bitter reminder of the Bhopal gas tragedy of 1984, everything spelt catastrophe. While these incidents were being analysed, somewhere in Goa, a robbery was in the works.

For now, Goa had just welcomed a new party-hopper. Nagendra was enjoying the music played by a world-famous DJ at a rave party. He was dancing like a child who cared only about the beats and not the steps. The rest of the crowd was passing around drinks, losing their minds over the booming music, hooking up and going to great lengths to have a good time, whereas Nagendra was already in his happiest zone. That night, he partied like a king while LSD looked after him like a servant.

At the break of dawn, the robbery was executed. He broke into the NIO for one specific artefact in the huge collection that was brought back from the deep waters of Dwarka. At first glance, the artefact looked like a pyramid. The astonishingly modern-looking prehistoric object had nine interlocking points. A detailed look at the pyramid revealed wavy symmetrical patterns that moved upwards towards the tip. The waves, lined in turquoise, and the rest of the pyramid, covered in gold, made it one of the most popular and mysterious archaeological finds. And now Nagendra had finally laid his hands on it as he stole the artefact from NIO before leaving for the submarine.

Chapter 3

The Flagbearer

Nagendra entered the submarine happily drunk as LSD quietly held him up straight, helping him walk. Nagendra's piercing eyes stuck to Parimal, for whom the developments in Nagendra and LSD's relationship were still new and difficult to digest. Still, he reluctantly met Nagendra's ravening gaze.

'You are very attractive . . . more attractive than your father,' Nagendra thought out loud. After a momentary pause, he said, 'Take me to our next word hunt.'

Parimal went ahead to take Nagendra's other arm and hung it over his shoulder, supporting him from the other side, as the three of them walked towards Nagendra's cabin. Once inside, Nagendra dozed off immediately, leaving LSD and Parimal standing in awkward silence. LSD wanted to seize this moment and talk to Parimal, but Parimal bowed to her and Nagendra and then walked off.

On the very night when Nagendra stole the artefact from the Goa museum and got back to the submarine,

Om was about to start telling his almost forgotten life story from the beginning to Ved Vyasa at Kailash. Just then, Ashwatthama entered.

'Parashurama will meet you soon and decide on your request.'

'Until then, we can listen to him tell us what he remembers,' said Ved Vyasa. Ashwatthama looked at Om, waiting for him to start.

'Thousands of years before both of you were born, the golden era of Satya yuga was untouched by poverty, greed, material wealth and even labour didn't exist. Whatever man desired, he achieved through sheer willpower, and that could be done only by cutting loose from the humdrum of life.

'Satya yuga was the yuga where humanity ruled supreme and every person was pious and meditative. A yuga free of diseases and disabilities, when people were born with innate supernatural qualities. Thus, out of the four yugas, Satya yuga held the highest significance.

'White was the colour of glory; illusion, fear, hatred, flaws and evil deeds had no place. It was simply the yuga of paradise where the fountain of contentment and completeness never ran dry.

'I was born in a small village on the banks of the river Tamirabarani, near a city that is presently known as Tirunelveli. The whole region was then called Dravida Desham, which is present-day Tamil Nadu. My mother's name was Lakshmi. At the darkest hour of one of the eeriest nights, my mother's water broke and only my father,

Vishnuyasha, was with her. He ran to fetch help. My mother
was the head of the village, so when news of her being in
labour broke, the villagers carrying fire torches scurried to
our house to support my mother.'

'Yes, I know that,' interrupted Ashwatthama. 'In our
astral forms, while we were in your past and you were
helping her deliver, I returned after assuring that the road
ahead was safe, and you were already inside the hut against
Kripacharya's orders. Kripacharya had seen the villagers
coming and warned you to leave immediately.'

'Yes! And I did leave immediately, but when all of them
returned, to their surprise, she had already given birth and
lay there unconscious and clean. The child, too, was lying
healthy and hearty beside his mother. No one knew who
did that.

'My delivery was the first mysterious miracle of my life
for the villagers, and they had no idea that it was just the
begi...i'ng of an endless chain of mysteries that they would
witness.

'The next morning, my mother opened her eyes and
held me in her arms for the first time. My father asked
her what had happened in his absence, and she told him
about the stranger who came in from nowhere to help
her deliver and then disappeared. My father suggested
keeping this story within the four walls of our house and
my mother agreed.

'Since my birth was miraculous, my mother believed
that I was godsent and thus named me accordingly. That's
how I became Devdhwaja, *the bearer of the flag of gods.*

'I grew up hearing from my mother that god himself had descended on earth to gift me into her hands. Every time I heard it, I thought it was merely a figure of speech she used to express her love for me and that most of it was a partially cooked-up story. Now I know it was not just a story and that the man was no godsend. That man was . . . me.'

Om turned towards Ashwatthama and continued, 'However, I did not remember my past when I saw my mother in the astral world with you and Kripacharya, that's why I had no idea what I was doing. Everything came back to me only when Ashwatthama shot Nagendra dead and his blood fell on my tongue,' explained Om, turning towards Ved Vyasa and addressing him.

'I had a golden chance to talk to my mother and tell her about my painful fate so that I could relieve her of some of her pain in the years to come. I wish I had known that I wasn't helping a stranger, but my own mother give birth to me. If only I had known this!'

Om mourned the lost opportunity of not being able to give his mother the closure she deserved. He knew that Ved Vyasa and Ashwatthama were patiently listening to the story of his past. Not wanting to make them wait any further, Om composed himself and continued.

'Life was peaceful, and the village was serene. The women had all the power and played a crucial role in leading, deciding and maintaining harmony in the village. My hamlet was matriarchal and our lineages were reckoned by the maternal sides. This matriarchal society was led by my mother while everyone lived like an extended joint family.

'As a child, I always wanted to become a priest. But a part of me also aspired to become a warrior. There was a constant tussle in my desires, therefore, I decided to master both. But as I grew up, *he* started showing signs of his presence in me.'

'He?' questioned Ashwatthama.

'Yes! He! A nameless, faceless, voiceless demon that lived and fed inside me. *He* had no physical presence, no voice, no face. *He* was the one everybody later knew as Nagendra until the day Ashwatthama finally shot him dead in Kuldhara. But back then, *he* had no name. *He* was only a frail little bug at the beginning of my noticing something else present within, but as I grew older, he grew stronger in me.

'I now remember one of the earliest incidents when I was playing with this beautiful pet rabbit of mine. We had been prancing around for hours till I finally sat with my pet under a tree. The rabbit, too, snuggled in my lap. While I was absorbed in caressing it with love, something took over me and I instantly twisted the rabbit's neck, snapping it into two within a fraction of a second. My actions were so barbarous that the onlookers were utterly disgusted and terrified. After that, several incidents happened in my childhood that showed a cruel side of me. All these were signs of *him* dominating me from within.

'My unpredictable behaviour resulted in kids maintaining a distance from me, so I would play with the animals but, at times, they too suffered the wrath of *his* anger which would be visible on *my* face. One day, when I was six years old, I was playing alone and walked outside the village. There, I found a huge dead creature that I knew was not from around these parts, as I had never seen anything like it before. The body was rotting, the stomach was cut open and parts of its body had already degenerated to bones. I tried to call out to someone older who could help me, but nobody showed up. However, my shouts were stirring something inside the enormous creature's stomach. I was curious, so I shouted again, and it moved in the same way, as if disturbed by an unfamiliar voice. It was amusing how it kept reacting to my voice every time. I peeped inside the open stomach and there lay the source of the movement: a scared little creature hidden in the corpse's womb, unaware that its dead mother was incapable of protecting it.

'At first, it looked like a bundled-up rainbow. A closer look helped me identify and distinguish between the blending shades. The frail little being looked as innocent and beautiful as a newborn baby. Though its features somewhat replicated the corpse, it was almost 1/900th of its size.

'It took me a few hours to win its trust. Eventually, it emerged from the body and sniffed me to confirm that I wasn't a threat. I was enthralled by this creature; it was truly something I had never seen before. It was a baby *navgunjara*.'

'Navgunjara!' repeated confused Mrs Batra and Prithvi simplified the meaning by saying. '*Nav* means nine, *gun* means qualities and *jara* means old. It meant that it was an ancient species that represented nine distinct qualities.'

According to Om, Navgunjara had the head of a puppy and four different kinds of limbs: a human child's arm and the legs of a tiger cub, an elephant calf and a foal. It also had the hump of a small bull and the waist of a lion cub. The tail was of a snakelet and the creature had two hearts, which were strikingly visible through its thin, almost translucent skin.

Om continued narrating his past, 'I decided to take it home with me. It took some time for the villagers to accept Nibhisha as my friend and a part of the village's family.'

'Nibhisha! The gift of God!' said Ved Vyasa.

'Yes! That's what it meant for me and soon would mean for the villagers too. Time moved at its own pace, and we became the best of friends. Nibhisha quickly started learning sign language and obeying my commands. I loved her as a sibling and she, too, reciprocated the same. But whenever *he* overpowered me, Nibhisha was always being ill-treated. As she grew, we learnt that she had some exceptional, unsurpassable powers. She could voluntarily amputate any of her body parts or completely transform herself into any of these nine creatures. Once, when I needed to climb a tall tree, she turned herself into a snake, to be my rope; and a full-grown woman when I needed an extra pair of hands to push, pull or lift anything. She would turn into a horse whenever I had to travel far and an elephant when I needed the kind of strength that was beyond human capability. What stood out the most was her ability to self-reproduce, a rare biological characteristic of Nibhisha. She had this quality called 'virgin creation', which would later be identified as 'female asexual reproduction' by scientists, wherein females can reproduce without mating. Instead, they use the method of faux fertilization to create an embryo using leftover egg cells in their reproductive system. This was a unique quality found only in navgunjaras back in the Satya yuga. The fact that she could raise and nurture a fierce and bold creature all by herself proved just how efficient she was.

'While good and evil continued to evolve simultaneously within me, Nibhisha grew along with me.

'I wasn't easily angered, but whenever I felt any rage bubble up, somebody was seriously harmed. No one could predict when and how something would switch within me. While Satya yuga was the yuga that was devoid of hatred, anger, jealousy and murder, I carried all these traits like a dormant volcano inside me. Whenever *he* took over, I felt caged in my own body as I would helplessly witness the mayhem unfold before me, fully aware that my actions were blatantly unacceptable. All that people could see was my face and body executing every heinous act that *he* desired. I used to read holy scriptures and I loved animals and fed them when I was me. However, I also learnt to wield weaponry and trained to become a warrior, only to murder the same pets with my own hands and eat them too, when *he* would take over. Even a madman had better control over his body than I did over mine whenever *he* would dominate me. I remember the eyes of that boy who saw me when *he* got the taste of blood and raw flesh after killing one of my pets. A boy from the village had witnessed it, but all he could see was me indulging in such a disgusting act.

'And then, finally, came the day when a sage visited our village. After meeting me, he told everyone that my birth happened in the wrong yuga. Though I was born in Satya yuga, I had all the traits of a man of Kali yuga.

'He said the mystery of my duality and unpredicted ruthless actions was hidden in the time at which I was born. Apparently, half my body had entered the world at the darkest minutes of the night, when the demonic powers are at their peak, and the remaining half entered in Bramha Muhurta, the most pious hours of the day.

'While the sage explained his contrasting presence within me, I sensed *his* rage building up. I knew *he* wanted to remain hidden, but every sentence uttered by the sage was revealing *him* bit by bit. *He* wanted to shut the sage's mouth while the sage continued to expose *him*. Suddenly, *he* overpowered me and the villagers witnessed me unsheathe my sword and behead the sage in broad daylight, not sparing the eyes of any man, woman or child. I didn't anticipate that *he* would kill him, but there I was with the bloody sword in my hand and the sage's head on the ground. He then compelled me to pick up the sage's head that rolled on the ground splashing blood all over. That was the day *he* had revealed himself willingly to all. Until that day, everybody had different notions to explain the mercurial changes in my personality. Some claimed to have seen me feeding on dead animals, others said I was the one who set their farms on fire. Before the public execution of the sage, there was no evidence of my violent deeds; those were just rumours that didn't merit any attention. Before that day, only some were suspicious of me, while the rest continued to support me because they had met the good part of me whenever they were in need. That day, however, all mouths in my favour were shut. In Satya yuga, where even the thought of evil and petty crimes that are so rampant today didn't linger, an era in which even stealing or lying was neither expected nor accepted—I stood there holding the head of the sage hanging from his long white hair in one hand and my sword in the other as a murderer. No one knew what to do with me because the concepts of imprisonment or death sentences weren't even thought of in Satya yuga.

'The sage's headless corpse had collapsed right in front of me, and no one dared to come close as *his* furious red eyes could be seen through my sockets. I felt like a mere mask. *He* mocked them by laughing at their petrified gazes. Soon, *he* had enough and seeing no threat, he calmed down, letting me regain control of my body. I threw the sword away and mourned for what I had done. I wailed uncontrollably and pleaded for punishment when some of the villagers began to walk towards me. I was ready to surrender but *he* was not. As they came closer, *he* took over again and ordered Nibhisha to attack. Nibhisha instantly obeyed, killing a few and injuring many within seconds. Everybody continued to see my face and hear my voice, which kept directing Nibhisha. I took over again and commanded Nibhisha to stand down. A state of heavy confusion had engulfed us. The villagers didn't know if they should accept my surrender, or be prepared to fight me. Nibhisha didn't know if she was supposed to attack or stay put. I was fighting a war with myself, changing my orders and temperament with every statement. The fear they felt towards me made me loathe myself. I simply stepped away from the chaos and went back home with my head held low.

'A few hours later, my mother came in. She, too, seemed afraid, but she knew I wouldn't let anybody hurt her. My mother was the only person for whom *he* and I shared the same thoughts.

'She caressed my head while I sobbed in her lap, trying to explain to her that I did not kill the sage and the villagers. My mother assured me that she understood me and offered me something to eat. I was hungry, so I ate it all, unaware that it was laced with a drug to make me unconscious.

'During the few hours I had spent alone waiting for my mother at home, the villagers had pondered upon the sage's verdicts and had decided that I was, indeed, an entity born in the wrong yuga.

'I was the first of those men that are too common in Kali yuga. Today, every other person can be heard saying, "I don't get angry that often, but when I do, I am unhinged." People with such traits were far away in Satya yuga; that's why it was easy to differentiate me as a man of Kali yuga. They arrived at a unanimous decision that I was a danger to mankind, and so it was imperative to divide me into two.

'When I woke up, I was tied up in front of a fire pit and many sages were circling me, ready to begin with the Prithak Vyaktitwa.'

'Prithak Vyaktitwa—the process of filtration!' Ashwatthama exclaimed in realization.

'Yes, this is the same process that Parashurama had performed on you to filter out all that is good in you from all that is polluted. I, too, have gone through it, long before you had,' said Om.

'Ashwatthama! Now I know how you must have felt seeing yourself suffering from leprosy, smeared in blood and pus all over your body, with furious red eyes that looked more powerful than your real self, struggling to get back inside like a snake tries to go back to its pit when pulled out by force. I know how you felt because I have felt the same. Once the Prithak Vyaktitwa was complete, I saw my reflection standing in front of me though I wasn't looking in a mirror. *He* who had been tormenting me forever, now stood in front of me, looking identical on the surface yet entirely different from within. All *he* wanted to do was to be absorbed back inside and take over me again. For *him*, I was nothing except the pit which *he* could cower in and feed on its prey, who was none other than me.'

The submarine closed in on the submerged parts of Dwarka. Clutching the stolen piece, Nagendra and Parimal took the submarine deeper into the haunting, pitch-black ocean to look for the next word. The large blade-like projections of the submarine's anchor dug into the sea while Parimal and Nagendra got ready with their diving suits and equipment. LSD kept an eye on their moves through the cameras on their helmets, directing them towards a massive underwater hole.

LSD's scrutinizing gaze was trained on the small monitor displaying the scans. She noticed a blank spot, as if the scanning machine had missed that part. She took the scanner back and realized that the scanner missed it again, because the blank spot didn't budge. It did not take her long to understand that it wasn't the machine missing the spot, but the spot dodging the machine. She immediately called Parimal and Nagendra and informed them of this strange scenario. Nagendra ordered Parimal to take a closer look at the blind spot. As Parimal swam towards it, LSD followed Parimal's heat signature moving closer to the spot on the monitor.

It was nothing less than a giant whirlpool surrounded by ocean currents that made it appear like a cloud. Beneath the clouds was present a mystical line going round in a circle, which seemed to be the perimeter of the big blind spot. Contrary to its outer appearance as a dark, dormant space, a dive inside revealed a whole new world full of life. Housing energies, matter, plankton and various other elements, it was as if it were a gateway to another deep ocean. Sunlight reached only the top layer and the farther one went, the darker it got; the only source of light would be some glowing substances that were scattered all over. These looked like fireflies but were precious stones. The atmosphere resembled that of billions of years ago. It was a well inside the sea!

Just like a black hole attracts all matter, this spot kept attracting Parimal as he continued to swim deeper and deeper. With dwindling visibility, oxygen and the increasing toxic layers, it was becoming difficult for Parimal to swim through. There were times when he felt like he had arrived at the bottom, only to realize within seconds that the bottom was still deeper. His heartbeat and his curiosity of finding what lay beneath were at the same rapid pace. Soon, his connection with the submarine was disturbed, then weakened and then was completely lost. Time was running out and he had to take a call. He decided to follow his instincts and went deeper, confident that even if something went wrong, Nagendra would follow him and bring him out of it since above the spot, Nagendra had already tied one end of the rope to himself.

When they got no response, LSD and Nagendra knew that they had lost connection with Parimal. Immediately, Nagendra jumped into the dark water and reached Parimal with the help of the rope he was holding.

In the wall of the giant well, almost at the bottom, Nagendra rubbed off the accumulated sand deposits and in no time, what looked like a stone wall showed a glimpse of a shining metal that looked like both silver and gold. It was around ninety feet high and covered the entire wall. The oxygen cylinder was rapidly emptying and the water pressure was making it tough for them to stay there longer.

Nagendra signalled Parimal to start scraping the surface to figure out where to fix the missing piece. They quickly got to work. LSD continued to watch it all on the monitor. As they kept rubbing off the deposited sediments, various figures carved into the walls began to emerge, indicating that it might have been a long-lost temple with godly figures and mythical creatures sculpted everywhere. These figures were nothing but all the Vishnu avatars.

Time was running out and so was the oxygen. While Parimal's hands frantically worked on the walls in search of the right place to fix the missing piece, LSD caught a glimpse of a real eye that blinked as Parimal's hand wiped past it.

'Parimal! I think I saw that eye blink!'

'What? Your voice is cracking. I can't hear you clearly!'

'There is something alive, mounted in the wall!'

Parimal still could not hear LSD but Nagendra understood her words and quickly turned towards Parimal. Parimal was still rubbing the wall and trying to hear LSD, unaware that he was about to be attacked by a humongous turtle whose face and body seemed like one of the engravings on the wall.

The moment Parimal turned around, he saw the turtle advancing towards him with its jaws wide open, ready to crush his face in a single bite. Due to his heavy diver's suit, Parimal could not fall back quickly. The turtle was entirely smeared in thick layers of algae, proving that it had been guarding the well, fixed in the wall forever, until now. Death seemed certain for Parimal but to his surprise, the turtle could not move further beyond a point that was just a few inches away from his face. Parimal breathed heavily as his heartbeat raced. He took the opportunity to distance himself from the turtle. That's when he saw Nagendra holding the turtle by its shell at its back end; he noticed just how enormous the turtle was, like none he had ever seen before. Nagendra had saved Parimal's life. The carved piece of stone fell from Nagendra's grip and landed on the muddy surface of the well. It was about to vanish in the soft sand because of the heavy movements of the turtle trying to free itself. Parimal's eye caught it and he instantly took the piece into his possession. Just then, he found a tunnel in the wall through which the turtle had moved out.

'Parimal, get inside the tunnel. That piece might have its place inside. Kill anything that comes in your way. Go!' screamed LSD.

Parimal looked at Nagendra, who was keeping the turtle busy and had drawn out an army knife, but before he could swim in, another turtle as huge as the first one came out, attacking Parimal. Nagendra took out his long, sharp dagger and slashed the most vulnerable part that was protruding from its shell—the neck. The one in Nagendra's grip was now bleeding to death.

Looking at the dying turtle, the second turtle went for Nagendra with the intent to kill. Parimal noticed the turtle's eyes and saw nothing but pain and threat. The eyes of every being speak volumes, and since Parimal originally belonged to a clan of snakes, he could read the eyes of animals very well. He realized that they were a couple.

'Parimal, go!'

Parimal swam into the long tunnel. As he progressed farther in search of the right spot to fix the piece, he came across a smaller turtle who seemed scared and lonely. It did not take Parimal long to predict that Nagendra was killing its second parent. LSD, too, saw the baby turtle, which was still bigger than the regular-sized adult turtles on Earth. Parimal could tell that it was just a child.

'Your orders are to kill it,' said LSD.

The turtle was cornered and had no place to hide or escape. Parimal saw the fear in its eyes and couldn't help but be reminded of his own unborn child. He decided to disobey the orders and instead, hid the turtle by moving a big rock in front of it, shielding it from Nagendra's eyes. As he rolled the heavy boulder to be placed in front of the baby turtle, he noticed the spot they had been looking for. The spot was actually on the rock and not on any wall. They had been searching for the key in the wrong place all this while!

Maybe mercy was the key to finding this spot, Parimal thought.

If he hadn't been kind, he would never have moved the rock to save the life of the giant baby turtle, which had lost its parents moments ago. He fixed the missing piece on the rock and a doorway opened for Nagendra on the outer wall. With the force of the water rushing into the vent, Nagendra, too, was propelled inside. Soon, the door closed itself, cutting off all the wires and connectors. Fortunately, the camera over the helmet and the microphone inside it was wireless, so LSD could still see and hear Nagendra. Parimal came out of the tunnel and found both the turtles dead and Nagendra missing.

LSD could see two different visuals on two different monitors now. One was Nagendra and the other was Parimal, both at the same depth but with different surroundings.

In Parimal's view, there were two dead turtles, a tunnel behind him and a ray of sunshine streaking across the mouth of the submerged well. He was looking around for Nagendra, who was on the other side, walking down a passage, and only LSD could see him. Astonishingly, the passage was as dry as a desert with not a puddle of water around. There was ample light but apparently, it was illuminating only the space around Nagendra. Everything ahead of him and behind him was swallowed by darkness. It was as if the light was focused on Nagendra and moved at his pace. The passage was broad, endless, eroding and hazy. It was an empty pit.

LSD could see that Parimal's oxygen would last only a few more minutes. 'Parimal, Nagendra is safe, but you are not. Your oxygen level is dropping rapidly. You need to get out of there.'

Parimal began to swim towards the surface. Nagendra had reached a dead end and ran out of oxygen. He took off his mask and realized that there was no oxygen in the tunnel and the oxygen cylinder was also empty. He began heaving for some air. In no time, Nagendra collapsed on the floor and stopped moving, as if dead. LSD saw Nagendra's vital signs pronouncing him dead again. This would be the end of the road for any mortal, but Nagendra was no mortal.

In a few seconds, he opened his eyes again. He was not breathing any more. The book of Mrit Sanjeevani had taught him that only immortals could claim this word and only then would it appear.

He stood up with determination and said, 'I am an immortal and I demand the word to appear.'

Fortune had favoured him for he was now one of them: the ninth immortal who would free the demons and their armies trapped by the nine avatars of Vishnu. This army would follow the ninth immortal against the remaining eight, fulfilling the prophecy recited by Ved Vyasa to the immortals of Gyanganj.

Nagendra's demand was granted, and the next word appeared for the ninth immortal. 'Tihu–Lau–Niyanta (तहिू-लो नियिता)' was now in Nagendra's grasp.

With this, the door was flung open and an explosion similar to a volcanic eruption followed. A huge whirlpool sprouted at the bottom of the well and began to escalate with a rhythmic rise and fall of the tides. Soon, it turned into a maelstrom with a speed of approximately 54 km/h. Breaking through all the barriers with steeply rising waves, it destroyed whatever remained of the submerged city of Dwarka, manoeuvring from crest to crest, hidden from the people at sea. It then proceeded towards the coast, ready to swallow whatever came in its path, willing to destroy the lives of millions, cause fatalities and transform into an uncontrollable, disastrous tsunami on the coast of Gujarat. Something similar rose thousands of years ago on the day when the sea consumed Dwarka forever.

Chapter 4

Messengers Don't Have Names

Parashurama came rushing to Ashwatthama and Ved Vyasa, calling out their names. The stress on Parashurama's face was enough to express his concern for thousands of lives that were only minutes away from death on the coast of Gujarat.

Parashurama suspected that the tsunami had emerged from the waters of Dwarka and said, 'If it's from the waters of the submerged Dwarka, it simply means that the hunt is still on.'

'But how? I killed Nagendra myself and was witness to his headless, dead body,' protested Ashwatthama, with a mix of certainty and confusion evident on his face.

The answer came from Ved Vyasa, who spoke hesitantly as he walked towards them. 'It must be Shukracharya behind all this. I had heard that Shukracharya and Nagendra were working together, but I didn't pay heed to it because Nagendra was dead. But now it seems that Nagendra was not the only asura working for him.' Ved Vyasa's remorseful words expressed his regret for being unable to comprehend it when he had heard Shukracharya and Nagendra's voices.

'Nagendra was never searching for the books of Mrit Sanjeevani for immortality. Immortality was just a by-product. He wanted the books to find the locations of these words and the process to extract them for Shukracharya,' added Ashwatthama.

'I need to save them,' Parashurama said with urgency and used his powers to teleport in front of Om for the first time before vanishing into thin air.

The immortals were now aware that Shukracharya was one more step closer to his mission after getting possession of the word from the submerged Dwarka. What they were yet to learn was that Dr Batra had Om's blood, and that's how Nagendra had come back to life, not only as young and fit as Om but also as an immortal like him.

Ashwatthama started walking behind Parashurama to accompany him to the coast of Dwarka, but Ved Vyasa stopped him. 'If Parashurama wanted your help, he should have taken you with him.' Ashwatthama looked at Ved Vyasa as he said, 'You are where you should be. If you want Om to trust Parashurama's decisions, you too will have to trust him.' There was nothing more to say after that statement of reassurance, and so both returned to Om's original story.

Om thought that they had come back with Parashurama's permission to let him visit Roopkund. 'What did he say?' he asked eagerly.

'Om, We could not put forth your request to him, but he will be back soon,' replied Ashwatthama.

Om was upset by the reply and Ved Vyasa sensed that he might retaliate, so before Om could argue, he said, 'We will have to give Parashurama a valid reason for you to go to Roopkund. For that, we need to know who you are and why you're so desperate to leave. Please, tell us what happened after you were detached from Nagendra.'

'His name wasn't Nagendra then.'

'What do you mean his name was not Nagendra?'

To answer that, Om continued.

'Once he was detached from my body, and I was acquitted of all his deeds, he was held captive, but the villagers did not know what to do with him. There was no concept of death sentences back then, so executing him was not an option. I was instructed not to be around him, not even see him from a distance and I agreed to never visit him. Eventually, they told me he was kept inside a dry well, covered with a lid that had a hole in it. Every day, they threw in some vegetables, fruits and other food through the hole, which was also the only source of air and water for him. Once, I had heard some men talking about his cravings for flesh and his pleas for a small chunk of meat every day.

'Sunlight never reached the bottom of the deep well. Once every fortnight, he was drawn out with handcuffs and bound in thick chains to be given a bath, followed by a change of clothes, before being suspended back in his prison. However, it wasn't easy because every time he was brought out, he either attacked someone or pleaded stubbornly to see me. But neither of his requests was honoured by the people in charge.

'Weeks turned to months that eventually became years, and never once did I see him again. Nibhisha and I carried on with our lives but found it difficult to forget him. He had made it hellish when he was within me, yet there had been a lingering sense of incompleteness ever since we had been detached, which never allowed me to lead a normal life again. It was like a childhood trauma that has such a lasting impact on one's personality that it leaves bruises of permanent side effects for the rest of one's life.

'I knew that expecting a normal life, with marriage and children, was out of the question for me. Hence, I chose to dedicate myself to the welfare of my village and fellow warriors. I decided to become everything that my big, joint family would ever want me to be. With all the knowledge and combat skills I had acquired, I became the guide who led and protected them. While I was busy paving the way for the betterment of my people, no one ever imagined that he was digging a tunnel with his bare hands through the wall of the well, connecting it to the Tamirabarani river, which was nearly 8.1 kilometres away from the village.

'"Devdhwaja! We took him out for a wash and he says he has some vital information to share, and that he will only share it with you," said one of the men who was assigned to take him out and put him back after the fortnightly chores, when he came to visit me.

"'He has done this several times. He's only deluding you. Everybody knows he has nothing to offer. Go back and please carry on with your task," I replied casually.

"'Deva! I don't think he is bluffing this time. I think he really has something to say."

'I honoured his instincts and decided to see him. I could never have imagined the impact of imprisonment that time had left on him. It was worse than expected. His hair was a long, tangled mess that went a little beyond his hips. His beard was another dishevelled bush that reached his abdomen. His teeth were rotting, and he drooled like a starving beast. Though he had never left my mind since the day of filtration, it was still a daunting experience to bear his presence even after so many years. I naturally **kept my** distance while his frail yet mysteriously strong **frame was** trying to reach me tirelessly.

"'You wanted to tell me something?" I asked, willing myself to look at him.

'He suddenly stopped struggling and stood motionless for a few seconds before replying, "Yes!"

"'What is it about?"

"'About the most important chapter of your life."

"'Most important chapter? And what is it according **to** you—my most important chapter?"

"'Your death!" he replied with a cynical smile. "And I know who is going to bring it to you!" he added confidently.

'By now, I knew it was nothing but another hopeless trick to seek attention, but I continued talking to him.

"'Who would that be?"

'"That will be the most important person in your life. Me!" he beamed with joy.

'I looked at the man who had come to fetch me, claiming how certain he was that Nagendra had something important to say. He simply hung his head low in a silent apology.

'"Put him back," I ordered him.

'"You are going to die, and I am the one who is going to kill you and your unique pet who once belonged to me too!" he screamed as he was dragged back towards the well, his voice echoing for a moment in the air, affirming his declaration. "I will devour your flesh for days after killing you! I lived inside you for so many years and I will pay your debt by absorbing you! I will eat you piece by piece.

'"I will kill you one day, and that day is not too far now. Do you understand that? I warn you today! Don't blame me later for not letting you know!" His body was chained but his voice was not. He was right; he had warned me then and was thrown back in the well. And I made the biggest mistake of my life by not taking his words seriously.

'The same day, a man came to our village seeking help. He looked weak and had a turban wrapped around his head. He knew a lot about Nibhisha and me, and of our capabilities as fighters. He told me about a word that was part of some verse and that it was a piece of the key.

'"Key? But where is the door?" I asked suspiciously.

'"I don't know. I am just a messenger. All I know is that it's a one-way door and souls can be trapped there to restrict them from entering the earth. It can only be opened with the key and I hold only a piece of it."

'The key was made up of words, but the door was unknown. He was ordered to deliver that word to someone in the Himalayas and he needed my help to take it to its rightful recipient safely.

'I asked him what the word was and expected him to say it aloud but to my wonder, he only showed it to me. He took off his turban and exposed his bald head, which was radiating a mystical glow, emanating magical colours of neon turquoise, bright saffron and even electric red. Everything was so bright that his head was glowing golden in the dark. The word was in the form of an energy chakra inside his head that I had never seen before. He said that he would tell me only if it was absolutely necessary.

'"What are you afraid of?" I asked.

'"The disciples of Guru Shukracharya. They will do anything to take it from me," replied the man.

'"What's your name?" I asked.

'"Messengers don't have names. Their names and identities are always just messengers. Only the face behind that identity changes," he answered humbly.

'As the messenger continued to explain, my mother overheard our conversation. He knew about Nagendra and me in great detail and his words validated his purpose of coming to me. Sensing credibility to his actions, my mother signalled me to instruct the warriors to prepare for the messenger's ultimate destination.

'The mission was important and the cause was pious, so I agreed to help him deliver the word. We planned to leave on the full moon, which was only a few nights away. Those were also *his* last nights inside the well. We packed our food and weapons and familiarized ourselves with the challenges that we might face on the way in the upcoming days. Deep inside the well, *he* had dug the last phase of his tunnel to escape. Nibhisha, my warriors and I bid farewell to our village and left for the Himalayas on that full moon night.'

As Om went deeper into the narration of his past, in the submerged Dwarka, Parimal had returned to the submarine and was taking off his gear.

'Where did Nagendra disappear?' he asked, and LSD took him to the control room with all the communication equipment and monitors that displayed the live visuals of what Nagendra was seeing. Parimal saw that Nagendra was safe and on his way back to the submarine. The monitor also showed the distance between Nagendra and the submarine. The estimated time of his arrival read 36 minutes on the monitor. They had acquired one more word. Nagendra was one more step closer to his destination and LSD had completed one more month of her pregnancy.

Looking at the visual, Parimal asked, 'What are they trying to achieve and who brought them together?'

The question he had asked LSD was answered by Nagendra, which took Parimal by surprise. 'Devdhwaja's death brought us together!' the familiar voice of his boss blared through the speakers of the room. Parimal did not realize that Nagendra could hear him, just the way he could hear LSD when he was in the deep well with Nagendra.

'The mother of your child does not have an answer to your question, and I believe she, too, has been wondering how I met Shukracharya. Am I right, LSD?'

LSD looked at Parimal but did not answer Nagendra. 'Oh! My love! You don't have to ask anything from me. I shall gift you everything before you demand it. After all, you love me. This long walk would seem shorter while talking to the both of you.'

'Parimal, do you remember what I said in Roopkund when we reached in search of the second word?' continued Nagendra.

'Yes! I do. You said, "The thought of a new life at the very place where you had killed a few so-called good men is strangely pleasant."'

'Exactly! I said that because if you had died at the hands of that big replica of Hanuman or the skeletons or the avalanche, your death wouldn't have been the first for me to witness at Roopkund,' said Nagendra.

'Being inside that well made me feel nostalgic today. It brought back all the vengeful memories and revived the rage and hatred for Devdhwaja that had been dormant within me. I spent years of my life inside that stinking, dingy, muddy well, all because of them!' It was evident in his every movement—Parimal and LSD could tell how vengeance was coursing through Nagendra.

'I had no track of time inside that shadowy pit, and I still have no idea how many years it took me to dig that tunnel with my bare hands to escape. It was a full-moon night when I emerged from that well through that tunnel. I walked back to the village, bent upon killing every man, woman and child; to just behead them, leave behind the heaps of their heads and headless corpses for Devdhwaja like a puzzle to be solved—which head belonged to which body? Then, eventually, I would kill him. I knew that the soldiers of the village, led by Devdhwaja, were to be identified and killed first while they were asleep so that by sunrise, when the villagers would realize the atrocity that had struck them, they would have nobody to protect them. Then, they would be at my mercy.

'Determined to put my plan into action, I cautiously entered the village, escaping the moon's light. However, I was astounded to see that many things as I remembered them had changed completely. The houses, the roads, everything. I could feel peace and harmony in the silent breeze of the night. No soldiers were patrolling the paths, which infuriated me further. It felt as though they were mocking me by showing just how perfect their lives were without me.

'But there was one thing that I always wanted to change which stubbornly remained the same—the matriarchy of that village. Those spineless men were still being ordered by their women. I silently entered a house, found a sharp piece of iron kept in a corner and slit their throats one by one. It was a blacksmith's house.

'Then, I went to the next house. A woman was fast asleep beside her two infant daughters. I grabbed one of the sleeping girls and that woke the mother. She snapped her eyes open, but before she could scream, I gave her a look that was enough to explain what would happen if she would let out a whimper. She didn't even know what to call me because that inconsiderate Devdhwaja and his people never gave me another name. My name was not Nagendra back then. The name that once used to be mine as well, now solely belonged to Om. I wanted everything back from him; my name, my face, my identity, my power, my life, and for him to return what was rightfully mine, he had to die.

'They did not kill me because ending another life in Satya yuga was beyond anybody's imagination; but not for me. I already had blood on my hands and tongue, and I loved its colour and taste. I asked the woman for the whereabouts of the soldiers. She told me that most of them had left the village a short while ago and were travelling to the series of Himalayas on a mission to deliver a man. Tracking them would have been impossible if I had let them go too far ahead. My hatred for Devdhwaja saved the rest of the village because nothing was more important to me than taking my body back from him. I left immediately and started walking northwards on the same night—of course, after killing the mother and packing both the infants as my meal for the road. Do you think that was the first-ever female infanticide? I sure think so.

'Anyway, it did not take me many days to find their convoy. If you want to go fast, go solo, but if you want to go far, go together. The bigger, the heavier, the slower.

He had to go far to reach the Himalayas and I had to go fast to reach him. The smaller, the lighter, the faster. It took me only a few days to track them and then started the series of deaths on the way to the Himalayas. They were many and so, facing them upfront would be foolish. That's why I followed them like a shadow, and every time I found anyone from his convoy alone, he died a lonely death. Nobody knew who was hunting them down till the night everyone reached Roopkund. Now you know why your death wouldn't have been the first one that I would have witnessed at Roopkund. Remember the skeletons protecting the word that had attacked us? They were all murdered by me.'

Parimal and LSD exchanged bewildered looks while Nagendra continued talking and walking, weighed down by the heavy underwater gear.

'The destination they were planning to reach was only a few weeks away, but before that, they had reached their final destination—death. Approximately two hours before dawn broke, when the darkness was my ally, I started killing the few remaining men as they rested peacefully at Roopkund. I killed many of them in their sleep and most of them died a silent death before they could even realize what had happened. But unfortunately, one of them yelped right before dying and the last four men, including Devdhwaja and the messenger, were woken up.'

Chapter 5

Messengers Have Names

Back at Kailash, Om pleaded one more time with Ashwatthama. 'I will be back in no time, even before Parashurama's return. In fact, if you wish, you can come along to ensure that I am not causing any harm or changing anything.'

Ashwatthama knew that whatever the reason was, he could not allow Om to leave. At the same time, he did not want to be rude to Om because, over the past few months, they had learnt a lot about each other and thus, developed a respectful bond.

So, to resolve his dilemma, Ashwatthama asked, 'Why do you want to go to Roopkund?'

'Because I was killed in Roopkund!' Om's answer piqued Ashwatthama's curiosity. Om continued. 'After walking for months and covering the large span between southern India and the Himalayas, we finally arrived at Roopkund.

'On our way, we encountered many asuras who tried to stop us. We fought bravely as a team and killed them all but also lost many of our warriors. While we were getting closer to our destination and the asuras continued to create more hurdles through their attacks, there was someone who was hunting us down wherever possible, stealthily following us like a shadow. At one point, there were only a handful of people left, but our greatest weapon was still standing. The most invincible of all—Nibhisha.

'The night was about to end when his final hunt began. We were a total of nine men at Roopkund, including the messenger.

'Upon hearing the piercing screams of one of us, we woke up instantly. We lit our fire torches to check on our fellow men but, unfortunately, found most of them lying dead. Five of our men were killed in their sleep and the last one had managed to alert us. We were now reduced to four, including me and the messenger, standing in the red snow drenched in the gross bloodbath of our warriors.

'All we could think of was, who could be behind this mass murder?

'I called out to Nibhisha and in the next instant, I saw one of my warriors being dragged in the dark, right in front of my eyes. I was the only one left to protect the messenger as the last warrior ran behind the dragged one to rescue him. My call was answered when Nibhisha, my most trusted and powerful friend, came into action. I was now confident that whoever showed up, no matter how strong, would be defeated. Dawn was about to break but before that, the murderer revealed himself. I was flabbergasted and couldn't understand how it was possible.

'I saw myself standing in front of me again. The disturbing sight sent shivers down my spine.

'He looked like a walking corpse, appearing so horrendous that even a demon would look civilized—rotten teeth, dishevelled and clumpy overgrown hair, long and filthy nails, and clad in bloodstained, ragged clothes. I had never been so afraid of anybody before but looking at that version of myself made me realize just how important it is to not lose control of one's self. I knew I had no control over him.

'He had been cruel since our childhood, but this time, the outrage and hatred he carried in his eyes against me seemed stronger than Nibhisha's prowess. The air felt heavy and unpleasant when Nibhisha found him standing there. It was so insensitive. The traumatic flashes of the past still occupied a part of Nibhisha's memory. I sensed fear in her body language and saw the pain in her eyes. She didn't know how to separate the two identities standing right in front of her because, for her, we were not two, but one.

'He said, "You were unfair to me at our last meeting and have been the same ever since we were separated. You could never prove your supremacy above me and yet, I was punished. Just because you did not have the spine to stand up for yourself, you let me rot in that dark pit and got everything including my share of happiness and affection. You took it all!

"'I kept wondering in the dark—on what grounds you were proven better than me! Perhaps, today, I will get all my answers. I don't want to kill this messenger or this imbecile pet of yours. They are not my enemies. Fight me fairly if you wish to see them alive."

"'Promise me you will let them go even if you win this fight and kill me." I tried to get assurance for their safety.

"'If?" he taunted and rolled his eyes.

"'Okay! I promise that I will let them go after I beat you. They are free to go after that. Then I will chop your head off and take it back to your people and show them how it will end for anybody who will ever stand against me. Then, they will know." Though he didn't laugh like a demon, his words were vile enough.

'I turned to Nibhisha. Despite being so massive, wild and fierce, she seemed innocent, gloomy, frightened and fragile. I cuddled her and caressed her as she reciprocated by rubbing her neck against me as usual.

"'Keep heading north, it's not too far any more. Nibhisha will help you," I said to the messenger. He still stood with his turban on, hiding his bright glowing head.

'I turned towards *him* and drew my sword while *he* picked up the sword of a dead warrior. I had a presumption that I might not win this smallest one-to-one bout, but I never thought that what I was about to fight would be the biggest war of my life. We were equals on every front. Our fighting skills were the same, so were our strengths and weaknesses, as were our moves. The difference between us was the rules of the fight and the rage *he* had against me. "Ethics" was beaten down to merely a word and that's when *he* turned everything ugly and lethal.

'Nibhisha and the messenger stood afar as spectators while we battled each other with fresh wounds that bled uncontrollably. Apparently, that's the result of good and evil fighting to coexist inside a body.

'His arms swung restlessly in attack as his hatred fuelled his aggression. I kept defending myself because I did not want to kill him. This went on for a while but eventually came to a point where his movements became a little lethargic. I took the opportunity to amplify my impact on his sword. All I wanted was for him to drop his sword and accept defeat, but with the way he was fuming with rage, he would rather die than be defeated. A moment came when I, too, lost my composure and unceasingly bashed my sword against his until it snapped in half. A broken sword was considered a sign of defeat and he knew it well. This was supposed to be the end of it—he ought to have accepted his fall with the broken sword in his tired hands. I saw the sense of acceptance on his face that he had lost. I stopped and turned towards Nibhisha. She came close and started licking my wounds, trying to comfort me. By then, the morning rays were growing brighter, slowly overpowering the dark sky. I was exhausted and closed my eyes for a moment, panting in relief. Suddenly, I heard Nibhisha growling and I instantly opened my eyes. I turned my head to see that he had the broken sword against the messenger's neck, looking at me with his ferocious eyes.

'"What would you prefer? This messenger's death or another round of fighting?" he asked.

'I straightened my shoulders and tightened the grip on my sword. He got his answer. I was ready to fight.

'"No! Not the sword. You have practised with weapons well enough while I was in that dark pit. We fight without any weapons this time," he sneered, still holding the edge of the broken sword to the messenger's neck.

'"You don't have to do this. You promised that you would let them go," I reminded him.

'Nibhisha continued to growl at him and hearing that, he loosened his grip on the messenger and said, "You growl at me, huh?"

'"Devdhwaja! I will let him go only if you punish her for growling at me."

'Helplessly, I looked at Nibhisha. She was aware that all the asuras she had fought till now had been to safeguard the messenger. She and I knew that the entire purpose would be defeated if the messenger died. Too many people had already martyred themselves to protect the messenger. If he were to die, it would nullify our dead warriors' bravery and sacrifice. So I was compelled to do whatever it took to save the messenger. I dropped my sword.

'"Tell her to turn into stone and remain that way till you call out her name again and free her."

'I stood there frozen. How could I punish Nibhisha so inhumanly when she had always been so loyal and ready to die for me?

'Unbothered by my dilemma, he pushed the sharp edge of the broken sword further into the messenger's neck till it created a slight gash that began to bleed. I turned to Nibhisha and looked at her affectionately. She, too, looked at me in sad agreement, as if she knew we were out of choices. We held each other's gaze and she allowed me to sin by commanding her to turn herself into a lifeless rock. I caressed her face and cuddled her, bidding her farewell.

'"I will soon call your name, my dear. Your time shall stand still till you live your deserved span and die a natural death."

'Looking into my eyes, Nibhisha curled up on the ground swiftly. One by one, her body parts, once heavy with vigour, slowly turned into a rock. Her last stare was as if she said, "I trust you, my friend, and I know you will bring me back soon."

'Watching my precious and only friend turn to stone boiled my blood. I turned back to the one whose command I had to follow unwillingly. The wrath coursing through me now was my fuel to defeat him again in this hand-to-hand combat.

'He dropped the broken sword and freed the messenger. We charged at each other and the moment he was within my reach, I flung my arm and punched his face. He returned a punch on the side of my ribcage. While my punch didn't even scratch his face, my side, where he had hit me, began to ooze blood. I then realized that he had the tip of a broken arrow hidden between his fingers, and that's what had stabbed my flesh, inflicting a deep cut.

The wound was below the right side of my ribs, making it difficult for me to even pick up the sword and attack. I was fighting hard to defeat him so that I could capture him and drag him back alive, but he was stronger now and fighting even harder to kill me. He picked up the sword and came charging towards me. Intending to help, the messenger intervened and tried to stop him, but was no match for his strength. In the blink of an eye, he cut off the messenger's arm and sprinted towards me again. I picked up the sword somehow, but both of us knew that I had already lost due to his pointed punch of betrayal on my ribs. He then stabbed my thighs, and I crumbled to the ground. As I screamed in pain, he caught my tongue, stretched it out and slit it off in a single motion.

'He went back to the messenger, looked at me and said, "I know the biggest pain I can give you is to show you how you've broken your promise. Your mission of keeping this man safe, whatever his name is, and delivering him to wherever he was supposed to reach has failed. You've promised Nibhisha that you will call out for her very soon, but I have your tongue now, and so you won't be able to fulfil that either. Never. That's another failure. You told your villagers that you would be back. But alas, you won't be returning to your people and they will never know how you died. Once more, you failed.

"'And now this messenger must die. Any last words to your helpless dying protector, Mr Messenger?" he taunted.

'The messenger was writhing in pain and with tear-filled eyes, he said, "You wanted to know my name before we left your village. My name is Nagendra. Thank you, Devdhwaja, for helping me this far."

'The messenger sat on his knees and closed his eyes. He held the messenger's forehead, showed him the sky and then slowly swayed his neck. The messenger struggled to breathe till he died. I remained a helpless and apologetic witness to his assassination. While I was looking at the dying messenger, he rejoiced at the sight of my feeble state, considering it a reward for his victory.

'And before I could comprehend all that had happened or predict what would happen next, he lunged at me. He raised his sword and stabbed me repeatedly in my stomach. With each thrust, he vented his frustration pent up over the past years, all the while delighting in my slow, excruciating death. My eyes closed eventually, and I was dead. His was the last face I had seen.'

'He loathed you so much that he did not hesitate to kill you. Then why did he take you to Dhanvantari to resurrect you?' asked Ashwatthama.

Back in the submarine, Nagendra had returned and continued his story while taking off all his gear.

'After I killed Devdhwaja, I felt like a conqueror, but physically, I felt very weak all of a sudden, as if someone was slowly sucking the life out of me. I fell on my knees due to my degenerating strength. That's when Shukracharya emerged before me for the first time.'

'But the question still remains!' Mrs Batra interrupted. 'What's the connection between Shukracharya and Nagendra? How did they form an alliance and for what?'

'This is exactly what Parimal wanted to know next, and Nagendra continued to explain,' Prithvi said, and Mrs Batra nodded, asking him to go on.

'I didn't know that one of us could not survive without the other, that killing Devdhwaja would be killing myself. Yet, I hated him so much that I was ready to die after defeating him. I closed my eyes and was ready to accept my fate when Shukracharya showed up as a saviour and guide.

'"Who are you?" I asked

'"I am the one who is going to save you from the death you have summoned for yourself by killing Devdhwaja."

'"What do you mean?"

'"You and Devdhwaja were meant to be one. Your bodies were separated, but your destinies were not. Your birth and death meant not two but one for the God of death—Yamraj. So, by killing him, you have not only reduced your strength and capacities but also brought your life to an end. It's just a matter of time now till death consumes you too. Your death, without Devdhwaja's life, is inevitable. After all, the God of death is also accountable and so he will set his accounts straight soon."

'"You said that you are the one who is going to save me. How and why?" I asked.

'"I am Shukracharya. All the asuras sent to hinder Devdhwaja's path to stop the messenger were my protégés and all of them lost. I wanted to abduct the messenger and bring him over to my side before he reached Dhanvantari."

'"Dhanvantari?"

'Looking at Devdhwaja's body lying beside the messenger's body in agony, he replied, "Yes! The demigod in the Himalayas who is compiling all the nine words that once strung together will become the key to open the door far in the southern end of the land. But now you have killed the messenger and paved the way to your death by killing Devdhwaja too. You have ruined my plan along with your petty, purposeless life, and now you are going to make it right for both of us," Shukracharya seethed at me.

"'How can I rectify anything now? They are both dead," I replied

"'Now you will take the identity of the messenger and drag Devdhwaja to Dhanvantari, where he will resurrect Devdhwaja so that you may live longer. Till then, I will work as your life support and keep you covered in the blanket of life, hidden from the eyes of the God of death," replied Shukracharya.

"'And why will you do that for me?" I asked.

'He looked at me with conviction and bringing his face closer to mine, he spoke in a low yet stern tone. "Because you did what none of my protégés could do. They were more powerful than you but none of them could kill Devdhwaja and bring the messenger to me. It's rare to find cruelty and evil in humans on earth in Satya yuga. And since all that is rare is precious, you are precious.

"'You have more to demand from the world and offer me by standing alive than by falling dead. Also, you will live because you must compensate for the loss you've caused me by killing the messenger who would have brought me the books of Mrit Sanjeevani, which Dhanvantari was going to write after this messenger brought him the word. Now, I will keep you alive until Dhanvantari resurrects Devdhwaja, and you will bring me the books as soon as Dhanvantari completes them so that I can have all the nine words to open the keyless door."

'I just wanted to live, so I said, "But I don't know anything about the messenger and the word he carried. Whoever Dhanvantari is, he is waiting for the word this messenger was travelling with, according to you. How do you expect me to tell him the word?"

'Shukracharya uncovered the dead messenger's head by removing his turban and the radiant, mystical hues of neon turquoise, bright saffron and electric red glowed, expanding into a small bubble that engulfed us in its glow. But soon, it began to dim. That was the last time it radiated before the magical colours turned completely dark.

'"I can read the word that hides beneath it but cannot extract it," said Shukracharya and sat with the dead body for a few minutes. He closed his eyes and suddenly, the dimming light of the messenger's head turned completely black.

'Shukracharya's eyes snapped open as he said, "Anadi!"'

'"This word will help you enter Dhanvantari's closed doors. They are waiting for him, and they know his name," Shukracharya said confidently.

'"Nagendra!" I said.

'"What?" asked Shukracharya.

"'Right before he died, he told Devdhwaja his name and I heard it. His name was Nagendra," I answered, looking at the dead messenger.

"'*Is* Nagendra!" Shukracharya corrected me. I frowned and Shukracharya explained.

"'For them, he is not dead. He is alive and his name is Nagendra. Your name is Nagendra from today onwards and you are the messenger carrying the word 'Anadi!'"

"'Why would Dhanvantari resurrect Devdhwaja?" I asked Shukracharya.

"'He will do that in exchange for the word that you'll give him. You will bargain and he will have to agree," Shukracharya assured me, but I still had my doubts.

"'Has he done it before? Bringing someone back from the dead?"

"'No! But he knows that he can. After all, he was the one who brought Amrit, the nectar of immortality, to the gods from the depths of the ocean during the Samudra Manthan, when Lord Vishnu had incarnated himself as a turtle named Kurma." Shukracharya didn't hesitate because he was certain of Dhanvantari's abilities.

'Why didn't Shukracharya resurrect Devdhwaja himself?' Mrs Batra asked.

'Because Shukracharya's powers were limited to bringing back to life only asuras. Unfortunately, Devdhwaja was not like me,' replied Prithvi.

'What happened next?' asked Mrs Batra.

Nagendra continued, 'I tied both his legs and dragged him all the way from Roopkund to the camp of Dhanvantari in the Himalayas. I fed on Devdhwaja's body parts in bits and pieces to keep myself energized and warm. His face was eaten away by frostbite and the rest of him was no better from being dragged upside down over rocks and through the snow. By the time I reached Dhanvantari, it was impossible to gauge what he had looked like before he had died and so, nobody could identify the resemblance between the one being dragged and the one dragging.'

Nagendra paused for a moment and suddenly threw a fit of rage, bellowing at the top of his voice. He pointed an aggressive finger towards his face and turned to Parimal.

'This is our real face! Since then, I have been the only one with this face. I am the real Devdhwaja, not Om!' he panted before gathering himself and continuing, 'With Shukracharya's guidance, I found Dhanvantari in the series of Himalayas where I first met her, the love of my life.' Nagendra smiled crookedly, pointing towards LSD.

He signalled LSD to come closer and gave her a passionate kiss. *LSD at Dhanvantari's camp!* thought a confused Parimal. It did not make any sense to him but he was just a helpless spectator and LSD, a married, four-month-pregnant woman, was more of an embarrassed victim. Both hopeless puppets looked at each other.

'Get out now. I need to rest,' Nagendra ordered Parimal.

Parimal bowed to his owner and left the room feeling emotionally bruised, heartbroken and wondering what Nagendra meant by meeting the love of his life at Dhanvantari's camp.

Chapter 6

The Fractured Past

While Nagendra was back inside the submarine, Parashurama had arrived at the coast of Gujarat where the disastrous tsunami was closing in. It had already swallowed several electric poles, vehicles and uprooted trees swirled in the inevitable whirlpool, as it grew bigger and taller at the seabed. People were running helter-skelter, and a stampede began as they desperately looked around for shelter trying to rescue their families and secure their belongings. Local authorities, the coast guard and disaster management forces had been deployed to rescue lives. The stormy wind was propelling everything in every direction, unleashing chaos never seen before. The rising water level was only a fraction of a second away from engulfing the beautiful coastline of Gujarat. Parashurama was running out of time!

He closed his eyes to concentrate and evoked a massive bow and arrow called the Sailastra. This powerful arrow was the counter to Vayuvyastra—the wind weapon. The Sailastra was mighty enough to calm the heavy winds immediately. As soon as Parashurama released the arrow, it surged with the energy of a thunderbolt, ripping through the wind and darting straight for the tsunami at an unimaginable speed. The blazing arrow pierced the gigantic whirlpool and the sight was supernatural. It was a war between lightning and water where the lightning emerging from a single arrow had tied the wind shut, overpowered the majestic sea and softened its harsh waves.

Thousands of lives were saved that day by an old stranger. The eyewitnesses gave their own definitions of the man they had seen and all of them sounded like imaginary, man-made tales, like the stories people had shared when they had spotted Vrishkapi flying a few months ago. Eventually, it became yet another failed trial of restoring mankind's faith in mysteries, magic and the Almighty.

Inside the submarine, LSD went to check on Parimal while Nagendra was asleep. Parimal's curiosity was becoming unbearable and LSD could feel that in every squirm.

'Ask whatever you want to, Parimal,' said LSD, and Parimal bombarded her with his questions as expected.

'We sail in the same boat, me carrying the boon of a lineage bound with a curse to serve him and you, a soul serving in exchange for the sworn salvation. I told you everything about me, but I am still getting answers in bits and pieces. What more must I do to gain your trust?'

'I trust you, Parimal,' LSD said softly.

'Oh! Do you, really?' He glared at her. 'You were LSD for me on Ross Island while we were interrogating Om.' Parimal was struggling to suppress his anger as he kept panting and pausing to maintain his composure and keep his voice low. 'At my mansion, just before we got married, you told me your name was Latika. When Nagendra died at Kuldhara and we returned with his dead body, I learnt that all the animals my ancestors ever had as their pets were you in different incarnations.' Parimal stopped himself from saying the next sentence but the way one can't hold one's breath for long, it flew out of his mouth despite his efforts.

'And now I come to know that you and Nagendra are soulmates! What are you really? Who are you?'

'I am a captive soul who is transferred from one body to another for salvation that was once promised to me but never granted.' LSD braced herself while she tried explaining everything to Parimal.

'I asked you a straight question and I expect a straight answer.' Parimal's blank face and stern gaze were something LSD had never seen. She held her stare with his and began answering him bluntly so that his agony could be put to rest.

'Everything started at the end of Satya yuga in the Himalayas when Nagendra showed up uninvited at Dhanvantari's camp one day. He somehow found our camp and came with a dead body that he had dragged along from God knows where. He looked exactly as you see him now after his resurrection; he was a handsome sight to behold, he looked aggressive but was calm in his words and his politeness disguised his purpose of coming to Dhanvantari.

'The dead body he had dragged all the way was tied at the legs. His face was unrecognizable from bearing the brunt of being dragged along the uneven surfaces along the mountain trail. He was frostbitten all over. The corpse's skull was mutilated in many places and appeared to have been treated by some amateur, kept in shape till it reached Dhanvantari's camp. Most of his blood had drained out of the several wounds he had, and whatever remained was frozen in his veins. That was the first time I had seen him.

'Although he looked unusual and different from all the others present, there was something in Nagendra that spoke about the calibre and persona he had acquired. He looked ragged but still, my eyes were stuck on him. His slender yet well-built body and sharp features were contradicting the expression he had when he arrived. Just like the way Nagendra looked was different from the way I saw him, I too had unusual fantasies and hidden desires that were completely different from the others in the camp. Maybe that's the reason when our eyes met, I felt like something was changing in me. Before I could realize it, a stranger had become my entire universe in a single moment.'

'You were one of those ten sages chosen by Dhanvantari!' Parimal gasped in realization as the story headed back to Dhanvantari's camp.

LSD continued, 'Yes! I was. Nagendra was a stranger and no one knew anything about him. The sages were not ready to share their huts with him. Each hut was accommodated by a pair of sages and my partner was Sushrut.'

'Devdrath!' Parimal's eyes widened as he tried to cope with another dropped bomb. He knew who Devdrath was. He had seen how Devdrath looked in the brain mapping process when Om had narrated his story during the interrogation at Ross Island, and the team was able to see Om's memories exactly how he remembered them.

'Knowing how accommodating and welcoming Sushrut was, I offered Nagendra a place to stay with me. Sushrut did not object to my proposal and that's how Nagendra entered my hut and my life.

'Our days began with Dhanvantari's teachings, and after that, we had ample time for ourselves.

'Sushrut, being Dhanvantari's best prodigy already, was always busy with him as they would experiment on the dead body Nagendra had brought. Nagendra and I started spending our leisure time together. We would go off to collect dry wood to cook and accumulate other things necessary for survival, which took us into and around the mountain. This gave us a lot of time to spend together. By now, he could gauge that I was head over heels in love with him. He also knew that I would never express my feelings because it was considered wrong for a man to fall in love with another man, especially for someone like me, who had given up all worldly desires, materialistic pleasures and societal life, and had taken an oath to dedicate my life to serving mankind. I was a man who would probably never accept his own truth explicitly.

'However, soon, everything would change. One day, when we were on our usual trail to procure daily resources, Nagendra nabbed the opportunity, cornered me in a cave and broke all my shackles!

'Until then, I was a *brahmachari*, a celibate. I had complete control over my body and mind through years of practice. I had voluntarily restricted myself from any sort of toxic elements or distracting thoughts. The efforts to be celibate were intentional because I was focused on empowering and motivating individuals, and serving people. I was following the path of Brahma and there was no looking back, until that day.

'In the dim corner of that cave, we trespassed all boundaries. His gentle touch flooded me with a wave of excitement, and I submitted myself to the currents of my newly discovered emotions. We made love like there was no tomorrow.

'Soon, I started believing that Nagendra had travelled all the way to the camp after battling such extreme conditions only for me, that the dead body he carried along was merely a medium for our union.

'Being Sushrut's hut-mate, sometimes we too assisted Dhanvantari as his second and third assistants and slowly gained his trust. Though Dhanvantari and Sushrut worked on the dead body rigorously day and night, we weren't informed of their progress. Most of the work happened only in Dhanvantari and Sushrut's presence. On the days we were not assisting Dhanvantari, we would spend the nights in each other's arms. We had our future mapped out for when we would leave the Himalayas.

'On one hand, I just wanted to attain salvation from the circle of life and death but Nagendra was desperate to open some door and rule the world. He never told me what he meant by the door, whether it was real or just a metaphor, and neither did I insist that he tell me. He was a man of few words and never shared much about his background or whereabouts. I, too, never probed much as I thought he was not comfortable talking about his past. Besides, I knew it was never easy for people like us to open up about our lives and for me, what mattered the most was the present I was living in, with the love of my life, above a silent mountain surrounded by thick layers of snow.

'Everything was perfect till Dhanvantari and Sushrut succeeded in reviving the dead body. I was there with Nagendra and Sushrut in the hut when he came back to his senses and opened his eyes for the first time.

'His body was covered in stitches and healing bruises. His bald head showed scars from the dreadful battle. One of his eye sockets had melted and the other had a dark patch. His right ear was missing. His face was still dilapidated, and it was terrifying to see his demon-like appearance.

'The man was named Mrityunjay after his revival, meaning victory over death.

'Everything I knew about Nagendra changed drastically that day. He seemed angry all the time, frowning, fiddling and speaking in bitter tones. He hated Mrityunjay, though Mrityunjay was just a kid at heart, and knew nothing about his past and the real world. All he knew were the sages he was growing up with.

'*We were his family, his whole world.*

'I tried to talk to Nagendra several times about what was bothering him, but he never expressed himself. Yet, despite everything, our love continued to grow, but with that also grew my fear towards him and his changed behaviour.

'After resurrecting Mrityunjay, Sushrut learnt medical practices with us all day and when night fell, Dhanvantari called him to his hut to compile his dictations in the process of creating Mrityunjay. Rumours were floating in the camp that even some demigods visited Dhanvantari at night to bless him with powers. Whenever Sushrut left the hut to visit Dhanvantari, and Mrityunjay would be deep in his slumber like a baby, I noticed that Nagendra would also leave the hut and return after many hours. I wanted to confront him, but could never gather the nerve, because not only was I afraid of him but also loved him too much to upset him.

'I had grown rather possessive and wasn't willing to share him with anyone. This fear had sprouted because of the suspicion that there might be someone else that he loved. So, one night, I silently followed him. It was such a relief to realize that I was wrong when I saw him sitting outside Dhanvantari's hut alone.

'Then, one night, after we made love and lay comfortably in each other's embrace, I asked Nagendra why he sat outside Dhanvantari's hut every night.

'He said he did that to eavesdrop on some words that he had come so far for, but it seemed that nature was against him. Sometimes, the wind blew past, whistling too loudly as Dhanvantari spoke, and sometimes, the wolves howled and the words he wanted to hear would be drowned out by these noises.

'After becoming aware of his hidden motive, I felt foolish to have so earnestly believed that the universe had conspired to bring us together.

'I thought I had more time with him in the Himalayas to get to know him better, but soon came the day when Dhanvantari ordered all the sages to go back to their provinces and impart the knowledge they'd learnt from him. This announcement was unanticipated and none of us were ready for it. Dhanvantari then ordered Nagendra and me to prepare the feast before everyone parted. Still, I was excited to move ahead and show him my world and see where he came from. After we would leave the camp, I was ready to go with him wherever he would have taken me.

'I had the rest of my life planned with him, but my imaginary world fell apart when I noticed Nagendra leaving the kitchen in the middle of preparations that day. From the small window of the kitchen, I could see him heading towards our hut. After a few moments, he returned and I pretended to be unaware, but when I saw him mixing some herbs in the sweet dish we had cooked, the dam of my patience crumbled. I questioned him just the way you questioned me today, Parimal. Nagendra wasn't expecting the interrogation and fumbled while answering. I did not want to support whatever he was up to, so I darted towards the door to go and tell Dhanvantari. But before I could step out, Nagendra blocked my way. He just looked deep into my eyes and smiled. I didn't know what happened then. I could not take my eyes off him no matter how much I tried. Within seconds, I was hypnotized. Never in my life had I known or experienced such manipulation. I was now totally under his control.

'"Now, go and serve it to all of them with a smile," was his first order.

'I knew what a heinous crime I was going to commit. Killing a sage was the gravest of all sins and I was about to kill seven. Reduced to being just a puppet, my body served the sweet dish to all of them with a smiling face. They reciprocated and accepted my offer warmly. Right before I started serving the sages, Sushrut and Mrityunjay were called in by Dhanvantari in his hut. I wanted to scream at them not to eat it, but I couldn't. I saw them collapsing, falling one after the other, and they saw me standing at a distance, still smiling at them like a sadistic monster hidden under the skin of a man.

'Later, Nagendra came out of the kitchen and said, "Go to sleep." I fell asleep instantly amid the dead sages. I don't know how long I was asleep, but I was woken by Nagendra's voice calling out my name.

'"Devdrath! Come here," he ordered. All the sages were still lying dead around me. I stood and walked into Dhanvantari's hut, possessed under Nagendra's spell.

'Nothing had ever shaken me to my core until I saw what was in the hut.' LSD choked on her own words as tears filled her eyes. She seemed to be reliving the horror and the guilt that came with the vivid memory. She took a deep, shaky breath and continued narrating with a heavy heart.

'I saw Nagendra feeding upon Sushrut's dead body like a carnivorous beast. He looked like nothing less than a vulture scavenging on the dead! Dhanvantari, who had been violently and mercilessly beaten up, was tied at the legs.

'I stood there like a statue when Nagendra looked at me, holding Sushrut's intestine in his hands and blood smeared all over his mouth. He ate in an uncouth manner and inevitably made a mess. He paused his barbaric act, stood up and walked towards me. Dhanvantari saw me and thought I was there to help as the ray of hope in his eyes was evident. However, he was not worried about himself. He was concerned about all the other sages.

'"Run, Devdrath, run! Save the others, help Mrityunjay, he is alone. Run!" screamed Dhanvantari.

'Nagendra closed the distance between us and kissed me in front of Dhanvantari. His blood-soaked mouth was pushed against mine as his tongue ran across my lips and face. The taste of blood and knowing where his mouth had been made me gag, but I was helpless. I could see Dhanvantari while Nagendra continued to expose my true self to him. What Dhanvantari had to witness so unwillingly was unimaginable to him. He was looking at two men involved in a sexual relationship during times when such a thing neither existed nor was even thought of. The blood on my face had marked me out as being just as sinful as Nagendra, making me an equal in all his deeds in the eyes of Dhanvantari.

'"Devdrath served the poisoned sweet dish to all the sages, and they are all lying dead outside. Come, I will show you," said Nagendra to Dhanvantari, dragging him outside the hut using the rope, his legs still tied in the same manner as he had dragged Mrityunjay's dead body when he entered our camp. Dhanvantari was sure of Nagendra's deeds and did not need proof. I knew that he wanted to steal the books of Mrit Sanjeevani but never in my wildest dreams did I suspect that he would murder them all. They didn't know that they were accepting their deaths from my hands. I wanted to yell at the top of my lungs, sobbing, demanding to know why he kept me alive, but I couldn't even shed a tear because even that was in his control.

'The pain of Sushrut's inhuman death and the ugly surprise of betrayal by two of his trusted disciples turned into rage as Dhanvantari found the corpses of other sages. The man who had dedicated his life to saving other lives was now surrounded by the dead bodies of his own disciples.

'"Smile, Devdrath," said Nagendra, and I involuntarily smiled again. Dhanvantari looked at both of us. Two men stood shamelessly in front of him with blood on their mouths.

'Dhanvantari squeezed one of his own wounds to draw out his own blood, cupped it in his palm, held it high and said, "I know you seek salvation. For killing your own people through such deception, I curse you to never be freed from the circle of life and death. You will never attain what you seek. You will take birth in all forms of life and die painfully in all yugas over and over again. You will remember this curse and you will remember every agony you go through in all your pitiful, ironic lives forever that shall keep mocking your decision of supporting this demon against your own people. You will experience nothing but pain in life and never die a respectful death. You won't be spared witnessing the misery and fate of your dead bodies after your deaths. You sold your soul for his love. I curse you that your soul shall remain his slave forever and you will find him and only him as the dead end in all your lives to come."

'The order was to smile. As if taunting him, I kept smiling impudently at Dhanvantari with Sushrut's blood on my mouth and face, and the deaths of all the other sages on my hands. Those were his last words to Devdrath.

'Dhanvantari was kept imprisoned for years in the nearby cave where we had made love for the first time.

'Devdrath's body became a prison for my soul. I was kept hypnotized for almost all of Devdrath's remaining life. Devdrath was just a living toy, a puppet in Nagendra's hands. He used Devdrath wherever he wanted, in whichever way he pleased. With time, Devdrath grew old watching Nagendra not age a day because of Shukracharya. He grew too old to even walk by himself, but Nagendra always carried him wherever he went.

'One day, after making love to Devdrath's rapidly perishing body, Nagendra sat by his side and said, "Have you ever wondered why I didn't kill you with all those other sages? Because I love you! You have gone through so much just to stand by my side and so, I decided to tell the truth to Dhanvantari today before coming to you. I told him that you were hypnotized and the death of all those sages was not your fault. I asked him to free you from the curse and he gave me the solution to break his curse and set you free to attain salvation. I can give you salvation and I will, but only after you promise to help me open the door and rule the world. My love! You will get what you want only when you help me get what I want. Your attainment of salvation now depends on the fulfilment of my desire. Once you promise me this, you will never be able to break it, even if you want to. I promise you salvation if you promise to do everything I ask of you till the door opens. I also promise to free you from my hypnotic spell right away if you agree to this.'

'I had been trapped in Devdrath's body for more than forty years and had no choice but to give him what he asked for. Then, I made the biggest mistake of my life. I promised him, knowing that I could not back out even if I wanted to. As he promised me, he freed Devdrath from his possession. Devdrath was too old to avenge himself or fight. Nagendra continued carrying Devdrath with him until Devdrath's last day of life, but Devdrath's death was not natural.

'His last day was the day when Nagendra saw a crocodile at a lakeshore. "I love you. See you soon," said Nagendra and served my body alive to the crocodile.

'I was too old to defend myself or even try to run away from my brutal fate. I remember the pain I went through when the crocodile ripped me apart and fed on my living and breathing self. I saw Nagendra pampering the crocodile, watching it eat me. I died and my soul stood there watching the crocodile crushing the dead body's bones and eating the flesh piece by piece. The crocodile ate to its heart's content and then left half the body on land before returning to the water. Nagendra had walked away as well. With no one to claim or cremate the body, whatever remained of the body was first eaten by vultures and crows, and then by insects. For several days, I was living Dhanvantari's curse by watching me decay and dissolve. I was a righteous man but this is what happens to your righteousness when you find love in the wrong person.

'After this cruel death, I opened my eyes as a small bird and the first face I saw was Nagendra's. The promise he had taken from me was just another trap. Every word that Dhanvantari had cursed me with was now becoming my reality. Devdrath, who was once Nagendra's lover, was now his pet as a small bird. I have had innumerable reincarnations ever since. I have been many trees in many lives and cut to death, branch after branch by Nagendra, sometimes to keep him warm, to make him a house and other essential items. He even made the handles of his axe from me to cut me! I have been almost all the living and extinct animals, birds and aquatic animals of this world but never have I ever gotten another human body after Devdrath's . . . till now, as Latika. Every time I was born, I found Nagendra there to rule me . . . or should I say, Nagendra always found me. Whatever I became, Nagendra had always been my dead end, just as Dhanvantari cursed. I remember all my lives and my deaths and my miseries and my pains. Most of my deaths were at Nagendra's hands, and every life truly ended excruciatingly. Sometimes, he fed me to other animals to put me in a new body, and sometimes he was the one who feasted upon me.'

Chapter 7

Births and Debts

Parimal believed that everything he had heard from LSD so far was enough to summarize the uncountable forms she had taken in her life. Yet, LSD wanted to go deeper and thus continued sharing every single detail that she felt was necessary for Parimal to know.

Glancing at Parimal and then averting her gaze, LSD said, 'I was there in Satya yuga and Treta yuga alongside Nagendra when he was tirelessly looking for Mrityunjay. The end of Treta yuga was followed by the beginning of Dwapara yuga in which Lord Krishna was born. I was a giant beaver—the largest rodent on the planet back then.

'One day, Nagendra saw a mystical lioness that was jet black and had a shiny coat. The lioness was pregnant and unable to hunt by herself. Nagendra had found his next pet. He killed me again and served me to her. Within moments, I witnessed my life turning into death and undergoing the process of reincarnation. For me, nothing seemed new;

neither the pain of dying nor the joy of rebirth. The giant beaver's suffering resulted in a charming black lion cub with the same bewitching lustre as the mother. Nagendra would cuddle and caress me, just the way he does now. Soon, I grew into a massive, adult lion.

'Nagendra rode on me, and the unusual sight compelled people to believe him to be a godsent man. His influence began to spread faster than wildfire and every province of present-day central India had heard of him. One day, when we stopped by a riverbank to quench our thirst, a woman approached him for help. She told him that she was in search of the godsent man who rode a black lion. She was holding her infant son swaddled in her clothes. Upon realizing that she had found Nagendra, she unwrapped the cloth and showed him her baby, ranting about the hopes she was fed by the people and how the godsent man was her last resort.

'At first, the baby seemed blind because he had no eye sockets, but when the woman uncovered him completely, we realized that the boy was half-man and half-serpent. His eyes were shielded by a layer of smooth skin, while the upper half of his body was of a man and the lower half of a python. The woman was Sarputi and the infant she carried was Lopaksh, the very first of your predecessors.'

Parimal was dumbfounded to hear this from LSD. He began to connect the new dots that she was gradually unveiling, but he sensed that she had more to add.

'Sarputi told us about Ashtavakra and why her husband Aghasura was killed by Lord Krishna, even before she had given birth to Lopaksh. She expressed the plight of her son being rejected by the world of snakes as well as that of humans and explained why she was desperately looking for us. She concluded with a promise to pay any price to save her son, even at the cost of her own life. Her vulnerability was an opportunity for Nagendra.

'He agreed to save her child, assuring her that she had come to the right place and only he had answers to her questions. His charisma and influential aura were working on her too. Nagendra laid down his conditions—that her child would gain vision and a complete human body only if Sarputi took an oath that would obligate her lineage to serve Nagendra for generations to come. This would continue as long as they served Nagendra and once their sons were fit enough to serve Nagendra, the generation that had been serving till then would eventually die in their original appearance of half-snake and half-human.

'Despite being wise and having eyes that could see through it all, Sarputi couldn't foresee the impending misery that would haunt her generations to come. Dazed by her love for her son, she accepted all the conditions. That's how Nagendra got his next servant.

'Remember when you told me about your past and how you are connected to Nagendra? And I told you that I knew about Sarputi and Lopaksh because I have heard about them from Nagendra as a bedtime story? I lied! It was not a bedtime story, but an incident I was an eyewitness to. I was there, right beside him as the black lion, when all that happened.

'Since then, your ancestors had been trapped in the mansion of boon, with the curse of serving Nagendra generation after generation, and I was their pet, serving Nagendra in all forms of animals that you now see in the frames hanging on your mansion's wall.'

With this, LSD looked into Parimal's eyes, which were already glued to her. All they could think was how intricately yet distantly their lives were interlinked beyond their mutual association with Nagendra.

'Another major event I've witnessed in the Dwapara yuga was Dronacharya's death in the Mahabharata,' LSD continued.

'Dronacharya! Ashwatthama's father?' Parimal gawked, trying to comprehend the new revelation, which was somehow related to everything else LSD had said till now.

'Yes! Dronacharya! The royal preceptor to the Pandavas and Kauravas, a man of exemplary military skills and knowledge, son of Sage Bharadhwaja and the father of Ashwatthama.

'During the Dwapara yuga, when Lord Krishna was on the brink of adolescence and the epic war of Kurukshetra was still some time away, your ancestors had begun to serve Nagendra and I had died as an old black lion. I then reincarnated as a fruit fly, which was the shortest lifespan I had experienced—fourteen days. Within just a fortnight, I transcended three different lives by dying as a black lion, being reborn as a fruit fly and then as an elephant calf.

'Nagendra had begun training me extensively right from the time I was a calf. He kept a good check on what

I was fed and paid close attention to my upkeep. I was trained to tolerate all sorts of blows from various weapons, safeguard my rider during a battle and follow commands that involved even harming the enemy's chariots, horses and other elephants. After a few strict years, I had mastered using all my body parts as weapons in battle. All the training turned fruitful for him when he rode me into Kurukshetra, where all the warriors and empires participated in the war. He joined the Kauravas' army as an ordinary rider in search of Om, who was then playing Vidur. But Nagendra didn't know that then. Vidur! One of the very few who refused to participate in the greatest war. Nagendra continued searching for Om's face in the dust storms of the war.'

'You participated in the Mahabharata?' questioned Parimal.

'Yes! I did, and I was killed by Bheem.' LSD's tone dipped in sadness.

'Bheem! The mighty and formidable Pandava that later killed Duryodhana?' Parimal probed.

'Yes!' LSD answered in a grim yet irritated voice.

'Why?' asked the curious Parimal.

'Dronacharya was one of the supreme, most relentless warriors. A warrior of such stature was impossible to defeat with simple strategies. But Krishna had come up with a plan that was beyond everyone's grasp. He asked the Pandavas to simply follow his instructions. His mischievously crafted strategy was to kill an elephant who was named Ashwatthama, the same name as Dronacharya's son, and then make Dronacharya believe that it was his son who had died on the battlefield. Bheem killed the elephant on the orders of Krishna.'

'Were you the elephant named Ashwatthama that was killed?' Parimal voiced his realization with eyes wide and curious to know more, simultaneously wrapping his head around the correlation between every aspect of her story.

'Yes! I was. Bheem did as was planned because that was the only way to defeat Dronacharya. He killed me and announced right away in his husky and bellowing voice, "अश्वत्थामा हतः इति।" That meant "Ashwatthama is dead".

'An apprehensive Dronacharya disregarded the rumours that were spreading in the middle of the day's battle and approached Yudhishthira, who was known for his adherence to honesty and dharma.

'"Is it true what I have heard? Is my son dead? Is Ashwatthama dead? Answer me!" Dronacharya questioned Yudhishthira.

'Yudhishthira replied in a low pitch and said "अश्वत्थामा हतः इति। नरोवा कुञ्जरोवा।।"

'That meant "Ashwatthama is dead. Know not whether man or elephant."

'However, Dronacharya couldn't hear the second half of Yudhishthira's justification, 'नरोवा कुञ्जरोवा' (know not whether man or elephant) because Krishna had instructed the warriors to blow the trumpets and bugles of victory so loud that it would distract the field and drown out the remaining words coming from Yudhishthira's mouth. All Dronacharya could comprehend was the first half of the statement, 'अश्वत्थामा हतः इति' (Ashwatthama is dead). A perplexed and disheartened Dronacharya stepped down from his chariot and sat on the blood-soaked field with his head bowed, mourning his son. It was then that the unarmed Dronacharya was beheaded. The ground rule of war was violated. News of betrayal and the death of his father through such deceitful tactics reached Ashwatthama, filling him with unfathomable vengeance and fury, which compelled him to commit mistakes so grave that eventually, he was put in a situation where he was cursed by Krishna himself.

'Back at your mansion, when you caught me standing in front of the frames with moist eyes just before our wedding, where I had also told you my name is Latika, I wasn't missing anybody. I was looking at my past life. I was pondering how far I had come, from Dhanvantari's camp to being born in different shapes and sizes, serving as a pet, and how much further I still have to go to reach that door that Nagendra wants to open. I still don't know what lies behind that door, but one thing I am certain of is that once it's open, I will be granted salvation. Until then, I must keep following the orders of my master, who is mistakenly thinking that he is my soulmate.

'You know, Parimal, I had always repented the ways I died and couldn't ignore that I was never cremated respectfully, until the day I died as your father's pet who was dear to you as well . . .'

'Baadal—my white deer!' said Parimal.

'Yes! The manager of your mansion, Shubendra, rightfully conducted the last rites for Baadal. However, he

was later punished by your father upon Nagendra's orders
because Nagendra loves deer meat and hence was looking
forward to relishing Baadal's flesh, but that couldn't happen.
I still remember the way you mourned when Baadal died.
You were only five years old when I was freed from a deer's
body, therefore, I am five years younger than you as I was
reborn as a human inside that very mansion.'

This alarmed Parimal and flashes of his people and
mansion ran vividly through his brain. He was trying to
sift through those memories and piece together someone
unusual who could have been LSD but before that, LSD
herself decoded it for him.

'I was born as a human after *chaurasi* lakh *yonis*, or 84
lakh incarnations. At the time of Baadal's death, Shubendra's
wife was in her first trimester and that became my path to
a new life. She died in labour and while Shubendra was
mourning his wife's death, Nagendra, being an opportunist,
stole me from him and left the mansion in the dark hours.
That is why I had chosen Shubendra to conduct the rituals
of kanyadan, the rite of giving away the bride, to honour
him by granting him what he deserved as a father. I had
heard somewhere that the one who performs a kanyadan
is sure to attain salvation. That was also my humble way of
thanking him for what he had done for Baadal.

'Milarepa, whom you recently saw burning to death in
Agra, was also Nagendra's accomplice a thousand years ago.
I knew him too. I was a butterfly that resembled a dead leaf
when Milarepa first met Nagendra. My name was Malti. At
the time, Nagendra went by the name of Nanshad and was

busy strengthening people's belief in Ravana, for whom he was also building a temple that still stands in Bisrakh, Uttar Pradesh.

'I was fed to a pregnant wall lizard in front of Milarepa and thus, I was reborn as a lizard and Milarepa named it Kark. My next birth was as a hyena named Kuroop and I was killed by Milarepa as part of his betrayal towards Nagendra. That day, he killed Kuroop and Dhanvantari before fleeing to Mount Kailash to inform Parashurama and Ashwatthama about Om's existence. Milarepa always wondered how these wild animals understood Nagendra's orders and obeyed his commands, spying on Milarepa for him, but he never realized that the dead-leaf butterfly, the lizard and the hyena were all the same soul—me.

'And that's my complete story, Parimal. Now, there's nothing that you don't know and nothing more I have to share. I hope I've answered all your questions.'

'Except one,' Parimal said.

LSD looked at Parimal, waiting for him to ask away.

'Who are we to each other now?' asked Parimal, looking into her eyes.

LSD stood mum. She had no answers for this one. At such a crucial juncture of their lives, when they were about to become parents, they were still unaware of exactly what kind of relationship they shared. Parimal waited for a moment, expecting an answer from LSD, but her long silence answered him instead. He then bowed his head in anger as a mark of respect from a servant, taunting her and walked off. LSD remained in the same emotional state, lost in her past.

Meanwhile, in Gujarat, the coastline was saved and protected but the submerged city of Dwarka had vanished forever. The media was brimming with the visuals of various dead aquatic animals and the heaps of fish that accumulated at the coast as a result of heavy winds and huge, leaping waves.

With another word lost and the havoc of another calamity, the threat on the world had intensified and those who knew the reasons behind this catastrophe were also aware of the deafening ticks of time. To end this mayhem and the hunt, it was critical to find out Shukracharya's next halt and where his protégés were headed next.

Parashurama had now returned to Gyanganj and rushed to see Ved Vyasa in the same hut where Ashwatthama and Ved Vyasa were listening to Om narrating his past. Looking at Parashurama, Om looked up expectantly, but before he could say anything, Parashurama called for Ved Vyasa and left. Ved Vyasa stood up and followed Parashurama. The right time for Om's answers had still not come.

'Ved Vyasa, I need your help. Do whatever you can and find out where Shukracharya is! We have lost five historically significant locations and with that, the asuras have already possessed five words. We thought it would stop with Nagendra's death, but we were wrong. Killing Shukracharya's asuras is not a solution. We need to find Shukracharya and stop him. We have to find him before he finds the next word, so you must start now!'

'I will do everything in my power to find him,' Ved Vyasa assured him. Watching Parashurama turn around to leave Gyanganj again, Ved Vyasa questioned, 'You have just returned. Where are you going now?'

'To meet an asura. Maybe he knows something,' said Parashurama with a hint of hope in his voice and left.

Ved Vyasa went back to Ashwatthama and Om and said, 'I've been given a task and I will not be around for some time.'

'Where is Parashurama?' asked Ashwatthama.

'He is gone.' Ved Vyasa noticed how his reply disappointed Om, but the complicated situation led him out of the room too.

Om had been patient enough and couldn't wait any longer for his request to be addressed and permitted. He decided that he would have to take some extreme measures if he wanted to walk out of Gyanganj again, but he wanted to try one last time to convince Ashwatthama before choosing rebellion. Considering that as his last peaceful resort, Om continued.

'I could neither save the messenger nor could I keep my word of returning to my village, but I believe Nibhisha still waits for me to call her back, as I had promised her. Ashwatthama, now you know why I must go, why I'm willing to take the risk and why i feel that this is the right time for me to go, otherwise, it will be too late. Please, please, let me go. I need to free Nibhisha! She has been punished for her loyalty towards me. Now that I remember my promise, I cannot make her wait any longer.'

Despite knowing and understanding Om's emotional turmoil and agreeing to the fact that Nibhisha deserved to be freed, Ashwatthama couldn't falter as he was bound by an obligation. 'My orders are to restrain you and not let you outside Gyanganj. You will have to stay here until Parashurama's next command.'

'I don't want to overrule anybody's orders, Ashwatthama. I have spent enough time explaining to you the urgency of reaching Roopkund. I cannot wait any longer,' Om said.

'You disobeyed Kripacharya in your past and the child was born . . .' Ashwatthama argued and before Om could protest, Ashwatthama rained his reasons down on him. 'Milarepa died. Vrishkapi almost lost his life. The world came so close to destruction all because of the birth of a child!' Om stood tight-lipped but matched Ashwatthama's gaze while Ashwatthama continued, seemingly riled up.

'You left Gyanganj once, but you are not doing it again on my watch. It does not matter what I think is right or wrong, I cannot let you out.' Ashwatthama's voice turned low and heavy.

Taking a deep breath, a disappointed Om said, 'Just the way whites have many shades, wrongs and rights have many shades too. Though neither of us is wrong, unfortunately, your right and my right stand against each other this time. I will do what is right in my eyes, and you do what is right in yours. I am leaving.' And Om began to walk out of the hut.

'Don't compel me to force my orders on you, Om, because then I will have to put you down in a manner which will not only hurt you physically but will also leave some dents in our respectful relationship,' warned Ashwatthama.

'I, too, request you the same, Ashwatthama. Don't compel me. I cannot sabotage an old relationship to save a dent in a new friendship. Please, don't try to stop me forcefully,' replied Om and walked out.

Ashwatthama followed him, voicing his last warning, 'Om, stop right there before I'm out of choices!'

Om paid no heed and continued ahead, which led to Ashwatthama's outburst. He sprinted after Om and attacked him. A fight broke out between the two immortals. His first attack was rather mild as it was meant to only neutralize Om, but Om had a befitting reply to his strike. Thus, he increased the intensity of the fight with every blow as nothing seemed to be staggering Om. Ashwatthama got a glimpse of Om's real strength, which he was deriving from the union of his intention and action. Ashwatthama was astounded to see such skills. He observed that Om could predict his next moves and countermoves and was skilfully dodging them all. These were attacks that Ashwatthama was yet to teach Om but there he was, fluent in them all.

'You seem to have transformed completely ever since you've remembered everything,' said Ashwatthama.

Not only was Om equally strong as a warrior, but he also had clever replies to Ashwatthama's words.

'Ashwatthama, I was only trying to respect the hierarchy while I was seeking your permission to move out. It was just a token of respect towards the position you held. Right is always right and if you believe what you are doing is the right thing, then you don't need anybody's approval, as I don't need yours.

'Ashwatthama, I hope you realize that I've only defended myself against your attacks till now, hoping that you will stop and let me pass silently. Please, don't make me attack you. I don't want to hurt you as I know that though you empathize with what I said, you are duty-bound to stop me.'

Om hoped that his words would calm Ashwatthama down, but they did the opposite and made him furious. Om knew that the only option left was to neutralize Ashwatthama if he wanted to leave. This time, Om chose not just to defend but also to fight back. As Ashwatthama walked towards Om, a sword emerged in his hands. Om closed his eyes as Ashwatthama saw a sword appearing in Om's hands as well. It was shocking for Ashwatthama as he had never taught Om how to summon a sword, yet he could do it. The sword reminded Om of Nagendra and the battle he had lost. Om got furious and Ashwatthama too held a sword by then. The battle of blades began, and the two warriors charged at each other with such fiery wrath that a single swing could have sliced a human body in half. In no time, Ashwatthama learnt that he was not fighting an amateur and matching up to Om's strength and skill was a challenge. The tables had turned. The one attacking all this while was now struggling to defend. Om's sword incessantly came down on Ashwatthama's as Om's arms seemed far from tired. Every blow left an impact not only on Ashwatthama's weapon but also on his mind and it continued till his sword as well as his willpower shattered.

Ashwatthama could not absorb what just happened.

'Enough of this madness, Ashwatthama!' Om growled.
Ashwatthama was on his knees, trying to comprehend
everything. 'Stay down. I know what I am doing. Don't
forget that I have been on this earth long before you were
even born.' Om was no longer requesting, but commanding
in a firm voice.

However, Ashwatthama was no less a warrior. He
stood up again, using all his strength, as Om walked away
from him. Ashwatthama closed his eyes and summoned a
bow and arrow now that the sword wasn't enough. To
Ashwatthama's surprise, Om had also summoned a bow
and arrow. All Ashwatthama wanted to do was to stop
Om without hurting him. Om, too, only intended to leave
without harming Ashwatthama. Yet, the clash of arrows
broke out between them. The power and speed of every
arrow Ashwatthama shot kept increasing, but Om was
easily able to counter them. When everything proved in
vain, Ashwatthama summoned the Naagpasha.

The Naagpasha could bind its target in coils of live,
venomous snakes. In the Ramayana, Ravana's son Indrajit
had directed it at Ram and Lakshman. When Om saw
the Naagpasha coming towards him, he did not shoot any
arrow to stop it. Ashwatthama was certain that this would
put an end to the battle and Om would be taken captive
but to his astonishment, only an inch away from Om,
the Naagpasha simply disappeared into thin air. The next
instant, it reappeared with its head now pointed towards
Ashwatthama. In the blink of an eye, Ashwatthama had
fallen, bound by hundreds of snakes.

Om calmly strode towards Ashwatthama and told him that the Naagpasha would free him in nine days and by then, Om would be far away from Gyanganj. Ashwatthama helplessly remained on the ground, entangled by the Naagpasha, watching Om leave, wondering how the astra that he had summoned and released had backfired.

Chapter 8

Pursuit, Promise and Power

Chapter 8

Pursuit, Promise and Power

Om was finally out of Gyanganj but not Kailash. He breathed a sigh of relief, looking southwards, where the way led to Roopkund, unaware that Ballhaar had his eyes on him. Just when Om had taken a few steps away from Gyanganj, Ballhaar charged at him with a big leap. Om was caught off guard and before he could even sense the danger, he was weighed down by Ballhaar's enormous body.

Struggling to free himself, Om saw Ballhaar towering over him as the Yeti growled and drooled all over Om's face. Ballhaar was a beast powerful enough to crush any human being with his bare hands. His grip kept tightening on Om's neck when Om suddenly started heating up to a temperature so hot that Ballhaar felt the burn on his palms, causing his grip to loosen. Om took the opportunity to escape quickly and got back on his feet as his body cooled down instantly. This was a characteristic of Om's body, all thanks to the black blood cells he had. Those few moments were enough for Om to prepare himself to fight again but he also knew that he couldn't waste more time wrestling Ballhaar here. He had to reach Roopkund as early as possible, so he decided not to indulge in the fight any more and started raking his eyes on Ballhaar from head to toe as if scanning him. Ballhaar was unbothered and rushed towards Om with the same aggression, roaring with the clear intention of tearing him apart as ordered by Kripacharya. Even when Ballhaar rushed towards Om, Om did not move an inch, showed no signs of defence and continued scanning Ballhaar.

Once they were close enough, Ballhaar punched him hard enough to have killed a normal human being but surprisingly, despite falling on the ground, Om's eyes didn't avert from Ballhaar. Ballhaar seemed a little taken aback by how little impact such a heavy punch had on Om. This offended Ballhaar even more, so he clenched his fists and roared in anger, ready to smash Om's head into a pulp in a single blow. As Ballhaar moved to make his final attack, Om closed his eyes calmly as if about to enter a meditative trance. To Ballhaar, it felt like a complete surrender to death, but in reality, Om was reaching out to someone. Ballhaar's determined arms spread out and closed in to crush Om's head, but just when they were an inch away from Om's head, another, bigger pair of hands gripped them. A dumbfounded Ballhaar looked up to find a much more humongous creature shadowing everything around him, looking at him with pure rage. Before Ballhaar could process what was happening, a powerful punch came flying to his face, giving Ballhaar a taste of his own medicine for the first time.

'Who was this creature and where did it come from?' asked Mrs Batra.

'It was Vrishkapi, who had been summoned by Om when he closed his eyes. After scanning Ballhaar from head to toe, Om could think of only Vrishkapi who was capable of overpowering and defeating Ballhaar. Thus, Om had called him so that he could keep Ballhaar at bay while Om would quickly escape from there.'

Om stood at a distance from Ballhaar and between them stood Vrishkapi, just the way he once stood between his sabretooth and Om when they had met for the first time.

While Om slowly began to follow the wind that was flowing towards his destination, Vrishkapi was focused completely on keeping Ballhaar there, making it difficult for the giant Yeti to keep an eye on Om and Vrishkapi at the same time. Bellowing in rage, Ballhaar came sprinting towards Vrishkapi and landed a punch on his jaw before jumping over him to reach Om. However, Vrishkapi was barely affected by the punch, so before Ballhaar could cross him, Vrishkapi grabbed Ballhaar's hand and swung him far away from Om. Despite being his heavy and colossal self, Ballhaar rolled away on the ground like a small toy. Vrishkapi now stood firmer, with his shoulders pulled back. His stance was enough for Ballhaar to understand that defeating Vrishkapi would not be easy and reaching Om without defeating Vrishkapi was impossible. All of Ballhaar's concentration was now aimed at Vrishkapi. The roar that both the giants let out in unison against each other echoed in the air and rumbled through the snow. They came charging at each other and thus began a hand-to-hand combat.

Om took advantage of this opportunity and walked away. Meanwhile, Ballhaar used all his stamina to match up to Vrishkapi's galloping frame. When their eyes were glued to each other, all their rage seemed to be boiling down to a mutual dilemma. Ballhaar was caught between the obligation of obeying his orders from Kripacharya and unwillingness to fight the one whose life he had saved. Vrishkapi couldn't decide whether he should fulfil his word, given to Om, even though it meant fighting the one who had saved his life by bringing his injured self to Gyanganj. Yet, none of them was ready to loosen their grip. Both of them turned to check on Om and saw that he had disappeared. Ballhaar was disappointed to see that he couldn't obey his command successfully and out of that frustration, he shoved at Vrishkapi so hard that he fell back a few metres. Vrishkapi exhaled sharply and landed multiple punches on Ballhaar's face until he fell on the snowbed.

A moment later, Vrishkapi came closer to Ballhaar and offered him a hand. Ballhaar took it and hoisted himself up.

'Forgive me, my friend. I was compelled to do this because I had given my word to Om that I would come to his aid whenever he demanded it. Just the way I've shown up for Om today, I will show up for you too whenever you call out to me. It's a promise from a protector to a saviour,' said Vrishkapi sincerely.

Ashwatthama was entangled in the coils of the Naagpasha. Kripacharya was gone again. Parashurama was in search of an asura. Milarepa was dead. Ballhaar had been defeated by Vrishkapi. Ved Vyasa was trying his best to learn more about the intentions of Shukracharya. But above all, Om's escape from Gyanganj was a disastrous turn of events that none of them had anticipated.

Unbothered by everything else, Nagendra and the team were moving forward in their mission. In the submarine, LSD returned from Nagendra's cabin to check on Parimal. Upon realizing her presence, Parimal stood from his seat and greeted her with a bow of his head. These stubborn, silent taunts were pissing her off and she snapped at him.

'Please, don't behave like a servant to me.'

'Any orders for me, madam? You could have called me to Nagendra's bedroom instead of coming here,' replied Parimal, still in his passive-aggressive behaviour.

LSD took a deep breath, trying to compose herself and maintain harmony, before calmly replying again, 'You asked me who we are to each other. I have come to answer it for you, Parimal. And anyway, we are both still servants, working for Nagendra, so I can always have more than one reason to come to you. Now, coming back to your question that you had put forth. Here's the answer—you are my husband, I am your wife and the child I carry belongs to us. That is who we are to each other.'

Parimal still held his ground and remained unresponsive. LSD stepped closer and stood in front of him. 'You wanted to know the whole truth and now you know everything. I never wanted to tell you all of this, because I never wanted to hurt you, Parimal.' She shortened the distance between them further as she said, 'I can feel you. I hear you, and I realize that my past hurts you, but there is one thing that you also need to understand. Being with him is a compulsion, not a choice. Coming here and standing in front of you is a choice, not a compulsion.' This was the first time LSD was not just reporting, but sharing her true emotions and expecting reciprocation from Parimal. 'Nagendra and I have made love but we never took vows of marrying each other, whereas you and I are married! I was betrayed, and I am still compelled to be with him. With you, even if I am forced to stay, it doesn't feel imposed. I have been punished more than I deserved for falling in love with a man like Nagendra, but to be punished by your hatred is not something I deserve at all.'

LSD kept her eyes on him, expecting a response, but this time Parimal's lips remained tight. This got on LSD's nerves as her vulnerable, moist eyes instantly turned dry and her tone changed from soft to firm. 'We go to Bheemkund next. Prepare for it.'

'Yes, ma'am!' came the curt response, less of an acceptance and more of an insult. Parimal seemed clearly unaffected by whatever LSD had said, while she left the cabin with tears brimming in her eyes.

'Bheemkund!' Mrs Batra frowned, wanting to know more about the intention.

More than 6000 years ago, Bheemkund was a natural water reservoir located near Bajna village in Chhatarpur district, Madhya Pradesh. It was a holy place and also went by the name 'Neelkund'.

Bheemkund was known for its fascinating turquoise water which was accumulated in red-clayed, jagged rocks surrounding the reservoir and created a mesmerizing contrast. The water of the *kund* (tank) was so clean that even the fish at the deepest end were visible from the top. Bheemkund was unique in its existence and easily surpassed one's expectations in terms of its beauty. The kund was situated inside a cave that had a Shiva linga perched at the left entrance. Though the tank was situated some 3 metres deep in the cave, once the first ray of sun hit the water, it illuminated the interiors in different hues of blue, indigo and turquoise. It was a truly enigmatic spectacle!

Bheemkund and its water held a special place in the Mahabharata era and for as long as it existed, it was a mystery for scientists too. While the Pandavas were exiled for thirteen years by their kinsmen and were wandering in the dense forests, Draupadi could no more control her thirst and fainted under the scorching sun. The five brothers searched in vain for a source of water. It was then that Bheem, with the strength equivalent to thousands of elephants, used his powerful mace to hammer the ground. The single blow created a hollow space and water surfaced from that spot, which was the roof of the cave, and later became the mouth of the kund. That is how Draupadi quenched her thirst, and the place was named after Bheem.

Mysteriously, the depth of the kund was unmeasurable. There had been several attempts by researchers and scientists from across the world to measure the depth of the kund, but no one had succeeded. Once, it was gauged up to 200 metres by some foreign scientists who installed underwater cameras, but beyond that, they were unable to trace the pool bed. Several attempts that followed simply failed to reach their desired objective!

There's enough evidence about how Bheemkund would turn into a foreteller whenever there was an impending natural disaster.

'What does that mean?' asked Mrs Batra.

The water level of the kund would rise exponentially before the occurrence of a natural calamity, even though the state of Madhya Pradesh is landlocked and has no connecting stream between the kund and the sea. Even before the earthquakes that occurred in Gujarat (2001), Japan (2011) and Nepal (2015), there was a tidal wave and a shifting of colours witnessed by locals, through which people could anticipate the disasters. Unfortunately, no one knew how to read the signs and predict them accurately.

Moreover, the water of the kund was considered as holy as the Ganga. It was believed that a dip in this holy water was enough to cure many skin diseases. Daily, several locals and visitors would take a bath in this kund, yet the water of Bheemkund was powerful enough to maintain its sanctity and purity and never got contaminated by any sort of algae or bacterial growth.

To deepen its mystery, the dead bodies of people who had drowned in Bheemkund never resurfaced, just disappeared.

While Nagendra and the team clearly knew the spot and were approaching the kund for their next word, Om could barely recognize Roopkund. Feeling darkly nostalgic, Om took nearly the same, and still the shortest, route from the series of Himalayas to the destroyed Roopkund, from where his dead body had been dragged away by the nameless Nagendra.

He believed that Nibhisha would still be there in her statue state but he also knew that the spot would be covered under piles of ice, even rocks, and it would take him weeks to search her out. He decided to look for Nibhisha in every inch and foot of Roopkund, though he had an idea of the designated periphery of the lake of skeletons as the never-claimed skeletons were none other than the warriors he once walked with. He reached the spot where Roopkund existed before the avalanche that was caused by Nagendra and his mates, wiping out the existence of the place forever and bringing Vrishkapi so close to death.

By then, Ashwatthama was back on his feet as the Naagpasha had set him free after nine days. Ashwatthama went into his hut and started preparations to leave Gyanganj to find Om and bring him back.

'You seem to be in hurry, Ashwatthama,' said Ved Vyasa.

'Yes, seer! I am going to bring Om back before Parashurama returns and I know already where to find him if I get there without any further delay.'

'You know where to find him because he is not trying to run or hide,' replied Ved Vyasa with a smile.

'You may be right, Ved Vyasa, but I am worried about Kripacharya being right about him. What if he really finds what he is now looking for? Because the world is not prepared to see what he wishes to bring back. I must go,' said Ashwatthama, and left.

Watching Ashwatthama leave, Vrishkapi walked up to Ved Vyasa and asked him, 'Where is Om now?'

Ved Vyasa closed his eyes to search for Om's voice and heard him screaming at the top of his voice, 'Nibhisha! Nibhisha!'

While the world was in search of the Covid vaccine, Parashurama was in search of Shukracharya, Nagendra of the next word, Ved Vyasa of the names of the remaining places, LSD of Parimal's hidden emotions and Ashwatthama of Om. Om was the only one victorious in his quest of finding the exact spot where he had lost Nibhisha. The rock that Nibhisha had turned into was more than just a boulder now. Time and nature had transformed it into a hill decked with tons of snow and hundreds of pine, deodar and fir trees rooted on it. He knew Nibhisha must be somewhere in the centre of the mountain but reaching it was a tedious task.

Disappointed but not disheartened, Om closed his eyes and tried to figure out ways to draw a path to the centre of the mountain. Just then, a greyish-white mace emerged from nowhere in his hand. Ever since he had regained consciousness and his memories, Om was continuously rediscovering his abilities whenever he was challenged by anyone or anything, even nature. The mace was made of tungsten, one of the strongest metals on earth. The carvings

on it were enough to make Om realize that it wasn't just
an ordinary mace but a very powerful tool. He struck
the mountain with the mace to see its impact and the air
resonated as if a cannon had been shot mid-air. The earth
beneath his feet rumbled, the mountain trembled, and
Om could see all the birds and animals on the mountain
fleeing from it. Without further delay, Om started breaking
the mountain from one corner. He knew he did not have
much time as nine days had already gone by in reaching and
identifying the spot, and Ashwatthama must be on his way.
Nine days was the estimated time of Ashwatthama's arrival
at Roopkund, before which Om wanted to fulfil his long-
forgotten promise. All Om desired was to rid himself of the
burden of his own promise by setting Nibhisha free before
Ashwatthama could reach him, so that he could silently
surrender and return to Gyanganj avoiding another conflict.
Om charged at the mountain incessantly and every single
blow brought him a step closer to the centre. The sound
of the strikes travelled far and loud, which would soon aid
Ashwatthama in locating Om.

Om tirelessly hit the mountain for days and
simultaneously called out Nibhisha's name. Then came the
day when his efforts were about to meet fruition. Right
before the next blow, Om stopped abruptly because he
felt that he heard something. Om focused on the sound
and realized that it was coming from within the mountain.
He kept his mace aside and stuck his ear on the rock to
hear it clearly. The sound was coming at regular intervals
in a proper rhythm. Om's eyes sparkled with joy as he was

able to recognize it. It was Nibhisha's heartbeat, and at that moment, it felt as if it was also the mountain's heartbeat.

'Nibhisha!' screamed Om with tears of joy brimming in his eyes. He picked up his mace again and this time began to pound at the mountain with twice the strength. The more he broke it, the louder became the heartbeats. Two long-lost friends, separated in Satya yuga, were about to reunite in Kali yuga. After a few more blows, Om saw a blinking eye from a crack that had formed due to the continuous thrashing. The eye was bigger than Om's entire head and he knew exactly whom it belonged to.

'The wait is over, Nibhisha. Here I am as I had promised, and you will be free in no time,' said Om as he stared into the hopeful eyes that had been waiting for aeons, not only burdened by the rocks but also by the assurance of the unsaid promise that she had once given to Devdhwaja that she would wait.

For Om, the search seemed to be coming to an end. But for Ashwatthama, it had only begun.

Chapter 9

The Deathless Divine Devil

It was the month of Ashadha (June) and the time of the crescent moon. The water of Bheemkund was illuminated with the amalgamations of several shades of blue and looked enchanting as the moonlight reflected from it and cast itself on the surrounding red walls. Standing on its edge was Nagendra, looking at the moon and the placid, glimmering water, which seemed ready to alert mankind and continue quenching their thirst till eternity. He took off the remaining piece of the same old sword, broken in the battle with Devdhwaja at Roopkund, and looked at the moon again. Parimal and LSD had no clue that it was the night of the lunar eclipse, and the shadow of the earth was about to cover the moon's light entirely. The eclipse had begun and slowly, darkness began to consume everything. As the moon lost its light and the reflection on the walls started disappearing, Bheemkund also began to lose its shimmer and beauty.

Nagendra stripped himself of all his clothes and stood naked. Then, the handsome naked man started cutting himself in several places on his upper body. By that time, the moon had been consumed entirely by the shadow and looked like a sphere of blood. Nagendra was bleeding profusely from his chest, hands and back. LSD and Parimal could not gather the courage to question his intentions or stop his actions. The rapid blood loss weakened Nagendra and he could hardly stand on his feet. Parimal tried to support him when a drop of Nagendra's blood fell on his hand. Though it was red enough to be called blood, it burned Parimal's fingers like acid. Nagendra then signalled him and LSD to not touch him. Within minutes, Nagendra fell into the kund lifelessly and disappeared into the depths of water. Bheemkund had a history of never letting the dead bodies come afloat, unlike every other water body on the planet. The moon started regaining its light but the water of Bheemkund did not shine any more. Parimal and LSD stood silently, witnessing Bheemkund lose its charisma. And then came Nagendra's body floating on the surface, contrary to popular belief. All his wounds and cuts were healed but he still looked dead.

Parimal looked at LSD for instructions and she said, 'Pull him out.'

He pulled Nagendra out and dragged him far from the waterbody. While he was trying to find Nagendra's nerves, LSD faced Bheemkund and said, 'Your purpose was providing water and saving lives by alerting the world. But from today, you have been contaminated forever, and anybody who expects anything from you will only end up dead if you choose to continue existing. Either you survive and keep killing every living being that may ever touch you, or consume yourself and have an honourable end. Liberate what you hide in your heart or be cursed and keep killing till eternity, nullifying your past good deeds with your own future curse.'

What happened was an unimaginable spectacle! A different Bheemkund had responded that night.

LSD vaguely saw the colour of fire spluttering inside the waters of Bheemkund. Before she could anticipate what would happen next, the temperature of the water started rising and the water started evaporating. The colour of fire was being emitted at the heart of the kund. It was a volcanic opening that was rising every minute, contrary to another belief that claimed Bheemkund to be a dormant volcano in its deepest groove, expected to never erupt. It wasn't difficult for her to understand what Bheemkund had chosen for itself. It chose to consume itself before harming mankind, just as Nagendra had planned and expected. As Bheemkund was dying, Nagendra was recovering. He got back on his feet and stood stronger right on the edge again. He minutely observed the white gas dissipating in thin air, as if searching for something in oblivion. LSD and Parimal stood silently beside him and noticed that Nagendra was neither blinking nor breathing. They wondered what he was trying to do and then they saw the words floating in the white vapour, readable just for a second. The word was 'Yasya Prapnoti (यस्य प्राप्नोती)'. Nagendra took a long, deep breath with his mouth open, sucking in the vapour that held the word and swallowing it. When he blinked his eyes after that, LSD could see the word floating inside his eyes, as if trapped and trying to be free.

Unaware of Nagendra's presence in central India, Parashurama too was in Madhya Pradesh, close to the next word location but for another reason. He was heading to Pataalkot.

'I have heard of Pataalkot but can't remember its significance,' said Mrs Batra, trying to recall.

'It's because the word *pataal* means the netherworld,' replied Prithvi.

Spread across the majestic valley in the Tamia tehsil of Chhindwara, Madhya Pradesh, from a bird's eye view, Pataalkot looks like a horseshoe. The height of almost 1500 ft only added to the valley's beauty. Pataalkot had hamlets that were abundant with medicinal plants and herbs. Doodhi River, which was the only source of water for the entire community, flowed through the valley, becoming the primary water resource for the flourishing flora and fauna. It was believed that the rocks around the valley had been there since more than 2500 million years ago. For ages, the civilization had been completely isolated from the rest of the world, but that gradually changed when schools and other public facilities were provided to the community. Pataalkot was so well hidden from the world that not many people knew about this place, thus maintaining its dense forests. Because the valley was so deep, sunlight would disappear a few hours after noon and thus, the village's days would turn dark quite early.

The tribes believed that Sita, the wife of Lord Ram, returned to Mother Earth's womb from this very place, hence, Pataalkot's depth was the result of the formation of the deeply engraved cavity.

The stairway to Pataalkot was believed to be the path to hell as it was the sole entrance to the netherworld. It is also home to serpents and demons as Lord Shiva often took mythical trips to the Pataalkot Valley to meditate.

The deep gorge was home to over 2000 tribes and thirteen villages that spread across more than 20,000 acres of land. The tribal community religiously worshipped Lord Shiva, the Fire God and the Sun God.

Parashurama was dressed in a white dhoti and cotton kurta, disguised as an ordinary old man. He reached the dense forest and moved cautiously to ensure nobody would see him entering. Nestled amid the tall and thick trees was a cave that was fascinating because its mouth was small but the interiors were wide and deep. The entrance was laced with a peculiar smell of carbonates and organic acids.

'You mean Parashurama had reached Pataal Lok, where the souls of sinners are sent after death, right?' Mrs Batra asked, seeming slightly confident of her assumption.

Prithvi explained, 'There are three worlds among which the universe is divided as per Hindu cosmology:

1. Swarga Lok: Heaven; the dwelling place of the gods.
2. Prithvi Lok: The earth or the land of mortals.

3. Pataal Lok: The underworld; the universe's subterranean
    realms that exist beneath the earthly dimension.

'The *Vishnu Purana* mentions a visit made by the divine
wandering sage Narada to Pataal. Narada described Pataal as
a place far more beautiful than Swarga.

Pataal Lok was believed to have clear water streams,
with the most precious and the rarest of jewels embedded
in the rocky surfaces. The air was perennially fragrant with
little herbs growing on the banks of the small water bodies,
and the soil glittered with shades of black, yellow and shiny
gold. The land there was an illuminating purple because
eroding precious rocks had blended with the ground
naturally over time.

The *Vishnu Purana* also states that Pataal Lok is 70,000
yojanas below the Earth's surface (1 yojana = 12.87 kilometres)
and is divided into seven realms that are layered on top of
each other. Their order from highest to lowest is: Atala,
Vitala, Nitala, Garbhastimat, Mahatala, Sutala and Patala.

'For a twenty-one-year-old, you have too much
knowledge,' said Mrs Batra in a tone of praise. Prithvi
continued without any expression in response to Mrs Batra's
compliment.

Parashurama was headed to the second-last layer
of Pataal Lok—Sutala. He had been walking for hours
following the trail in an underground tunnel. The cave was
quiet except for the ambient echoes of the swimming fishes,
hopping frogs and buzzing insects. Parashurama reached a
door that looked weakly guarded, with only two demons

who didn't allow any trespasser to stand there for too long. Looking at the stranger, one of the demons made scary faces to scare off Parashurama, who simply kept walking towards them because he knew that they were nothing more than mere living scarecrows.

Parashurama stood strong in front of the guards and said, 'Tell him, Parashurama wishes to see him.'

Hearing Parashurama's heavy voice, the demon guards squealed in fear, realizing that the stranger was not scared of them. One of the two feigned bravery and repeated Parashurama's words. 'Tell him, that Parashurama wishes to see him! Who says so?'

'Parashurama!' replied Parashurama, annoyed by the idiocy.

'Parashurama says that Parashurama wishes to see him. Him? Who?' asked the comically grisly demons.

'King Bali.'

'Parashurama says that Parashurama wishes to see King Bali,' repeated the demons at the gate.

'Yes!' affirmed Parashurama.

The guards were naively ignorant of whom they were talking to despite learning that he was Parashurama. One of the two continued barring him as the second went inside to pass on the statement while repeating it continuously.

'Parashurama says that Parashurama wishes to see King Bali. Parashurama says that Parashurama wishes to see King Bali.'

'King Bali!' asked Mrs Batra in wonderment, curious about the man whom Parashurama had travelled so far to meet.

'King Bali, the pious demon, is one of the seven immortals who rules the kingdom of Sutala in Pataal Lok,' Prithvi said.

Back at Kailash, Ved Vyasa smiled with a sigh of relief and said, 'It's time. Parashurama is about to meet King Bali.'

'How do you know from here that Parashurama is meeting King Bali?' asked Vrishkapi.

'Because I have the ability to hear every word ever said on earth. Sound is an energy that floats for eternity in the cosmos, and I can hear and search for any voice and every piece of information that was ever spoken by anybody in the past or present. Shukracharya knows that I hear what he says and that's why he never tells the men under him his full plan, to keep it hidden from me. He only orders his next move after reading it in the books of Mrit Sanjeevani. Now, let me hear the conversation between Parashurama and King Bali,' said Ved Vyasa and closed his eyes again.

Parashurama was respectfully taken to King Bali and both stood facing each other.

Battle-trained and with the toned physique of a warrior, covered in precious jewels over his bare chest and shimmery clothes below the navel, King Bali was the king whose powerful character, knowledge and inherent potential gave him the recognition of 'Mahabali' or 'Mahabalwaan'.

'Greetings, Parashurama! What brings you to Pataal Lok?' asked King Bali humbly.

'I need your help, mighty Bali. The past few months have been extremely difficult. Mankind is in danger. We have lost places like Mansarovar and the submerged Dwarka and, the hunt still continues as we speak.'

'O, dear Parashurama! I believe that earth is safe in the worthy hands of a strong avatar like yourself with the alliance of immortal warriors like Ashwatthama and Kripacharya, and need I mention, Lord Hanuman, whose presence alone is enough to end the war?'

'The end of Kali yuga is not near yet, so the return of Lord Hanuman is still centuries away, according to the prophecy that Hanuman and all the immortals would rise to help Kalki, the final avatar of Lord Vishnu. Perhaps their motive is to end the world before time, I believe.'

'That brings me back to my first question. What brings you here to Pataal Lok?'

'Shukracharya!'

King Bali held Parashurama's gaze, silently urging him to elaborate.

'We believe that upon the orders of Shukracharya, some asuras are hunting for hidden words that form the key to an unknown door. No one knows where this door is and what lies behind it. Guru Shukracharya is the guru of asuras, and you are an asura too. You can help us find out what he is trying to do and if needed, stand by us to stop him. Someone from your clan must know something and being the king of Sutala, you have the right to information from other asuras.'

King Bali pondered over it for a moment before saying, 'I will try to reach Shukracharya but standing by the immortals to save the earth would bring me to a moral dilemma. Supporting the immortals in this case would put me against my own clan if Shukracharya is involved. Dear Parashurama, I cannot promise my allegiance to you, but I can promise you that if your prediction turns into reality, I will not stand against you on earth. My ancestors, Hiranyaksha and Hiranyakashipu, have done enough harm to the world in their time which I repent till date, and so, I will not participate in anything that is against the earth protected by you and the other immortals. However, I don't wish to kill my own people either. For me, my war ended long ago with my ancestors but my remorse for their deeds will last till the end of Kali yuga.'

'If you get any information about the hunt or Shukracharya or whatever lies behind the door that he wants to open so desperately, just say it aloud and we would know,' said Parashurama, with disappointment ringing in his response.

'Oh! That means Ved Vyasa is awake already,' affirmed King Bali.

'Yes! Just speak and it will reach us through him.'

'Greetings to you, Ved Vyasa,' said King Bali joining his hands and smiling in the air, listening to which Ved Vyasa smiled too in Gyanganj.

'And I assume Kripacharya and Ashwatthama stand strong by your side as ever.'

'Yes!' replied Parashurama, as the king had expected.

'So, the asura immortals, Vibhishana and I, are the last ones you have called for the cause?' King Bali's tone was of disappointment.

'I am not going to meet Vibhishana only to have my request turned down again. You were the last one. If we can do without you, we will be able to do without him too.' Parashurama and King Bali greeted each other respectfully before Parashurama left Pataal Lok, unaware that Nagendra was nearby.

Half of Bheemkund had drained through the vent of the volcano and half of it had evaporated. It was like a broken pot that couldn't inhabit any element of life any more. Bheemkund lost its existence and at the same time, Cyclone Nisarga hit the western coast of India.

The tragedy of Bheemkund's disappearance shook central India as earthquakes that measured high in magnitude on the Richter scale struck the terrain, which had been deemed unlikely to experience such a calamity. Because the epicentre of the earthquake was at Bheemkund, which was quite close to Pataalkot, King Bali, too, felt the tremors in the walls of his empire and so did Parashurama as he left Pataalkot. Looking at the trembling Pataal Lok, King Bali immediately called some of his strongest asura spies.

'Go to Vibhishana as messengers and tell him that I wish to meet him immediately.' The asuras bowed their heads and turned around to execute the order. 'Return only when he comes along,' bellowed King Bali before they left.

An exhausted Nagendra had reached the submarine and went directly to see Shukracharya, leaving LSD and Parimal in the same room again.

Parimal knew that LSD was not with Nagendra by choice but was rather caught in an inescapable trap. He sympathized with her because he, too, was bound by an oath that, if he dared to break, would grant him the ultimate punishment of non-existence. He wanted to live for his unborn child with his traditionally married woman, but sympathy was not the only emotion that he had for LSD. There were many emotions he carried within him that occasionally surfaced on his face. This time, what was visible to LSD was anger towards Nagendra, but she thought it was for her. An awkward silence engulfed them every time Parimal and LSD stood face to face.

That was one such moment when she spoke. 'I have always felt sorry for myself since yugas, but for the first time, I feel sorry for someone else, and that is you, Parimal. I am sorry.'

She stood there saying nothing and waited for Parimal's response. Parimal knew she was hoping for a reply but he chose to keep mum again. Unfortunately, they were stuck in the vicious cycle of expectation and disappointment from each other; always short of words to explain themselves, yet somehow understanding and knowing almost everything that the other wanted to say. The irony was that their emotions never revealed themselves verbally any more. Whenever one tried to express, the other chose to remain unresponsive. They knew that they wanted to speak and hear the same words from each other, yet they were stubborn enough to not lay it out. They knew they were in love, but even declaring this would be disheartening to both as they were cursed by the awareness of their own miseries, which had left them utterly helpless.

Realizing that Parimal wouldn't break his silence, she said coldly, 'Your next orders are to reach Ellora,' and walked out.

'Bheemkund was next. We have lost one more,' Parashurama declared after reaching Gyanganj and meeting Ved Vyasa.

'We don't know how many more there are, but one thing is noticeable. The first was Mansarovar, followed by Roopkund in Uttarakhand, Agra in Uttar Pradesh, Kuldhara in Rajasthan, Dwarka in Gujarat and now Bheemkund in Madhya Pradesh. They are moving from north to south. Ved Vyasa! We need to know what other places they are going to raid and why. Only you can answer that.' Parashurama looked at Ved Vyasa with a dim ray of hope evident in his eyes.

Ved Vyasa responded immediately, 'I believe there are a total of nine locations, six out of which are lost. You are right. They are moving from north to south. The remaining three locations ought to be south of Maharashtra.'

'South of Maharashtra?' Parashurama echoed, as if he had understood something.

'They are moving towards the Ellora caves next,' confirmed Ved Vyasa, putting an end to Parashurama's curiosity.

Hearing that, Parashurama was fuming and shaking with rage. 'If they dare step inside my temple, I will kill them all. I will not think twice before beheading them. They will face their worst nightmare before leaving their bodies.' His eyes were fired up, reflecting the aggression bubbling inside him. 'Vrishkapi! Bring Ashwatthama to me.'

'Ashwatthama is not here. Om defeated Ashwatthama and left Gyanganj. Ashwatthama has gone to bring him back,' Vrishkapi spoke in a fearful tone that only multiplied Parashurama's anger exponentially. Om had disobeyed his orders, Ashwatthama couldn't stop him, and now the countdown for the next word had already begun as Ved Vyasa spoke.

'I will return to Gyanganj only after I have eliminated the threat of Shukracharya's asuras forever,' were Parashurama's last words before he left.

Chapter 10

The Celestial Betrayer

On 5 July, in Ladakh, an earthquake of the magnitude of 4.7 on the Richter scale struck Kargil, but this time, Bheemkund could not warn anyone of the catastrophe.

While Ashwatthama had arrived at Roopkund and was following the loud echoes of Om's hammering mace coming from miles away, Parashurama was moving towards the Ellora caves, and Parimal was sailing towards the coast of Maharashtra as ordered by Nagendra.

Just then, a crew member came to Parimal and informed, 'You are being called, sir.'

Parimal followed the crew member and after taking a few turns in the narrow corridors of the submarine, he opened a cabin door for Parimal. Parimal peeped in cautiously before stepping inside.

'Welcome, Parimal! Come meet your child!' Nagendra's joyful voice rang through the room.

Child? But it's only the sixth month, thought Parimal before entering the cabin in confusion. He saw Nagendra holding the probe and sliding it across LSD's pregnant belly. The ultrasound screen showed a growing foetus whose features were quite prominent now, owing to the accumulating fat, growing organs and the developing muscles and bones. Its face looked sharper and clearer, giving a fair idea of the facial outline. The body as a whole looked much more proportionate compared to the previous ultrasound, conducted before LSD and Parimal had gone to Shetpal, where Parimal's ancestral property was. What caught Parimal's attention was the striking and evident shiny line around the foetus that seemed to be protecting it. He ruled it out as just normal foetal development in a mother's womb. Responding to the vibrations and sounds from outside, the foetus moved its hands and legs frequently while its limbs remained tucked into its curled-up body.

Upon seeing his child in LSD's womb, the silence of his overwhelming emotions could only be felt. LSD's gaze was stuck on Parimal. As their sharp gazes continued to assess each other, they spoke in silence until Nagendra's voice interrupted their quiet conversation.

'Why am I suddenly feeling so claustrophobic and choked here? I wonder how claustrophobic the child must be feeling inside you when I feel so suffocated despite being outside. Should we relieve the child by bringing it out right now?'

Parimal and LSD both skipped a heartbeat in terror and were petrified to hear his suggestion. If the child was taken out, it would instantly die and so would LSD. Nagendra's stare bounced between the two as if waiting for their permission. When their expressions didn't change, he said, "Come on, guys! Immortals have the power to joke. They just don't use it," and burst into demonic laughter. LSD and Parimal had no idea how to react.

Suddenly the laughter stopped and Nagendra said in a serious tone, 'Parimal, don't you feel like walking away from this room right now?' That was enough for Parimal to understand the order. 'Perhaps fewer emotions in this room would generate more life. What do you think, little master?' Nagendra winked, putting a ear to LSD's belly, trying to feel Parimal's child. LSD was embarrassed and apologetic again as she watched Parimal leave. They finally had the moment where they had the opportunity to express themselves together, but Nagendra's presence had destroyed that chance. Just before walking out the door, Parimal turned to look at LSD and gave her a warm smile that conveyed what he would have otherwise said to console her: *Everything will be all right. I love you.*

'Phew! I feel so free! Now I feel the space and air. I feel better,' Nagendra said, taking a deep, dramatic breath and sighing loudly.

Someone else at Roopkund also released a sigh of relief, feeling the space and air again after aeons. While LSD's child still had time to come out of the womb, Nibhisha had served her time in the womb of the mountain and was ready to move out of the trap. After days of relentless hammering, Om finally laid his last strike. Chasing the unstoppable hammering noise from miles away, Ashwatthama had also reached the spot to witness the last of it. He was almost a hundred feet away from Om when he saw the enormous being breaking through the remnants of the mountain and emerging like a butterfly from its cocoon. The mace in Om's hand disappeared the very moment the work was done.

The way a flower blooms gradually, Ashwatthama could see Nibhisha growing to a new height with every movement. Though Ashwatthama had heard a lot about Nibhisha, at that moment, he was smitten by her mesmerizing looks. He recalled how Om had described her when he had found her as a baby navgunjara. 'Nav meaning nine, gun meaning quality and jara meaning old. That means the old creature represented nine qualities,' were his exact words.

It was intriguing for Ashwatthama to see how the amalgamation of nine different body parts of nine different beings had resulted in something so divine. Her soul seemed to be the most innocent one, even after she had outgrown all labels that defined her magnificence. And it was her pure soul that Ashwatthama could feel vividly as he scanned her from afar.

It was an overwhelming moment for Nibhisha and Om, and a breathtaking one for Ashwatthama. Gigantic and humongous were understatements to define her size. She was far more enormous than what he had imagined while hearing about her from Om. The moment she was free, Om and Nibhisha embraced each other as an elephant or any other giant animal hugs a human being. The wait was

over for the two and their affection for each other saw no
bounds. However, in no time, Nibhisha sensed the presence
of another human being through her smelling abilities and
turned vigilant. Looking at her suspicious demeanour,
Ashwatthama chose to hide behind a rock till he could
gauge her complete calibre and strength because she would
surely attack him to save Om if she felt even the slightest
threat from him.

'Nibhisha! What's wrong?' asked Om.

Nibhisha stood in front of Om as if trying to guard
him against an unknown threat. She furiously looked
everywhere in search of the invisible.

'Calm down! It's all right. Look at me,' said Om,
caressing her.

'It was because of me that you were trapped since yugas
and so I had to liberate you. It was a forgotten debt that I
finally repay today, my friend. Though I will never be able
to compensate for the loss of your time and your loyalty to
me, one thing I can do is free you. I must now return to a
place where I cannot take you along.'

Ashwatthama could hear his words and realized that
Om had all the intentions to return to Gyanganj.

'Times have changed, Nibhisha, and the world is
different now. The days when you could walk freely beside
me are long gone. You only exist in myths and folk tales now,
and humans' acceptance of anything they don't understand
or resonate with is nearly nil. You are a brave warrior, and I
cannot ask you to hide. I will fail Ashwatthama if I stay with
you and if I return, I will fail you. After what has happened

to you, I have no right to even ask you to stay here till I return from Gyanganj after requesting the residents of Gyanganj to allow you in there. I wish I had someone who could tell me what should be done.'

'You must return with me and bring her along too,' said Ashwatthama, revealing himself. Hearing an unfamiliar voice and looking at the weapons on Ashwatthama's body, Nibhisha turned aggressive, ready to attack Ashwatthama to defend Om.

Om looked at Ashwatthama, who kept his gaze on him. Without looking away, Om said, 'He is a friend. He is not going to harm us. Calm down, Nibhisha.'

Nibhisha softened a little but remained on her toes.

'When you described her, I never thought she would be this huge,' said Ashwatthama, cautiously progressing towards Om and Nibhisha.

'She wasn't fully grown when we were separated. I know because I had seen the size of her dead mother in my childhood,' replied Om.

Ashwatthama came closer to Nibhisha and carefully raised his hand to caress her. She, too, reacted calmly towards the friendly touch.

'He is right! I am not going to harm him or you. I am a friend,' said Ashwatthama.

'My apologies to you, dear Ashwatthama, for binding you with the Naagpasha and leaving you like that without your permission,' said Om.

'I wouldn't have accepted your apology had I not witnessed Nibhisha alive,' Ashwatthama spoke humbly and continued, 'Had I been in your place with the conviction that an old ally was still alive and waiting, I, too, would have done what you did. Nibhisha is also extinct now and so she deserves a place in Gyanganj, but the problem is that she is too large to be taken to Gyanganj without being noticed by humans.'

'That is no problem, Ashwatthama,' assured Om.

'What do you mean? She is almost twice the size of an elephant. There are villages we have to pass by, and it is simply impossible to take her along without being seen.' Ashwatthama was confused by Om's confidence.

Om smiled and looked at Nibhisha. Nibhisha read his eyes like in the good old days and despite having been in the world for thousands of years, Ashwatthama witnessed something he had never seen before. The snake-faced tail of Nibhisha that was hissing at Ashwatthama suddenly started taking over the rest of her body. The hump of a bull, the four legs, of which one was of a tiger, another of an elephant, one of a horse and the last a human arm, the head of a female puppy and the waist of the lion, all squeezed and transformed into her new body of a snake, so that she could easily pass the crowd of hundreds without alarming anyone.

Om could read the question on Ashwatthama's face and as the snake wrapped itself around his arm, he explained. 'She has the ability to transform into any of the nine animals she is made up of, depending on the need of the hour.'

'Nine animals? But I can sense only eight!' questioned Ashwatthama.

'She had two hearts like the octopus, but now she has only one. She lost the other to Nagendra.' A moment of silence ensued, which Om broke by saying, 'The need of this hour is to lay low and so, here she is!'

By then, Nibhisha was all set in her snake form, coiled and covering his hand from wrist till elbow. It was time to return to Gyanganj.

As they began to walk their way back, Parashurama had already gone alone to defend Ellora, leaving behind a terrified Vrishkapi with his questions after seeing Parashurama's rage.

'I have never seen Parashurama so angry. What lies in the Ellora caves?' asked Vrishkapi.

Back then, the Ellora caves were just another tourist spot for humans that drew travellers from all over the globe, being the world's largest rock excavation.

The Ellora caves, situated 29 km from Aurangabad in Maharashtra, were a series of cave complexes firmly entrenched in the rocky mountain face of the Charanandri Hills, comprising an assortment of twenty-nine caves that represented great historical significance.

One of the most mysterious caves in Ellora was cave number sixteen, which housed the Kailash temple. No one knew who built it and when. According to a legend, this temple was thousands of years old. No one had any information about its creator, nor did it have a carving date. The rocky mountain itself was 6000 years old, making the discovery of this temple unthinkable, unique and exceptional for that period.

Uncovered using the vertical excavation method, the Kailash temple represented one of the best examples of

constructional and structural innovation. The creators built
it from the top of the rock, descending their way to form
this great temple complex. One of the oldest rock carving
complexes in the world, it was composed of a multi-
storey building. To build anything out of a mountain, the
common approach followed was to break the mountain
from the back and sculpt it accordingly. It was called the
'cut-in' technique. However, the Kailash temple had been
built using the exact opposite, and a much more difficult,
technique called the 'cut-out' technique, where the sculptors
carved a single stone and crafted it into the Kailash temple.
Many scientists claimed that it was impossible to build the
same structure on any uneven mountain, even while using
the latest construction technologies. Yet, millennia ago, it
was built perfectly using only chisels and hammers. It was
the greatest achievement of its time and stood out as a
marvel in terms of its architecture, techniques and history.

'I am confused,' Mrs Batra said. 'Kailash is the name
of the Himalayan mountain range in which a camouflaged
town named Gyanganj exists. This is also said to be the
home of Lord Shiva, so how come there is a mysterious
Kailash temple in Maharashtra?'

Prithvi replied, 'The Kailash temple of the Ellora
caves was white in colour and was constructed using a
pyramidical design to resemble Shiva's abode in Mount
Kailash. The temple was so divine that its pious aura was
felt in its surroundings. It was a symbol of the piety and
the purity of the Hindu culture and aptly represented the
Vedic rituals. A sculpture of Ravana lifting Mount Kailash

was engraved in the cave, which was a historical milestone in the field of architecture. Archaeologists, researchers and enthusiasts from the relevant disciplines believed that the construction of these structures would have required discarding approximately 4 lakh tons of rocks. Yet, for some unknown reason, such a hefty mound of rocks was never seen piled up anywhere. Being in the most technologically advanced year of 2041, it's still an impossibility for architects to make something like the Kailash temple of cave number sixteen with the same perfection. It was believed that it took almost 150 years and the work of days and nights to carve the Kailash temple. None of this could be executed in practice today, thus reinforcing the belief that sages had blessed the construction of the temple.'

'So, was it constructed by some other, much more advanced civilization and not by humans?' asked Mrs Batra.

Replying to which Prithvi said, 'Vrishkapi had posed the same question, to which Ved Vyasa replied, "Because Parashurama was the one who carved the Kailash temple in approximately 351 years as his penance and devotion towards Lord Shiva. He did it after he was relieved of all his negativities. Parashurama was known to be constantly furious and ready to attack or kill, but after the Prithak Vyaktitwa Yagya, all those traits were separated from him, just as they were from Ashwatthama and Om. When he had undergone the process, he had learnt it and later performed the same on Ashwatthama to release him from his cursed body of leprosy and revenge.

"'Following the Vedic tradition and rituals, he conducted a *mahayagya* before commencing the construction of the

Kailash temple. After seeking blessings and permissions from the mountain for building the temple, he purified the rocks by chanting the mantras for purification and ignition of energy. It is believed that these mantras resonate in the caves even today. The temple and the place as a whole were blessed by sages, something which can be felt in the structure of the temple.

"'Many of those sages now live here in Gyanganj. They had performed the mahayagya before Parashurama started to build it inch by inch with his chisel and hammer. He worked night and day, chanting 'Om Namah Shivay' and eating rocks as he believed that not a piece of the mountain that he was carving for his idol could be thrown away as waste—hence, he consumed every piece of rock he had chiselled out.'"

While Ashwatthama and Om were heading back to Kailash with Nibhisha comfortably clinging to Om's arm, Ashwatthama asked, 'Where did you get that mace from?'

Om pondered over it for a bit. 'I, too, wonder how I summoned it. I just thought that I needed something strong to set Nibhisha free and there it was, emerging right in my grip. Ever since I woke up after Nagendra's death in Kuldhara, I've been experiencing many changes that I am still trying to comprehend.'

Ashwatthama and Om reached Gyanganj's door, where Ballhaar awaited Om. Ballhaar charged at Om the moment he saw him. Om had already made up his mind not to hurt Ballhaar and only defend himself. However, just as he put up his guard, Ashwatthama roared to stop Ballhaar. It worked, though Ballhaar was still panting with the anger of failing to fulfil the orders given by Kripacharya.

'Let him pass, Ballhaar! You will not do any harm. I command it.'

Ballhaar unwillingly stepped back as Ashwatthama entered Gyanganj with Om and Nibhisha. Ashwatthama called out to Vrishkapi.

'Vrishkapi! Meet Nibhisha!' Ashwatthama said and Vrishkapi flashed an innocent smile, reaching out to the snake wrapped around Om's hand. Om let Nibhisha off his hand and she started transforming back to her original form. It was a visual treat for Vrishkapi as he was awestruck by the phenomenal sight. He had never seen any creature like her before, yet he wasn't afraid but overjoyed to see a creature so stunning and adorable at the same time.

After Nibhisha had turned into her gigantic self, Om said, 'Nibhisha! He is your guardian from now on and he will take you to the land where you are free to move in your original shape and be as you wish to be. You must obey him and be a good girl. Now, go along. I will visit you soon.'

Nibhisha greeted Om with her usual embrace and looked at Vrishkapi to lead the way. An enthused Vrishkapi bowed his head and led Nibhisha under his supervision, like a child bringing his friend to show his home.

Ashwatthama let out a sigh of relief, looking back at how events had unfolded but had now come to a positive closure in Gyanganj. However, the relief was short-lived.

Ved Vyasa came rushing to him and informed him of Parashurama's whereabouts and that he was looking for him.

Without wasting another moment, Ashwatthama left for Ellora and took Om along because this time, he was confident that Om was ready.

In the middle of Shravan (July), the number of confirmed Covid cases had touched one million in India. People's movements were restricted as a strict lockdown was imposed, and to millions in the world, it felt like the wrath of the gods against man's ill-treatment towards the greatest gift bestowed unto him, that is, nature itself. Monsoons had begun to drench the country and tourism was diminishing owing to the endless lockdowns and ever-changing Covid-19 guidelines issued by the government.

Parashurama had reached the Ellora caves. Unlike the regular days, when it was full of tourists and devotees, it was as vacant as an undiscovered terrain. The sheer silence of the place was alarming. Parashurama decided to stay in the caves to keep an eye on and guard the temple night and day, till the month of Shravan was over.

In Odisha, the asuras sent by King Bali, with orders to summon Vibhishana, had reached the Jagannath temple in Puri. They were disguised as policemen so that their movement on the roads of Puri and inside the Shree Mandir (Jagannath temple) wouldn't be restricted. Only a handful of priests were present inside the premises for the daily rituals, an unusual sight compared to the otherwise crammed pavilions with hundreds of priests sitting there and offering their services to the tourists during the pre-

Covid times. The asuras took off their shoes outside the
temple and walked in. Because they were serving the
righteous demon King Bali and keeping themselves away
from all evil deeds, they all managed to step into the temple
unharmed. Though Vibhishana looked as ordinary as every
other member there, the asuras could easily identify one
of their own clan. Vibhishana was barefoot, wearing the
same off-white clothing as every other priest. He was
cleaning one of the statues and chanting prayers. As they
started approaching him, he too, identified them despite
their disguises and walked towards one corner of the temple
where no one could see them. The asuras silently followed
him and found him standing at a dead end behind the main
block of the temple. All the asuras bowed in front of him.

'What brings you here?' asked Vibhishana, trying to
read their faces.

'King Vibhishana! We have come on the orders of King
Bali. Because he cannot step out of Sutala and on the surface
of the earth before Onam in the month of Ashwin (August),
he has summoned you urgently to Sutala,' said one of the
asuras with the highest degree of respect and submission.

'Hmm . . . I am aware that he can only walk on land
during the festival of Onam on the orders of Lord Vishnu.
I am between my prayers, which will take a few days to
complete. Give my regards to King Bali and assure him on
my behalf that I shall come and visit him once I am through
with my prayers,' said Vibhishana, ordering the messengers
and expecting them to leave, but they continued to stand
with their heads held low.

Realizing that none of them was budging despite his assurance, he asked, 'What is it?'

'Our orders are to return with you, King Vibhishana. We shall wait here for you,' said the asura hesitantly.

Anticipating something more to the situation, Vibhishana asked, 'Is there anything else I should know? Speak freely.'

'Lord Parashurama visited King Bali right before we were ordered to bring you to Sutala,' replied the other asura.

This was unexpected for Vibhishana and so he asked again to be certain. 'Lord Parashurama himself came to Sutala in Pataal Lok to meet King Bali?'

'Yes, King Vibhishana! And right after he left, we were ordered to find you.'

Lord Parashurama's visit to the underworld was enough for Vibhishana to understand how critical and urgent the matter must be.

'Let's go!' said Vibhishana before closing his eyes and bowing down in apology for leaving the course of prayer midway and seeking permission from his lord to go. Crossing all the asuras, he then walked towards the main gate of the temple. All the other priests wondered what crime he had committed to be arrested by the police and taken from the temple.

Vibhishana left to meet King Bali as Ashwatthama and Om trudged their way to Parashurama at Ellora. It would take a few days for Ashwatthama and Om to reach Parashurama but by then, on the other side, Nagendra and the team were inching closer to the coast of Maharashtra, headed towards the same destination. LSD's baby bump and Parimal's concerns for her were prominently growing and were obvious to Nagendra as they stepped on land again, unaware that Parashurama awaited them in Ellora.

Chapter 11

Tricked

Nagendra and the team had stepped into the Ellora caves. A cautious Parimal, leading the way for LSD and Nagendra, spotted Parashurama from a distance, sitting with his eyes wide open like a vigilant combatant scanning every minuscule movement around him. Parimal recognized Parashurama from the Ross Island battle, when Ashwatthama and Parashurama had attacked the interrogation facility to rescue Om. He instantly stopped LSD and Nagendra, asking them to step back.

'What's wrong?' asked Nagendra.

'We can't go any further. Parashurama is waiting for us.'

'He's seen your faces, not mine,' answered Nagendra confidently.

'Ashwatthama and the others might be around as well,' warned Parimal.

Nagendra gave it a thought before pulling out a tattered piece of folded paper and handing it to LSD. 'Your death is certain this time if he spots either of you, so split up and be hidden. Keep an eagle's eye on him. If he suspects your presence, your end is inevitable.'

Listening to these words, Parimal could only think of his wife and their unborn child and posed a request to Nagendra. 'Don't let her be here. We should simply send her as far away from here as possible. Let me do this alone.'

'She is stronger than you are and sharper than you think she is. She is not going anywhere,' said Nagendra, turning down Parimal's request. LSD handed an advanced micro-Bluetooth device to both and kept one set for herself.

Parimal was angry, LSD was happy to see his concern for her and Nagendra was determined to achieve his target. They split up and went in three different directions. LSD and Parimal took their positions to keep a check on any movement from Parashurama while also searching for other immortals around.

As they parted to take up their positions, LSD and Parimal heard Nagendra's voice in their earpieces.

'The Ellora caves are over 2 km long and the only advantage we have here is that Parashurama does not know the exact location of the hidden word that he is here to save. Parimal, launch your drone and scan if there is any other immortal in or around the temple premises. LSD, once Parimal confirms the positioning of other immortals, if any, make your way inside the temple without being seen and keep the paper I've given you safe. It will guide you to the spot of the next word and you are going to extract it for me. I shall take advantage of the fact that

Parashurama has never seen me before and keep him distracted.'

Parimal and LSD received their orders as Nagendra walked straight towards Parashurama. Nagendra looked young and handsome and showed no signs of an asura, which was what Parashurama was expecting to deal with. Nagendra was not even on Parashurama's radar as he had been told that Ashwatthama had killed the old Nagendra and seen him dead with his own eyes in Kuldhara. This made it easy for Nagendra to walk in plain sight and get close to Parashurama. LSD kept an eye on Parashurama as Nagendra approached him while waiting for Parimal's clearance to walk into the temple. To ensure LSD's safety more than anything else, Parimal launched the drone to scan the entire vicinity and the premises of the Ellora caves in search of any other immortals that may be hidden anywhere else.

And then, Parashurama saw a young male walking towards him. Nagendra was dressed like the average young man and was ambling towards Parashurama with a smile as if he wanted to ask him something about the place or was perhaps looking for directions. Yet, Parashurama couldn't ignore the suspicion bubbling in his mind as he thought, *who is this young man and what is he doing here when even tourists are not allowed?*

'Stop! Who are you?' asked Parashurama.

'हा माझा तुम्हाला प्रश्न असावा, आजोबा!' (That should be my question to you, Grandpa!)

Nagendra argued in the local Marathi dialect, still walking confidently towards Parashurama, appearing like an ordinary mortal who was clueless about the man he was addressing as Grandpa.

'लॉकडाउन लागू होईपर्यंत सर्व गुहा बंद आहेत हे तुम्हाला माहीत नाही का?' (Don't you know all the caves have been closed since the lockdown was imposed?)

Parashurama re-checked his outfit. A simple shirt, jeans, basic chappals and two kukris, the knife-like weapon that the watchmen usually carry with them were what he saw, so he played along and replied like a tired old man. 'I am sorry, son. I was walking towards my home town with a group of young people like you, but my old legs could not match up to their speed and I lost my way and reached here.'

'तुला इथे कोणी पाहण्याआधीच जा नाहीतर माझी नोकरी गमवावी लागेल (Get going before anybody sees you here or else I'll lose my job),' Nagendra said in a cautious tone, pretending to be the guard of Ellora, because that was the only way Parashurama would comply.

'Oh! You are the caretaker,' said Parashurama.

'नाही! फक्त एक रक्षक. आता जा! (No! Just a guard. Now get going),' replied Nagendra, still in character.

By then, Parimal was sure that there was no other immortal accompanying Parashurama.

'LSD! You may proceed towards the temple,' ordered Parimal.

LSD had her orders and she immediately began moving stealthily towards the temple, taking cover behind walls so that she wouldn't be spotted.

Parashurama also turned and pretended to leave. Just when everything was going as planned for Nagendra and the team, a bird attacked the unidentified flying object in its territory. The blades of the drone injured the bird, and it was about to crash but Parimal somehow controlled it. The injured bird flew away, but there was a constant knocking sound from one of the blades that had a part of the bird's wing stuck on it.

The noise made Parashurama's ears perk up! He looked up, spotted the drone and immediately began looking around to search for the man who must be behind the drone stunt. Still pretending to be an ordinary old man, he turned to Nagendra, who stood right behind him, as close as his shadow.

Anticipating that his cover was blown, the moment Parashurama turned around, Nagendra pounced on him, stabbing him ruthlessly with two identical *khukri* knives in his hands. These knives were sharp enough to slash through anything in a single swing.

By the time Parashurama realized he was under attack, he had already sustained several deep cuts due to the 'wedge effect' of the khukri, which was lethal enough to kill an ordinary human. Young Nagendra was too agile and swift for an ordinary human being, and Parashurama had noticed it.

Nagendra was still close to Parashurama, stabbing and slitting him all over. Parashurama shoved at Nagendra's chest so hard that the cracking of his ribs echoed through the air. By then, LSD took the opportunity to enter the temple, avoiding Parashurama's sight. Parashurama's hands were enough to throw Nagendra a few feet away. Thrown to the ground, Nagendra could feel his broken ribs piercing his heart as he tried to move. Parashurama was bleeding profusely but it hardly seemed to faze him. He was still unaware that the one attacking him was Nagendra, but seeing him lying on the floor like a dead sack, he decided not to waste any time on him and quickly moved towards the door of the temple.

Parimal could see it all from the camera of his drone and knew that he had to intervene before Parashurama could enter the temple and harm LSD. Parimal chose to engage directly as he sprinted after Parashurama, shooting at him. Parashurama turned from the temple's door and faced Parimal. Seeing the man shooting and running towards him doubled his rage as he recognized Parimal from the battle of Ross Island, where he had missed out on killing him.

Your death is certain if he sees you this time. Nagendra's words rang in Parimal's ears. The mortal Parimal was colliding straight with the mighty Parashurama, whose single blow was as lethal as any astra. Still charging at him, just a step before coming within Parashurama's reach, Parimal threw a smoke grenade between them. The time it took for Parashurama to come out of it was enough for Parimal to vanish and Nagendra to heal. When the smoke cleared, while searching for Parimal, Parashurama noticed the mole on the foot of the young man who had unbelievably healed as he began to get back on his feet.

Astonishingly, the young man showed no signs of the damage that Parashurama had done to him moments ago.

First Parimal, and now a young man with a mole on the exact spot as Nagendra's foot that Om had told them about. This was enough for Parashurama to comprehend the situation he was in.

Nagendra got back on his feet, dusted his clothes, picked up his khukri again and said, 'We have never been introduced properly! Hi, I am Nagendra! And I am one of you now! An immortal. Won't you guys throw a fresher's party for the new mate?' Nagendra's tone dripped with sarcasm and confidence.

Enjoying the look of disbelief on Parashurama's face, he slowly and calmly walked towards him to buy as much time as he could for LSD. 'I was the one who attacked Kripacharya and trapped both of you in Om's memories. Because that past, where you had your little vacation, was not only his to claim. It is equally mine,' Nagendra winked, deliberately annoying Parashurama.

Parashurama summoned his axe in anger, assuming that he would keep Nagendra from entering the temple, clueless of the fact that LSD had already infiltrated the temple and was searching for the spot indicated on the piece of paper. Moreover, she was receiving live instructions to gauge how much time she had to steal the word.

'I found the spot!' said LSD, and it reached her team.

'You have already met Parimal on Ross Island. Right?'

As Nagendra said that, the drone, still hovering over Parashurama, swooped down and clung to his back before electrocuting him. Parashurama trembled violently as an extremely high voltage ran through his body. This gave them some more time against Parashurama, but only till he grabbed the drone by its edge, pulled it in front of him and smashed it into pieces. As was his habit, Nagendra latched on to Parashurama's back, in the same way he had done to Vrishkapi at Roopkund and Om in Kuldhara. This time, he stabbed both the khukris into Parashurama's collarbone. While Parashurama was trying to dislodge the clinging Nagendra from his back, Parimal was trying to cut off his legs with a chainsaw he pulled out of his bag, but could only injure him.

Covered in several wounds, Parashurama was on his knees. In all these years of life and experience in combat, for the first time, he was witnessing the modern and utterly unscrupulous style of warfare that simply defined the ultimate quote of Kali yuga, 'Everything is fair in love and war'.

Oblivious of the havoc at Ellora, Ashwatthama asked Om, 'How did my own arrow backfire on me when we were fighting? Who taught you how to use the Naagpasha?'

'I don't know how it turned back on to you, and no one taught me how to use the Naagpasha. I just know it,' replied Om.

'What other weapons can you summon?' Ashwatthama was curious and the answer he received was startling.

'All of them,' Om shrugged.

'All of them! What other astras are there?' asked Mrs Batra.

Prithvi started explaining them. 'The list is endless, and it could take many lifetimes to possess all. I will tell you some that you must have heard of before and some that you ought to know as we proceed.

'Agneyastra, whose deity was the god of fire, was a fire missile and had divine powers that could shower fire following the natural cosmic principle. Almost all the warriors of the Ramayana and the Mahabharata possessed this astra, including Ashwatthama.

'Varunastra was the water weapon, used as a counter for Agneyastra. Once released, it would unleash a copious amount of water that could wash away everything. This astra, too, had been obtained by many in the Ramayana and the Mahabharata.

'Paraswapastra had the power to put the opponent to sleep on the battlefield. Only Bhishma possessed this weapon during the Mahabharata, and he was stopped by the gods when he tried to use it against his guru, Parashurama.

'Naagastra was a destructive, serpent-shaped weapon that was deadly enough to spread poison in the body. Many warriors possessed it during the battle of the Mahabharata.

'Naagpasha, as you know already, was a weapon that, once released, would entangle its target in hundreds of venomous snakes. In the Ramayana, Indrajit used it against Lakshman and even Om used it against Ashwatthama when he tried to escape Gyanganj.

'Only the Garudastra could release someone from Naagastra and Naagpasha. This was possessed by Lord Ram and Arjuna, although Om also had Sauparna, which would release bizarre birds and is another counter for Naagastra.

'Vayuvastra had the capability to create high-pressure winds that could sweep away thousands of soldiers in the blink of an eye.

'Suryastra had the power to dry up any water body and chase away any sort of darkness with the blazing light emanating from it.

'Indrastra, as the name suggests, was directly linked to Indra—the king of demigods in heaven, who had the power to release, control and execute thunder, storms, lightning and rain, and even decide how the rivers would flow.

'Twashtra-astra could create confusion within an army and make them fight amongst each other as enemies. It was once used by Arjuna during the battle of Kurukshetra.

'Sammohana-astra rendered the target unconscious and had the power to put them in a trance. Arjuna used it against the Kauravas' army.

'Parvatastra, if summoned, could cause the fall of a mountain straight from the sky and on to the targeted army.

'Anjalika-astra was the personal weapon of Indra. It had the power to behead the opponent. This weapon was used in both epics. Laxman had used it to kill Indrajit, Ravana's son, and Arjuna killed Karna using the same weapon.

'Sharanga was a bow that belonged to Lord Vishnu, which was also used by the Vishnu avatar Ram, and later by Krishna.

'Nandaka was the ethereal sword of Lord Vishnu with an indestructible blade that could kill countless demons.

'Sailastra was the counter to Vayuastra; this weapon was used by Parashurama to prevent the destruction during the submersion of Dwarka.

'Brahmastra was the most powerful, most lethal and the most captivating astra, capable of destroying an entire army in one blow. Apart from the warriors from all eras, during the Mahabharata, Kripacharya, Bhishma, Drona, Parashurama, Ashwatthama, Arjuna and Karna had all mastered the knowledge to kindle the power of Brahmastra whenever required.

'Bramh Shirsha astra was more magnificent than the Brahmastra: it had the power to shower meteors and was terribly dreadful.

'Narayanastra spluttered millions of blistering, fierce missiles. There was no way to escape except surrendering and lying low so that it would spare its target.'

Ashwatthama and Om were stepping closer to Ellora. While Nagendra and Parimal kept Parashurama engaged and away from the temple gate, back inside the temple, LSD was following the instructions to sequentially find the letters carved and hidden in different corners of the temple. She arrived in front of a specific stone carving of Ganadev, the troop deity, as mentioned in the paper and burnt the piece of rock that held the carving. After burning for a moment, most of the rock extinguished itself, leaving behind only a burning letter. The letter was 'अ (a)'. A few seconds later, the letter stopped burning, and LSD traced her thumb over it as if overwriting it. The moment she finished the trace and turned, she saw another carved figure of Vidyadharas, the demigods, catch fire. She walked towards it and once the next letter emerged, she repeated the same thing as instructed on the paper. One by one, it happened five more times on five different statues carved on the walls and pillars, and eventually, she had obtained the full word: 'अष्ट संग्रह (Ashta-sangrah)'.

Parashurama summoned his unconquerable and indestructible divine axe. The wind speed which accompanied the axe was so powerful that Parimal and Nagendra could not move an inch closer to Parashurama. The time it bought Parashurama was enough for him to revive. While he got up on his feet with his axe, Parimal was ordered to hide again. Parashurama was sure that Parimal had not entered the temple as he had kept an eye on the door all along. Now, the only one standing in front of him was Nagendra. Parashurama rushed towards Nagendra and went for his waist, cutting him in half with a single slice of his axe. In no time, Nagendra was lying on the ground divided in two but in the blink of an eye, he was back on his feet.

This was the first time that Parashurama was fighting another immortal and the second time in the past few minutes that Parashurama felt a sense of failure. Nagendra continued to challenge Parashurama to kill him, which Parashurama already tried twice, but Nagendra came back to life every time, laughing at him.

'We can do it till the end of Kali yuga, Grandpa,' said Nagendra, mocking Parashurama.

Parashurama was all set to strike again but a loud sound from inside the temple grabbed everybody's attention. He immediately ran towards the entrance of the temple. Parashurama was one step away from entering when he was suddenly thrown away by an invisible force. Parashurama fell a few feet from the door, wondering who had pushed him away. As he was getting back on his feet, he saw LSD leaving the temple. Just when he was about to charge at her, he saw a figure forming itself in thin air. Nagendra went closer to the emerging figure and stood there. Within moments, Parashurama saw Shukracharya standing between LSD and himself. It was clear to Parashurama that he would have to go through Shukracharya to reach LSD, who was walking away from Parashurama. In no time, she was nowhere to be seen and Shukracharya, along with Nagendra, stood at the temple's entrance. Parashurama was ready with his weapons to charge at both, but before he could, Shukracharya turned back and entered the temple and Nagendra ran to the side from which he had come. Parashurama's priority was the temple and therefore, he chose to follow Shukracharya.

Parashurama entered the temple but Shukracharya was nowhere to be seen. *He had vanished into thin air as he had emerged from it*, thought Parashurama and hastily looked everywhere to ensure that the temple was safe. He noticed that the temple was turning back into a boulder from one corner, slowly consuming the whole structure. As he turned towards the only door of the temple, he saw Shukracharya standing there, blocking the exit. Shukracharya's heavy voice roared through the temple and suddenly, several asuras unleashed from his body and cornered Parashurama, attacking him collectively.

Parashurama began to slay them all, but more continued charging at him endlessly. Some reached for his hands, while some grabbed his legs. Others piled on to him to stop him from reaching Shukracharya. Right in front of his eyes, Shukracharya walked out the door, turned around and stood there watching. Parashurama, who was still trying to free himself, could see Nagendra, Parimal and LSD joining the audience as they stood beside Shukracharya. Parashurama realized that it was the perfect opportunity for him to attack and finish all of them. However, what he did not realize was that the asuras weren't holding him tight to keep him away from Shukracharya but were restricting him from leaving the temple. The asuras were distractions who were there just to keep Parashurama captive till the whole temple structure turned back into the giant mountain that it was before Parashurama had carved it.

Even before he could have slaughtered them all and reached the exit, the door had returned to its original form from centuries ago, when it wasn't sculpted. The whole temple had transformed into the enormous mountain that it used to be, consuming Parashurama and all the asuras. The weight of disappointment, disbelief, defeat and dejection pushed Parashurama down to his knees again as he felt choked by the emotions of losing what he had built. He screamed out his location to Ved Vyasa in agony and in the pain of losing the temple. Nagendra, Parimal and LSD stood calmly with Shukracharya outside and witnessed the entire transformation before leaving.

Chapter 12

The Nine Avatars

The increasing death toll due to the persistent pandemic was a sign from the gods that the end of the world was nearing. Moreover, Mansarovar being consumed by Rakshastal, an avalanche destroying Roopkund, the Taj Mahal turning black, the ghost village of Kuldhara vanishing overnight, the destruction of the submerged Dwarka and volcanic lava evaporating Bheemkund added to the anxiety of every ordinary person that the gods were furious and that this was the expression of their wrath on mankind. The new addition to the misery that was fuelling the unfaltering fire was the unexplainable phenomenon of reverse engineering at Ellora.

Ashwatthama and Om had to leave empty-handed, wondering where Parashurama was. Soon, experts, scientists and researchers were flocking to the site to understand the unknown.

Back in Sutala, Vibhishana appeared in front of King Bali.

'Greetings, mighty king!' said Vibhishana.

King Bali smiled, stood up from his throne and hugged Vibhishana as an elder brother. Vibhishana reciprocated the gesture warmly.

'Come! Sit!' said King Bali, offering a seat to Vibhishana beside him.

Vibhishana sat and silently waited for King Bali to initiate the conversation and share the reason for which he had been urgently summoned.

'Vibhishana! I need your help in locating Shukracharya.' King Bali's voice was heavy with worry.

'I was informed that Parashurama had visited Sutala and now you are in search of Shukracharya. What's the matter, King Bali?' asked Vibhishana.

King Bali explained, 'It all started after someone named Nagendra got his hands on a book named Mrit Sanjeevani that was concealed since eternity. Parashurama believes that Nagendra is Shukracharya's prodigy and that Shukracharya is the one responsible for these catastrophes. Ashwatthama had killed Nagendra in Kuldhara but the destruction continued. Ved Vyasa is awake and believes that nine places contain the secret words, which, when put together, would serve as a key to some mysterious door that Shukracharya intends to open. Five out of those nine places have been destroyed because the words they held had already been stolen when Parashurama had visited me. Two more have been lost since he left, and last I heard, Parashurama has been missing too, ever since the Ellora temple turned into a rock.'

'And you wish to meet Shukracharya through me?' confirmed Vibhishana.

King Bali continued, 'Vibhishana! Shukracharya and his protégés are up to something so ruinous that Parashurama had to visit me, and I requested your immediate attention. Out of the seven immortals, only two of us are asuras, and that, too, successors of those who became the reason for four of the nine Vishnu Dashavatars till now.

'Dashavatar! Who is that?' asked Mrs Batra.

'Dashavatar is a Sanskrit word and can be simplified by breaking it into two. "*Dasha*" means ten and "*avatar*" means "incarnation". Thus, dashavatar denotes the ten primary avatars of Lord Vishnu, who is one of the three superior gods in Hinduism. Lord Vishnu was known to balance the astral order for the betterment of mankind and whenever the balance was disturbed by any adversity, Lord Vishnu would descend to earth as one of these ten avatars that I am going to tell you about now.

'King Mahabali and Vibhishana are the only members alive of the families of those asuras who were confronted by Lord Vishnu several times. In fact, out of the ten avatars of Lord Vishnu, four avatars had descended to earth because of Vibhishana and King Bali's ancestors and their deeds,' replied Prithvi.

'Four! That's quite a number!'

'Yes! Those four avatars were Varah, Narsimha, Vamana and Lord Ram,' said Prithvi as he proceeded further to explain the incarnations.

'Satya yuga saw these four incarnations of Lord Vishnu at different junctures of the yuga. Matsya avatar, being the first, symbolized the presence of life on earth, which was first found underwater. The purpose of Matsya avatar was associated with King Satyavrata, one of the biggest devotees of Lord Vishnu. One day, when the king was washing his hands in a nearby stream, he noticed a tiny fish quickly settling in his cupped hands, pleading with him to save it from the bigger fish. The king, as he was kind-hearted and benevolent, carried the fish back with him and put it in a vessel which it outgrew very quickly. Hence, it was shifted to another tank which became too small for her again. It continued to grow bigger than every container it was put in, until one day, the king ran out of options and was forced to take it to the ocean. Once the fish was free to swim in its new abode, it revealed itself as Lord Vishnu. The giant fish cautioned the king about the impending natural calamity that would destroy the entire kingdom. The fish also instructed the king to build a boat and carry the Vedas, along with the seven sages, the king's family and every important living creature to the other side.

'The second avatar that followed was the Kurma avatar, which depicted the struggles of life and how there's one chance available to set the record straight by staying determinedly on the righteous path. During the Samudra Manthan, the gods and the demons churned the ocean to obtain the elixir of immortality. A serpent named Vasuki aided the process by becoming the churning rope which was tied around Mount Mandara, which was the churning wedge. As the churning continued, it simultaneously eroded the mountain till it was about to sink. That's when Lord Vishnu agreed to transform into a giant tortoise and carry the weight of the mountain on his back. The descendants of the same tortoise paid the price of their life while guarding the well from which Nagendra and Parimal had extracted the word from the submerged city of Dwarka.

'After the Kurma avatar stepped the Varah avatar, which represented various aspects of sacrifices borne by a boar to uplift the earth from its darkest phase. The predecessor of King Bali, Hiranyaksha, once displaced the earth from the solar system and carried it to the galactic ocean. To stop Hiranyaksha and save the earth from being lost, Lord Vishnu appeared in the form of a boar. The Varah or the boar fought with Hiranyaksha for almost a thousand years and ended the battle after he massacred the demon, lifted the earth held between his two tusks and restored the planet to its orbit.

'The last incarnation seen in Satya yuga was the Narsimha avatar, the fiercest incarnation among them all. Hiranyaksha's younger brother, Hiranyakashipu, had been blessed with a powerful boon by Lord Brahma himself. The boon stated that Hiranyakashipu could not be killed in any of the *pancha bhoothas*,[5] i.e., neither be killed by a human nor by any animal, neither inside a shelter nor outside it, neither during the daytime nor at night, neither on the earth's surface nor in space, neither with a living weapon nor with an inanimate object.

---

[5] The five elements of creation and nature.

'Lord Vishnu incarnated the Narsimha avatar to stop Hiranyakashipu and his sins. Narsimha had the body of a man and the head and claws of a lion. His protruding teeth made him appear even more intimidating whenever he roared. Narsimha eventually stripped the demon Hiranyakashipu down at his courtyard door which was neither inside nor outside the house. He did so at early dusk which could be considered neither day nor night. His pointed and sharp claws ripped the demon apart, thus killing him with neither a tool nor a weapon. And throughout, Hiranyakashipu was forcibly laid on Narsimha's thighs, thus keeping him neither on land (earth) nor in space. Despite the protection promised by the boon, the way he was killed showed how Lord Vishnu neutralized the demon when he continued to threaten mankind.

'After Satya yuga ended, Treta yuga commenced. This era saw three more incarnations: Vamana, Parashurama and Lord Ram.

'Vamana avatar was the first avatar of Treta yuga and the fifth in the chronology of the ten incarnations. This avatar was also the first time where Lord Vishnu appeared in a complete human form, though as a dwarf, and was often referred to as Trivikrama—the one who conquered the three worlds. Lord Vishnu descended on earth as Vamana to save the demigods and to do that, he had to meet King Bali and subdue his pride. King Bali was the fourth heir of Hiranyakashipu.

'With his sheer devotion and atonement, Bali was able to expand his authority over all the three worlds, also known as Triloka. Lord Vishnu had incarnated as a dwarf brahmin with the intent to end the rule of King Bali. When he met Bali, he demanded three feet of land, equivalent to the size of his own feet. The moment Bali agreed to Vamana's request, the dwarf became so humongous that he covered heaven in his first step and stepped upon the netherworld in his second.

'Witnessing this phenomenon, Bali understood that the dwarf brahmin was none other than Lord Vishnu. To fulfil his promise, Bali put forward his head as the third and the last place for Vamana to put his feet on. Vamana put his last step on Bali's head, sending him to Sutala and blessing him with immortality, thus including him in the list of the seven immortals.'

Understanding the back story of King Bali and his connection with the old demons, Mrs Batra repeated, 'Hiranyaksha, Hiranyakashipu and King Bali come from the same lineage that compelled Lord Vishnu to incarnate as Varah, Narsimha and Vamana.'

Prithvi nodded and continued, 'The sixth incarnation is Parashurama himself. By now, I believe you have a fair idea about Parashurama and his accolades, and how he proved to be the best mentor.

'He was followed by Lord Ram, the seventh incarnation, who was a symbol of morality and the embodiment of truth. An unprecedented warrior, Rama was meant to end the reign of King Ravana, Vibhishana's brother. Since Vibhishana was a true devotee of Lord Vishnu, he chose to differ from King Ravana's ideologies and met Lord Ram to put forth his thoughts, unbothered about going against his own blood. This gesture and Vibhishana's undivided support granted him immortality, making him the second asura after King Bali to be an immortal.

'Treta yuga ended with the end of Ravana and his rule. This paved the way for Dwapara yuga where two more avatars, Lord Krishna along with his brother, Balarama, graced the earth. While Lord Krishna had descended to counter the wicked, Lord Balarama was the harbinger of wisdom, honesty, faith and simplicity.

'Eventually, Dwapara yuga ended and Kali yuga began, anticipating the final incarnation of Lord Vishnu. This avatar would demolish all evil and defy every unethical practice, and that would conclude the unrighteous events that have taken place in Kali yuga. This incarnation of Lord Vishnu would be able to end the existence of the most destructive era out of the four yugas and rejuvenate the world

'Nine out of the ten avatars that have occurred till date have slain numerous demons such as Madh, Kaitabh, Kumbhakarna, Meghnaad, Khar, Dushan, Mahiravan, Tadka, Haygreev, Banasur and even Kuvalayapid. Out of these asuras, Kumbhakarna was Vibhishana and Ravana's brother.' With this, Prithvi looked at Mrs Batra as if saying that his explanation had answered all her spoken and unspoken questions.

King Bali further elaborated to Vibhishana on why he felt they shouldn't get involved from either side.

'We come from a lineage of demons, but our loyalty is towards the gods. I told Parashurama that we would not stand against him, but neither would our armies fight against Shukracharya. I don't want to contribute to our ancestor's mistakes by allying with Shukracharya; however, I don't want our clan to become the reason for the end of the world as well. We are still burdened by the deeds of our predecessors and that is why, despite our boons, we are still asuras. We are still paying for our ancestors' deeds. This is not our fight, but we stand at a junction where we belong equally to both sides. I need your help to prevent it and it seems that only Shukracharya can do that at this point, being the guru of the asuras. So I want your help to locate him as he was once very close to your family.'

Ruminating on Bali's dilemma, Vibhishana said, 'That's true! Guru Shukracharya has been closest to my family once and has always been against the gods. Everyone is aware of his personal vengeance against Lord Vishnu. He trained and educated Meghnaad, the eldest son of my brother Ravana, and made him so powerful that Meghnaad defeated Lord Indra to conquer heaven. His victory over Indra earned Meghnaad the title of Indrajit. In the battle of Ramayana, Meghnaad had even bound Ram and Lakshman with the Naagpasha, bringing them to the verge of death. Shukracharya was the guru of my family, but he would never listen to me. He still holds me responsible for Meghnaad's death and Ravana's defeat at the hands of Lord Rama.'

King Bali insisted, 'Just help me find him. Some asura you know might be aware of a way to reach him. I will take the responsibility of convincing him out of this madness, but for that, it's imperative to find him. We will not partake in the war if it occurs, but we must attempt to prevent it.'

'I agree, King Bali. I will see what I can do to find him,' assured Vibhishana. 'For this, I request you to permit me to return to my kingdom in Lanka. I need to meet my army and the asuras and order them to prepare for what the future might bring to us. I need to brief my asuras before they leave Lanka in search of Shukracharya in all possible directions.'

While King Bali and Vibhishana were clueless about Shukracharya's whereabouts, he along with his triad were entering the submarine, exhausted after their fight with Parashurama. However, another surprise awaited them. At the entrance of the submarine and in all the corridors and engine rooms, they found a whole new crew of faces they had never seen before. Strangely, none of the crew members were humans.

'Don't worry!' said Shukracharya. 'These asuras had been controlling the crew by possessing their bodies to learn how to navigate the submarine as well as the machinery. They don't need those human bodies any more.'

'So where are the crew members now?' enquired LSD.

'They are stored in the cold room along with the provisions,' replied one of the asuras as he greeted Shukracharya.

LSD and Parimal exchanged a slightly worried look. They were the only two remaining humans on board.

Shukracharya said, 'We are very close to our final mission, and so, to remain hidden is our best weapon from now on. Congratulations, Nagendra, on your flawless plan to trap Parashurama. It was your idea that an immortal cannot be killed but imprisoned. For some time, the immortals will be a ship sailing directionless, without a captain. LSD needs rest and extensive care. From now on, she won't walk out of the submarine. Parimal! You are still the commander of the ship and all these asuras will follow your orders. Now go, resume your responsibility.'

Shukracharya handed him a slip that had the coordinates for the next two locations. 'Don't say it out loud!' alerted Shukracharya. 'Ved Vyasa will be listening. Just read the note and do the needful silently.'

'What was written on the note?' Mrs Batra asked anxiously.

'The instruction was to take the submarine from the western coast of Maharashtra to Mypadu Beach on the eastern coast, and their next destination was 370 km from Mypadu Beach—the Veerabhadra temple situated in the Anantapur district of Andhra Pradesh—which would take nearly nine hours by road,' replied Prithvi.

Veerabhadra Temple was the most intrinsically secured sculpture. The eternal art in the form of murals and depictions narrates the epic sagas from the Puranas, the Ramayana and the Mahabharata.

The temple was enshrined with a mound of Lord Shiva, almost 200 metres away from which was the big bull, Nandi, carved out of a single rock as per common belief. The Veerabhadra temple, locally known as the Lepakshi temple, was believed to be a marvel of Indian architecture and carving skills in ancient times. Its pictorial depictions of the country's immense history only added to the temple's exquisite charm.

In the temple premises, just beyond the Kalyana Mandapa, was a gigantic imprint of a foot. It always looked moist, irrespective of the weather, and symbolized the stomping of a footstep, which supposedly belonged to Goddess Sita. This temple had served as a pit stop when King Ravana was on his way to Sri Lanka after abducting Sita.

The water in this footprint was considered holy and a mark of respect for Goddess Sita.

Another astonishing element inside the temple was a unique hanging pillar among the seventy pillars on the premises.

'Hanging pillar?' asked Mrs Batra, trying to imagine and understand the physics of such a pillar.

'Yes! The hanging pillar. Out of the seventy pillars, this pillar was a testament to the engineering genius of that era. The sixteenth-century temple made of stone had this one pillar suspended from the ceiling, with only a paper-thin gap between the pillar's bottom and the floor. The tour guides used to prove the marvel of this pillar by sliding a piece of cloth through that gap without touching the floor or the bottom of the pillar.

'Once, in 1910, a British engineer named Hamilton, startled and awestruck by the incredible structural marvel, tried to look for architectural aberrations. In that process, he managed to alter one corner of the pillar, due to which there was a sudden structural shift in the exterior hall's ceiling with a tilt in the roof alignment, and pillars all around leaned on the adjacent one, thus disfiguring the series of the murals in the temple. The engineer understood very well that one more move would cause the entire temple to collapse. This led to a slight disorientation in the position of the hanging pillar. The attempt of the British engineer was concluded to be unsuccessful and after that, no one could unfold the mystery of the hanging pillar.'

In Aurangabad, Ashwatthama and Om were in Om's hideout, planning their next step. They couldn't decide between going back to Gyanganj or waiting there for further instructions. 'There is a question that often strikes me about you. Please allow me to ask,' requested Ashwatthama to Om. Om turned and seemed keen to know what Ashwatthama wanted to ask.

'Vidur was Ved Vyasa's son who was born in Treta yuga but you were born thousands of years before him in Satya yuga. How did you claim to be the half-blood brother of the fathers of the Pandavas and Kauravas?

'Vidur was the son of a handmaiden to the queens Ambika and Ambalika. Queen Ambika was the mother of the blind King Dhritrashtra, the father of the Kauravas whereas queen Ambalika became the mother of Pandu who later became the father of five brothers called the Pandavas. The father of all three kings was Ved Vyasa. He knew that the Kauravas and Pandavas would eventually fight each other in the battle of Kurukshetra and the war would consume everything. So he wished to have one son away from this and chose Vidur. Ved Vyasa knew about my existence; he met me and requested me to replace Vidur as nobody in the Kingdom knew what Vidur looked like. Because of being the handmaiden's son, Vidur was not brought up with Dhritrashtra and Pandu but was directly introduced to the kingdom while he was in his forties. The one who was taken away from the kingdom in his childhood was Vidur but the one who returned with his name was me on the request of Ved Vyasa to replace his son Vidur.

'Who you met before being cursed was me and nobody ever saw the real Vidur because he never returned to the kingdom. After the end of the Mahabharata war, I made a hut for Dhritrashtra and Gandhari, the parents of the Kauravas, and Kunti, the mother of the Pandavas, and then vanished into the jungle. What happened to the real Vidur and how his life ended can only be answered by Ved Vyasa now but I never questioned him. Because death is death after all, irrespective of how it consumes a mortal. But I have a question for you now,' said Om to Ashwatthama. Now, Ashwatthama was keen to know the question. Om said, 'How did I mistake your identity with the great Subhas Chandra Bose in 1945 when I saw you after the end of the Mahabharata?'

'You were not mistaken! As you did for Ved Vyasa, I replaced Subhas Chandra Bose on the flight to give him a safe passage. I have been a warrior all my life and he was a true patriot fighting for the land that belonged to me too. In other words, he was fighting for me and my land, and I dressed like him and took the flight so that the world could believe that he is gone. There was a pact that I still respect and so I don't want to open any more threads. In short, what I did for him is what you did for Vidur,' answered Ashwatthama.

This conversation stopped when Om saw the muted news flashing on a channel that showed three faces captured on a door's CCTV footage, walking out of the Ellora temple right after it had turned into a rock.

He instantly unmuted and the news anchor announced, 'Look at these three faces, walking out right after this tragic yet mystical incident of Ellora. Two of them have been identified. One is Parimal Nair, a PhD in Indian history and a professor. The other is Latika, who was born and brought up in a small village with her grandfather. There is no record of the death of her grandfather and the villagers thought that both were either killed or abducted from the village overnight. Since that day, she was never seen, but today, she was spotted with this history professor. However, the third young man in the footage is yet to be identified and no government records could be found on him as yet.'

Om instantly recognized Nagendra. Seeing his own face after yugas, knowing that Nagendra was still alive and now an immortal, too, was a feeling that Om could not describe in words. He had never felt as lost as when he saw Nagendra more real than himself.

Silent, depressed, yet adamant to stop him, Om said to Ashwatthama, 'Nagendra is alive! Look at the news. You recognize the two faces from Ross Island and Kuldhara; the one that you cannot recognize is him. That was my face before Dhanvantari gave me this life and Sushrut gave me this face. I suggest we request Kripacharya to lead our way. Can you call him here? Maybe he can guide us in the absence of Parashurama.'

Looking at the young Nagendra and realizing that he was still alive after being beheaded, Ashwatthama felt a mixture of shock, fury and failure. Without another word, he silently agreed to Om's suggestions and closed his eyes to summon Kripacharya once again.

Back at Gyanganj, Vrishkapi came rushing to Ved Vyasa. 'I need your help.'

Ved Vyasa looked at him and said, 'Tell me. What's bothering you, Vrishkapi?'

'I am bothering myself,' replied Vrishkapi.

'Vrishkapi, this is a very bad time to play riddles. If there is something serious, say it straight and clear,' said Ved Vyasa in a tense tone.

'Ever since Om has cured me, I am experiencing changes in myself,' said Vrishkapi with a genuinely confused expression.

'What kind of changes?'

'I can take more giant leaps than earlier. I can fly with an unmatched and unscaled speed. I sometimes feel I am weightless and sometimes, even the tiniest part of my body feels like I'm carrying the weight of a mountain. While meditating, I experienced flashes of powers that are elevating my height more than usual and sometimes even shrinking it to the size of a pebble. My soul, I feel, is now connected to another spiritual soul. My ability to recover from any injury didn't exist earlier when I was brutally wounded at Roopkund. I am fascinated by these changes I have been noticing, but I'm worried about losing control.'

'You come from the clan of Lord Hanuman himself and perhaps, these traits were always dormant within you. They seem to have been activated now after Om helped you recover. Maybe in true meaning, you are now blessed by Hanuman.'

Vrishkapi blankly stared at Ved Vyasa and asked, 'What do you mean?'

'The changes and the supernatural powers that you are experiencing are called Siddhi, and they can only be obtained through meditation and hard work, Vrishkapi. Lord Hanuman was granted eight such Siddhis that are reflecting in you.

'Verse 31 of the Hanuman Chalisa says, '*Ashta siddhi nava nidhi ke dātā, asa bara dīnha jānakī mātā*', which means Mother Janaki (Sita) granted Lord Hanuman a boon to become the bestower of eight siddhis (supernatural powers) and nine nidhis (divine treasures). Those supernatural powers are Anima, the ability to reduce his size; Mahima, the ability to increase his size; Laghima, the ability to become weightless; Garima, the ability to increase his weight; Prapti, the ability to travel anywhere and acquire anything; Parakamya, an irresistible willpower; Vastiva, mastery over all creatures; and Isitva, the ability to become godlike with the power to create and destroy.

'Your displays of supernatural powers are proof that not all but some fragments of Lord Hanuman's siddhis are now bestowed upon you since Om helped you recover. This is what you might need in the coming days, Vrishkapi,' said Ved Vyasa.

'So what should I do?' asked Vrishkapi.

'You are the warden of all extinct beings here, Vrishkapi, because you know how to tame them, keep them in control. Learn to control your powers. Train your powers to help you as and when needed. Learn yourself better, Vrishkapi. This would help you to defeat any threat, any adverse circumstance. I assure you, there is nothing for you to worry about at all. No one teaches a fish to swim or a bird to fly. They just know it and practise it regularly, and so should you. Practise understanding all that you are capable of.'

As Ved Vyasa guided Vrishkapi, he heard Parashurama's voice informing him of his location.

Ved Vyasa stood up hastily and said, 'Vrishkapi! You said you can fly now! How fast can you fly to Ashwatthama? I have an urgent message for him.'

Chapter 13

Boon or Bane?

The month of Shravan (July) ended and Bhadrapada (August) began. Unexpected challenges and catastrophes continued to knock on India's doors while the government and the citizens struggled on various levels due to Covid-19. The latest tragedy was the crash of Air India Flight AI344 at Calicut International Airport, Kerala, which had claimed nineteen lives. Kerala also had to bear the brunt of heavy rain that caused landslides, killing twenty-four people, trapping many and rendering several others homeless. Farmers began an intense protest against farm bills in northern India. India's GDP for the fiscal year 2020–21 had dropped dramatically by 23.9 per cent. The prime minister had laid the foundational stone of the Ram Mandir at Ayodhya, which covered the front pages of every newspaper, but far north at Kailash, before Vrishkapi could decipher what Ved Vyasa had asked him to do, he noticed perplexity on Ved Vyasa's face as he heard Shukracharya's words.

'Congratulations, Nagendra, on your flawless plan to trap Parashurama. It was your idea that an immortal cannot be killed but can be imprisoned.'

'This was all planned,' murmured Ved Vyasa, in dismay at not being able to understand it before.

'What happened, seer?' a concerned Vrishkapi asked.

Ved Vyasa looked at Vrishkapi and said in guilt, 'Vrishkapi! They used me against all of you. They had planned everything, every small step. They knew our reaction even before we reacted. They had anticipated every single move of ours from the very beginning. Once they had obtained the books of Mrit Sanjeevani, they knew we wouldn't stay quiet but would chase them. They deliberately left the trail evident so that we would follow it and be trapped. They knew I would try to locate them by tracing their voices, therefore LSD intentionally spoke of Ellora to Parimal, so that I would hear it and Parashurama would be there to defend it alone. They knew that dividing our strength would make it easy for them to handle us. Sending you to Roopkund was also a part of their strategy, not ours, because they knew that you can't be sent beyond that point and among humans, that is why they let me hear those first few locations so that we chose to divide our warriors and individually try to save each place.

'From trapping Parashurama and Kripacharya inside Om's past to capturing Parashurama in Ellora now, every bait was cleverly placed. By not letting us attack them together, they succeeded. They first tried to kill you alone at Roopkund; the wounds were fatal. Then, they attacked Milarepa alone in Tejo Mahalaya and burnt him alive. Meanwhile, Kripacharya was trapped alone in Om's past and then Ashwatthama was left alone to stand against all of them in the battle of Kuldhara. Nagendra, knowing himself well, was certain that after Om recollected his past, he would go in search of Nibhisha to fulfil his ancient promise and somebody would accompany him back to Gyanganj. That would leave Parashurama defenceless when he would head to Ellora.

'They were certain from the beginning that even if two immortals came together to stop their word hunt, they would fail, and so they cleverly kept all of them occupied or trapped. I was merely a puppet in Shukracharya's hands, telling Parashurama and Ashwatthama what he wanted to convey for the smooth functioning of his plans.'

Ved Vyasa looked highly disappointed in himself at not being able to anticipate this. Hearing all this, Vrishkapi was furious, recalling the heinous Nagendra who had so deviously killed Milarepa and attacked him from behind. 'I told Om that they are cheaters. They don't fight fair. See! I was right. They've been doing this all along. What are my orders, seer?' asked Vrishkapi, all pumped up.

'As I asked, how quickly can you reach Ashwatthama without being noticed?' Ved Vyasa asked.

'I discovered a few days ago that I can shrink to the size of a tiny insect, which means I can fly above the clouds in my normal form and then transform before I land among the humans. I will then recall my original self only when I find Ashwatthama and myself in a secluded space,' Vrishkapi gushed about his newfound abilities.

'Like Lord Hanuman! Very good! What else can you do?' asked Ved Vyasa.

Vrishkapi pondered for a moment, innocently comparing his powers to Hanuman, and said, 'I don't think I can lift a mountain.'

Hearing that, a small smile tugged at Ved Vyasa's lips. 'Until you experience it, manifest it.' He walked towards the exit of Gyanganj as Vrishkapi followed, hearing his instructions. 'Tell Ashwatthama where Parashurama is so that they can release him from Ellora. Tell him that no one should attack Nagendra alone. Also inform him that they're left with only two last chances to stop Nagendra and that now, neither do I know nor will I be able to tell further where they are headed for their next word. I am unaware of the final location too, but both these places must be south of Maharashtra. I am sure of that. Lastly, convey to him that Vibhishana and King Bali have decided to stay neutral.'

By then, Vrishkapi and Ved Vyasa were standing on snow at the exit of Gyanganj under the open sky.

'May Lord Hanuman be with you, Vrishkapi.'

Vrishkapi bid Ved Vyasa farewell and shot up into the sky with a sonic boom. The snow below and around Ved Vyasa's feet melted due to the energy that was radiated.

Parimal captained the submarine, surrounded by asuras who did everything exactly the way they had learnt from the men who now lay motionless in the cold storage room. He was concerned about LSD's health as she was now seven months along in her pregnancy. This was the time when she needed more care and attention, but there was no other woman in the submarine to attend to her in the last trimester. Parimal had so much to say to her and so he wished to be around LSD but could not see her unless he was permitted to. The only one who could allow him was Nagendra, who was busy embossing all the extracted words on to a two-foot-long and six-inch-wide copper sheet, in LSD's cabin.

The submarine sailed off the coast of Maharashtra towards a spot close to the coast of Sri Lanka, while the king of Lanka, King Vibhishana, reached his kingdom. The one who was dressed in ivory-coloured clothes and was merely a servant at the feet of Lord Jagannath in Puri was now decked in gold ornaments and clad in the robes of ancient kings as he entered his courtyard. Hundreds of asuras awaited him and greeted him in unison as he sat on his throne. He gestured for everyone to remain silent and then spoke in a grim voice.

'I have called this meeting for a vital purpose. I want our messengers to visit all our spies scattered across Hindustan and hand over my sealed letter to them within a week. This is an extremely critical matter and they should all be sent in search of the one mentioned in the letter. If they fail, we'll see the end of the world.'

Ashwatthama, too, was committed to preventing the war, as he sat down to meditate to summon Kripacharya. Hours passed, but Kripacharya was nowhere to be found. Although there was no progress in his search for Kripacharya,

Vrishkapi had succeeded in finding Ashwatthama and Om. He descended from the sky, shrunk himself to the size of a fly to remain out of sight and entered the hideout from the gap beneath the door. Then, through the window, he entered Ashwatthama and Om's room. Vrishkapi saw Ashwatthama in a deep meditative state and Om guarding him.

Vrishkapi decided to break his trance and said, 'Parashurama is trapped at Ellora, and you must free him. Ved Vyasa doesn't know where Shukracharya is headed next. We have two more chances to stop them and Vibhishana and King Bali will not participate in case the battle breaks, even if we need them.'

Ashwatthama opened his eyes as he could hear the voice loud and clear, but could not see anyone. Om was just as mystified to find no source of the voice. They exchanged vigilant looks and drew their weapons out.

'This voice resembles Vrishkapi's,' said Ashwatthama with a hint of uncertainty.

'Not just my voice, but my body too resembles Vrishkapi. I *am* Vrishkapi, sent by Ved Vyasa to bring this message to you,' came the reply in a strained voice, making Om and Ashwatthama raise their eyebrows.

'Show yourself immediately! Or else be ready to fight it out,' said Om.

The tensed voice said, 'That's the problem! I can't! I recently discovered that I could shrink myself and I did this to keep myself hidden from humans, but now I don't know how to get back to my original size. The last time it happened on its own. I shouldn't have tried this! Will I be stuck in this size forever? Oh, no! Please, help me both of you! This is driving me crazy. I am so tiny, and you both are so big!'

'Vrishkapi, stop panicking! Tell us where you are first,' Om asked, interrupting his ramble.

'Look here! Above the round thing fixed on this wall near the door,' said Vrishkapi, waving his arms.

They followed the instructions and came closer to inspect the wall. They noticed the tiny Vrishkapi standing above the fan regulator on the switchboard.

'Please help me!' Vrishkapi pleaded.

Om extended his palm, helping Vrishkapi fall on to it, and asked him to explain why Ved Vyasa sent him to them. Vrishkapi repeated everything and they realized that every tragedy since Mansarovar was just a part of Shukracharya's plan to keep the immortals divided and occupied.

A sudden knock on the door grabbed everyone's attention. Om helped Vrishkapi into his shirt pocket and Ashwatthama opened the door. Kripacharya stood outside the room in the attire of an ordinary man.

Kripacharya entered the room and was visibly displeased to find Om as he still didn't trust him. Om greeted him respectfully, but Kripacharya rudely ignored him and turned to Ashwatthama, 'You were looking for me?'

'Yes!' Ashwatthama confirmed and addressed the pressing issue without wasting any time. 'Three more locations have been raided since you left, only two spots remain to be hunted down and Ved Vyasa has sent strict orders to stick together while searching for Shukracharya. We must unite.

Please guide us in the absence of Parashurama,' requested Ashwatthama with joined hands.

'Om goes back to Gyanganj and we proceed from here to bring back Parashurama. After that, we shall figure out the locations of the next two words as well as of Shukracharya's protégés,' ordered Kripacharya with a rigid, expressionless face.

'And what do I do? Where do I go?' came Vrishkapi's voice from Om's pocket.

Before Kripacharya could utter his doubts, Ashwatthama updated him on Vrishkapi's state and posed another request. 'I got a glimpse of what Om and his powers are capable of when I saw him breaking a mountain in Roopkund recently, similar to the one at Ellora, and I believe he can do this quicker than us. I urge that we focus on the locations below Maharashtra and let Om and Vrishkapi free Parashurama.'

'I won't be answerable to Parashurama for any actions of Om and Vrishkapi, and you will be held accountable if anything goes wrong. This is on you,' said Kripacharya, tenacious about his perception of Om.

'I take complete responsibility for their actions,' Ashwatthama replied in a heartbeat and looked at Om. The trust between Ashwatthama and Om had not only been restored but was also strengthened further with Ashwatthama's confidence in him. Kripacharya agreed to Ashwatthama's suggestion, and they decided to stay there to shortlist some of the places while Om and Vrishkapi were free to rescue Parashurama.

Before leaving, Om took out a mobile phone, gave it to Ashwatthama and said, 'We will keep you posted and also track your location.' Ashwatthama agreed and kept the phone.

As Om and Vrishkapi left the room, Vrishkapi asked, 'What did you give to Ashwatthama?'

Om explained to him what a mobile phone was and what purpose it served in the modern world. Vrishkapi wondered why Ved Vyasa sent him so far to give a message and why he didn't have a mobile phone, too, to contact them in Aurangabad! It would be too complicated to explain the mechanism of network towers and their non-availability in Gyanganj, so putting that aside, Om said, 'Because Ved Vyasa does not like carrying a mobile phone. Besides, he doesn't need one as he can hear everything without a phone.'

'Yes! But he can only hear us, and his voice can't be heard without a phone. Now, after learning about the phone thing, I feel like a messenger pigeon sent to deliver messages. Even pigeons are bigger than me. What have I done?' asked the innocent, tiny Vrishkapi, disappointed in himself and slightly upset with Ved Vyasa.

After Om and Vrishkapi left, Ashwatthama asked Kripacharya, 'Where were you? I was unable to locate you.'

'Right after the incident at Ross Island, Dr Batra, an expert who was there during the interrogation, made many breakthroughs in medical science and suddenly vanished from the face of the earth. A few weeks ago, he was found dead on one of Gujarat's seashores. The DNA reports confirmed that it was Dr Batra's body, and that his death was due to drowning. I believe he had Om's blood and that played a vital role in Nagendra's immortality and in his own death too. What I can't understand is how his body reached the waters. While investigating that, I learnt that his dead body did not float its way there, but he was taken to the sea alive and what returned to the shore was a dead Dr Tej Batra.'

Ashwatthama understood what Kripacharya was trying to point out and confirmed, 'You think Nagendra is operating from under the ocean?'

'Had he been hiding on land, I would have caught him by now. Dr Batra was brought alive to Nagendra with Om's blood sample, in some ship or submarine, forced to give the sample to him and then released alive underwater for the fish to feed on. No man can swim back to the surface dead or alive from the depth of a submarine but fortunately, the tsunami that arose after the destruction of the submerged Dwarka brought the dead body from the deep waters to the coast of Gujarat. His wife was nowhere to be found, so his last rites were performed by the locals after the autopsy and DNA sampling.'

'The books of Mrit Sanjeevani ought to be where Nagendra is,' said an angry Ashwatthama.

'Yes! Nagendra is hiding underwater. During the investigation, I found an unknown speedboat that was spotted at Digha Beach a few months ago. Later, the same boat was spotted at Mandvi Beach and in the Gulf of Kutch when the incidents of Kuldhara and Dwarka happened.

Then it showed up recently in Goa and the coastal areas of Maharashtra, when the raid and the hunt at Ellora occurred.' Kripacharya showed the photographs of the boat to Ashwatthama, which validated everything Kripacharya had just shared.

Seeing the photographs, something dawned on Ashwatthama. 'This is Parimal's boat! It is the same boat that Parashurama and I chased from Port Blair to Ross Island to rescue Om.'

Kripacharya explained Nagendra's modus operandi: 'Nagendra and his team arrive at the beach closest to their location, carry out their search for the word and then hide in deep waters before silently travelling to their next location, completely hidden from the world. They take the speed boat from their vessel to the shore and return to it after their work is done.'

'So this means that if we find the vessel, we find them.'

'Yes! Now that they have left Ellora, there are only four coastal states south of Maharashtra and Goa that they could move to.' Kripacharya opened the map of India and pointed out the possible states: Andhra Pradesh, Karnataka, Tamil Nadu and Kerala.

'Instead of trying to find the location of the next word, we should find the submarine. If we find them, their quest is already over because this time we will be together, and our attack will be more lethal and more organized than before,' Ashwatthama agreed with Kripacharya.

It was a total of 2730.6 km of the coastline south of Maharashtra that they needed to search. As they began their 'Mission: Find Nagendra', the submarine was already closing in on Mypadu Beach in Andhra Pradesh, which was at a distance of 370 km from the Veerabhadra temple.

By then, Om and Vrishkapi had reached Ellora. Om stood in front of the massive rock and closed his eyes to summon the same mace that had helped him free Nibhisha. While Vrishkapi was still struggling to get back to his normal height, he saw the emergence of the mace in awe.

'How did you do that? This mace is awesome!' Vrishkapi gasped.

Om took him out of his pocket and asked him to stay away as he began breaking through the rock, which would send shards flying. Vrishkapi did as he was requested and waited at a distance to see what this magical mace could do for Om.

Om started hammering the rocky mountain with full force and every blow created a new crack, denting the mountain heavily. Looking at Om, Vrishkapi, too, desired to lift the mace and look like Lord Hanuman but for that, he had to regain his original self.

Om could sense his agony and while pounding at the rock, he said, 'You are physically the strongest among us, Vrishkapi. Right now, your weakness lies in your willpower and determination. Ellora is the place that Parashurama created with sheer will and determination and there could not be a better place for you to meditate and gain what is yours to claim.'

Om's words hit Vrishkapi deeply, as Ved Vyasa's words about how Parashurama had created the temple with a single hammer and chisel rang in his ears. Hence, Vrishkapi sat meditating in a corner in front of the huge yet weakening rock, with the sounds of Om's mace hitting it aiding his meditative state.

Back at Gyanganj, Ved Vyasa could hear the conversation between Ashwatthama and Kripacharya along with the striking of the mace on the rock to free Parashurama.

Several days passed as Nagendra and the others remained hidden underwater, as ordered by Shukracharya. It was time for the next move, so they reached the beach on the same boat. Less than half a day after reaching Mypadu Beach, Parimal and Nagendra were at the gates of Veerabhadra Temple, waiting for the priests to leave the premises at night, as the temple was open from 5 a.m. to 12.30 p.m. during the day and 4 p.m. to 8.30 p.m. They prepared to enter when they saw the last priest closing the doors of the temple and leaving.

Sticking to the plan, nobody uttered a single word about the place to each other, thus feeling confident that they could hunt for the word uninterrupted. Nagendra and Parimal broke the chains on the gate, entered the temple and identified the hanging pillar out of all the other pillars. In the dark of that night, Nagendra took out the same copper sheet that he was carving while they were hidden underwater. The copper plate had all the words they had extracted so far, from Mansarovar to the Ellora caves.

अविनासी अनादि अनंता | सकल जगत तिहुं-लो नियंता ||
यस्य प्राप्रोती अष्ट संग्रह |

He placed the sheet under the hanging pillar and moved it back and forth as if scanning it through the pillar's base. Moments later, light was reflected from the pillar on each word. It felt as if the pillar was inspecting whether all the words were correct and in sequence. This went on for a few minutes, after which the next word after Asht Sangrah (अष्ट संग्रह) began to emboss itself on the copper sheet, carved exactly like the rest of the words. The new and penultimate word they acquired was 'Sah Bhavishyati' (सह: भविष्यति).

In the next instant, all the pillars started to melt like burning candles, and the two of them walked out of the temple unquestioned and unchallenged, as if it was child's play. While Nagendra and Parimal made their way out of the temple, Parashurama, too, was getting closer to his hour of liberation. It would take half a day more of constant hammering to set Parashurama free, but before Om could free Parashurama with the power of his magical mace, he had already freed Vrishkapi with his magical words. The impact of Om's advice worked miraculously on Vrishkapi. At that moment, Vrishkapi grew not only physically but spiritually too. He opened his eyes and found himself in his original state. Looking at that, Om stopped the hammering. Vrishkapi stood up from his spot, trudged towards Om and asked for the mace. The subtle shift in Vrishkapi's energy was evident to Om, so he handed over the mace to him without any question. As Vrishkapi held it, it shone brighter than before, as if it was drawing unlimited power from Vrishkapi. After a few seconds, both Vrishkapi and the mace looked fully charged. This time, it was Vrishkapi's turn to request Om to step aside so that the shower of rocks wouldn't hurt him. Om complied and Vrishkapi laid his first blow on the rock, which was at least a hundred times stronger than Om's. What was going to take half a day a while ago, was done and dusted in minutes. The whole mountain crumbled down to pebbles and Parashurama stood tall in front of them. Vrishkapi walked to Om to return the mace, but Om refused to take it back.

'This mace suits you, Vrishkapi. While you held it, it looked as if it belonged to you more than to me. Consider this a gift from a friend. May this mace be with you always.' Vrishkapi accepted the gift with humility.

Nagendra and Parimal reached their speedboat before the break of dawn and left for their submarine in the dark. Once they entered the submarine, they handed the copper sheet to Shukracharya. As they left Shukracharya's cabin, Parimal dared to ask Nagendra, 'May I visit her? I just want to ensure she and the child are okay.'

'Good that you remember that you are not allowed to visit her cabin without my permission, Parimal. This is what I like about you. You learn things at once,' Nagendra said, but this time, Parimal wasn't enjoying the appreciation. He was rather annoyed by the unnecessary sugar-coating because he only wished to hear, 'Yes, you may!' But what Nagendra gave him instead was a 'No'.

Nagendra walked closer to Parimal, kept a hand on his shoulder and said, 'I understand that you're worried about her health, especially now when you know that she is surrounded by asuras and is the only female on board in your absence . . . and mine too. But I assure you, she is absolutely fine and resting, and for now, you should too. You have not slept all night and you look terrible. Go take a shower, sleep for a few hours and then visit her.'

Parimal was helpless. He couldn't do anything but bow his head and follow the order, which he knew was wrapped in fake concern. He went back to his cabin, ate and took a shower, and lay on his bed, instantly slipping into a deep slumber. He must have been asleep for a few hours when he was jolted awake by somebody's screams. Immediately he knew it was LSD's voice. He got up instantly from his bed and took out his gun from the drawer of his bedside table before rushing out of his cabin barefoot and shirtless, just in his pyjamas. While he ran towards LSD's cabin, her screams continued, and his fears, worries, assumptions, everything played in front of him like a movie. He was desperate to be next to LSD as quickly as possible. He reached her cabin but realized that the screams were emanating from another room, so he immediately rushed towards that door and flung it open.

The sight in front of him was unbelievably horrific.

There lay LSD on a stretcher with her hands cuffed and tied to the pipes above her head, while Nagendra stood beside her with a knife in his hand. LSD was crying for help, struggling to free herself. On sheer instinct and without another thought, Parimal aimed the gun at Nagendra, causing several asuras to surround Parimal with the intent to kill if he moved even an inch or tried to pull the trigger.

'Stand down! All of you!' shouted Nagendra, looking at the asuras behind Parimal. The asuras obeyed but remained alert. Nagendra then calmly looked at Parimal and said, 'You too, Parimal! Stand down!'

Parimal was sweating with anger and nervousness but refused to lower his gun. 'Wh-What are you d-doing to her? What is g-going on here?' asked Parimal, stammering in reality and not as he had once acted at Ross Island.

'Ohhh! Dear Parimal! Why do you think I asked the two of you to conceive after the raid at Mansarovar? So that you could fall in love? This was all done for the keyhole pupil-shaped eyeball that every child in your family brings to the world. I need neither your love nor your child. I just need that eyeball. Simple!'

Heart racing, and still stammering, Parimal spoke again, trying to dissuade Nagendra out of this madness. 'Ye . . . yes! Sure, y . . . ou can have it when the child is born but right n-n . . . now, it's just the beginning of the eighth month. The ba . . . baby is premature. It's not time yet for the child to be bo . . . born.' With his eyes wide open out of fear and concern for the unborn and LSD, Parimal tried hard to persuade Nagendra.

Nagendra gave it a thought as he did some mental calculations. Parimal started to lower his gun and LSD heaved a sigh of relief.

Looking at the asuras standing behind Parimal, Nagendra said, 'Sometimes he is driven by his emotions but overall, he is an obedient boy, and he will understand. Right, Parimal?' Nagendra looked at Parimal.

Parimal was willing to do whatever it took to bring LSD out of that cabin unharmed and so he agreed to every word Nagendra said. 'Right!'

To which, Nagendra said, 'Good! So the bilateral talks are over here. Now I am going to cut her open to take the child out alive,' and penetrated the knife into LSD's swollen abdomen.

Parimal could not believe his eyes and ears. Piercing through the abdominal walls and making a deep vertical incision, LSD's belly was now ripped and left open as she screamed her lungs out in excruciating pain. Blood gushed out with unimaginable force as her intestines, as well as the bladder, went under the knife. The congested cabin of the submarine, along with Nagendra and Parimal's faces, were coated with blood splattered all over.

With a cut so deep and so fatal, the water inside the uterus overflowed like a stream and the umbilical cord could be seen connecting LSD to a hard coating. This hard coating was the same thin and shiny layer that was visible in the previous ultrasound scans of the foetus. When Nagendra attempted to take the baby out, which was still nowhere to be seen, he noticed that the hard coating was actually an eggshell that was as big as an ostrich egg.

Nagendra drew the egg out of LSD's womb just the way he had been extracting words from different locations, causing catastrophes and bringing the very existence of those places to an end. As he placed the egg beside the dying LSD and cracked the shell open, everyone in the room was startled by what was unravelling before them!

A bright emerald liquid oozed out of the egg. This was the same liquid that LSD had previously consumed when the representative of Goddess Bhagavati had descended in the form of a giant snake with wings and gills to bless her at Parimal's mansion. As the liquid flowed from the shell and continued to spread on the floor, everyone saw an infant connected to the shell and the mother by the umbilical cord. All the asuras broke into a loud cheer upon seeing a human child inside a snake egg!

Parimal stood still as if frozen in shock and was too stunned to speak. LSD was bawling in pain, but her cries were drowned under the loud celebrations of the asuras.

On top of it all, Nagendra held the child and scornfully said to LSD, 'Shh! You are shouting right in my ear, Devdrath. Look how close I am. My eardrums might just burst. It will be over soon. You'll die in a few minutes, darling.'

And Nagendra was right. LSD gave up within minutes as the final scream escaped her lungs along with her last breath. A weak and premature infant drenched in blood cried out loud in Nagendra's arms. The asuras stopped cheering the moment they heard the baby crying.

Holding LSD's child in his hands, still attached to its dead mother through the cord, Nagendra spoke to Parimal as if nothing had happened. 'You were right! It wasn't the time for the child to be born, the baby is premature, but you see the keyhole pupil he holds in his palm has matured completely and is ready to serve its purpose. It is time for us to leave the submarine. We must surface the submarine to open the door.'

Nagendra seemed no less than a lunatic as he put the crying infant inside the open womb of his dead mother and prepared to detach the pupil from the infant's hand.

Parimal had lost everything with LSD's last breath, as all his thoughts about spending a peaceful life with her and creating a beautiful future for their child once they were out of this madness shattered right there.

'I feel sorry for you,' were her last words to Parimal. He did not want to see anything after he had witnessed his wife's dead face. He thought of all the words he had extracted with Nagendra and realized that there was no difference between the extraction of those words, which left the structures dead, and the birth of his child, killing LSD.

Before anyone could brace for it, Parimal aimed his gun at Nagendra and pulled the trigger. The bullet went straight through his head. Another fountain of blood painted the room red as Nagendra collapsed with a thud. The asuras grabbed Parimal tightly before he could shoot again. The infant continued to sob in LSD's open body, surrounded by her scattered internal organs.

Parimal had broken his oath and ended his loyalty to Nagendra. It was time for Parimal's boon to end and his human body to fade away. Suddenly, Parimal's vision began to blur and his eyeballs bulged out of their sockets and fell to the ground, to be crushed under the feet of asuras beating him. A layer of skin grew rapidly over his now hollow eye sockets. While Nagendra was regaining his composure, Parimal's lower half body was turning into a snake. While Nagendra's strength was returning, allowing him to stand again, Parimal's body was losing all balance, eventually falling in front of Nagendra. While one collapsed, the other rose again. Half of Parimal was now reduced to a helpless blind man and the other half of him was a spineless, crawling snake; all that he was now was a man without vision and a snake without venom. The asuras holding him began to claw and tear at him. All Parimal could hear and feel was his crying son and the pain in his entire being.

And as the child's cries intensified, Nagendra opened the baby's clenched fist and saw the eye embedded in his left palm. Without further delay, he pulled out a small khukri and made a circular incision around the pupil. The screams of the infant were deafening and would send shivers down any human's spine. But just as the submarine remained invisible to the naked eye, the baby's sobs were also meant to remain unheard by anyone, anywhere.

Nagendra then pinched into a corner of the eye with the sharp tip of the khukri before digging deeper to gouge the pupil out. His tiny little palm began to bleed profusely as the flesh was scratched out along with ruptured veins. The sight would have been grossly horrifying to any normal being, but to Nagendra, it was just another day. The moment he had safely extracted the pupil, the delicate skin of the baby's palm, which had been swollen till then, flattened instantly as if a door had closed.

Once he had obtained the most awaited and precious element, Nagendra's focus shifted from the infant to Parimal and the asuras. He signalled the asuras to stop torturing Parimal.

'You kill him, you gift him his freedom from all his suffering. You leave him half dead here, and he dies slowly, regretting shooting me despite knowing that I am invincible. Let him be,' said Nagendra and left, followed by the other asura crew members.

Chapter 14

The First Name and the Last Word

The asuras left for the other areas of the vessel, locking the cabin's door from the outside. Parimal was on the verge of death and the baby's wailing filled the room, resounding beyond the walls—the corridors also rang with its cries. Parimal was unable to lift his torso and reach his crying child, in part because of the deep injuries he had sustained and in part because his lower body had transformed into a snake. All he could do was stay on the floor, just underneath LSD's blood-soaked corpse.

Throughout his life, Parimal had secretly felt crippled by the boon his dynasty had been given, but today, he experienced true helplessness as he understood what it meant to be feeble and chained by one's disabilities. The baby's cries went on for a while and suddenly stopped.

Could I have done better? thought the blind Parimal, lying there in the pitch-dark, bleak cabin. The momentary silence disappeared when Parimal burst into violent sobs, gasping, screaming in agony, as he felt the heart-wrenching pain of reality. *No eyes to even shed tears,* he added to himself, screaming in pain. Bruised by the last few gruesome visuals of his life and weakened by excessive blood loss, Parimal, too, lost consciousness.

Just when he thought everything had come to an end, not one but two sounds pierced his ears and brought him back to his senses for a while. One was the sound of LSD's blood still dripping from the corners of the stretcher, and the second was of his child crying again, with the umbilical cord still attached to the mother's open belly. The dripping sound was a symbol of death whereas the crying was a symbol of life. Parimal felt liberated from the deception of blind love for LSD and was now imprisoned by the blind future of his child. With the realization that his baby was still alive—he could at least hear his child's voice, if not see it—another effulgent flash of realization struck Parimal: that Ved Vyasa could hear them too.

'Ved Vyasa! The final destination is Padmanabhaswamy Temple at Thiruvananthapuram!' screamed Parimal at the top of his voice, hoping to be heard and identified amid the sounds of the whole world that reached Ved Vyasa's ears.

He kept repeating the name of the location over and over again till he could barely utter another word. When he came close to his last breath, in a frail voice, he finally murmured, 'Save my child in this submarine closest to the beach near the Padmanabhaswamy temple. Save my child . . . in the subma . . . rine closest to the . . . beach . . .'

And with that, Parimal died! LSD and Parimal lay dead in the same cabin, never united, as the infant continued to mourn.

'Padmanabhaswamy Temple?' Mrs Batra interjected.

'Yes! The final destination,' replied Prithvi.

Staggered by the revelation, Mrs Batra grew more attentive as Prithvi continued to describe what was so special about the temple.

'Sree Padmanabhaswamy is one of 108 Divya Desams,[6] situated at Thiruvananthapuram, in the state capital of Kerala, India. "Thiruvananthapuram" in Malayalam stands for "the city of Lord Vishnu" (holy abode of Lord Vishnu). It was considered the richest place of worship in the world. The presiding deity, known as Padmanabhaswamy, depicts the emergence of Lord Brahma (the creator), seated on a lotus, from Lord Vishnu's navel. Hence, the name Padmanabhaswamy, where *padma* means lotus, *nabha* means navel and *swamy* means Lord. Here, Lord Padmanabhaswamy is seen in a reclining position or as the *Anantha Shayanam* (meaning in a posture of eternal sleep)[7] on the Adi Shesha,[8] the five-hooded serpent (also known as Shesha Nag).

'The temple often attracted people's curiosity due to the mysterious secret it held in a never-opened room of the temple known as Vault B.

---

[6] One of the 108 abodes of Lord Vishnu.

[7] The state of eternal sleep.

[8] The five-headed serpent also known as Shesha Nag.

'In 2011, it so happened that a retired IPS officer who lived very close to the Padmanabhaswamy shrine filed a plea in the Supreme Court to take stock of the temple's unaccounted treasury. The apex court appointed a seven-member committee to record and bring into account the hidden and unknown treasure. After the officials started looking for the treasure trove, they found six chambers and labelled them A, B, C, D, E and F. But opening the doors of those chambers proved to be a difficult mission. However, as they continued, the team apparently found gold, diamonds, rubies, sapphires, emeralds, intricately designed ornaments, precious gems and stones that had been donated by various dynasties over time. Statues and thrones of gold and precious metals worth rupees one lakh crore were also on the list. However, Vault B, traditionally known as "Kallara", remained untouched and intact, owing to the belief that whenever someone attempted to open the vault, it invited misfortune, jeopardizing the efforts. This belief was cemented when news of the untimely demise of the petitioner started making the rounds within just a few weeks of attempting to open Vault B.'

'What made Vault B so special? There has to be more to it than precious jewels, right?' Mrs Batra tried to dig deeper as Prithvi continued.

'Several myths and legends sprang up about the Kallara vault and its undiscovered treasure. The vault door looked heavy and impossible to open—if at all it was opened someday. It was also engraved with massive, detailed carvings. Yakshi, the ferocious and enchanting vampire, could be seen at the top of the vault, whose temperament, if disturbed, could invite misfortune. The carvings of two enormous serpents facing each other guarded the vault. Supernatural powers protected the door and thus, there were no latches that served as a restriction.

'Centuries ago, when the temple management attempted to open the Kallara vault, they heard sounds that resembled rushing waters and harsh waves. They were so vivid and frightening that the inspectors had to step back and abort the attempt to open the door. They are not alive to know that the sound they heard was not of waves but from other worlds. Since ancient times, the door was believed to have been sealed by the chants of an invincible mantra, and only an immortal of high calibre could obliterate the Nagas carved on the door with an accurate counter-chanting of the mantra, thus opening the mystic door. So everyone only wondered what lay behind the closed doors of Kallara.'

'Hmm, so you are saying that they tried every possible way to open the chamber, but everything was in vain, and only that one mantra has the power to crack it open? Wait a second! The words that were being collected . . . do they constitute the mantra that could open the door?' Mrs Batra was trying to piece together everything she had heard so far with the legends Prithvi was narrating about the temple.

Prithvi didn't immediately react to her doubts and continued.

'The Kallara door of the Padmanabhaswamy temple remained a mystery till the month of Ashwin (September) in 2020. By then, Nagendra was only one word short in his quest to complete the mantra,' Prithvi paused to look at Mrs Batra, affirming her budding doubts. 'These words were meant to be woven into a mantra which, when said aloud after offering the eyeball extracted from the infant's palm, would open the doors of the inscrutable, enigmatic Kallara.'

When the news of the collapsed Veerbhadra temple reached the ears of the immortals, they realized they needed to search a smaller area as Andhra Pradesh had been ruled out. The chances of finding Nagendra now were narrowed down. While Ashwatthama and Kripacharya were yet to search the coastlines of Kerala and Tamil Nadu, covering 569.7 km and 906.3 km, respectively, to locate the hidden vessel, Parashurama, Om and Vrishkapi were on their way to reunite with Ashwatthama and Kripacharya.

As Nagendra's submarine moved closer to the land near the Padmanabhaswamy temple, Parimal's voice caught the attention of Ved Vyasa back at Gyanganj, as he heard his own name in the wretched voice of a dying Parimal, with an infant crying inconsolably in the background.

'Ved Vyasa! The final destination is the Padmanabhaswamy temple, Thiruvananthapuram. Ved Vyasa! The final destination is the Padmanabhaswamy temple, save my child . . . in the subma . . . rine closest to the . . . beach . . .'

Ved Vyasa could not waste another second in giving the immortals their last and only good chance at stopping Nagendra and Shukracharya. He had to inform them of the new revelation before it was too late. He hurried to the other sages and ordered them, 'Get the Pushpak Vimana ready.'

'Pushpak Vimana! The one Ravana had used when he kidnapped Sita?' Mrs Batra asked, joining the dots between the airborne vehicle and the Ramayana.

Prithvi replied, 'Yes! People think it is a myth because they want people to think that way. Everything written in the Vimana Purana about how the heavy vessels flew at that time using mercury as their fuel is true. After defeating Ravana, Lord Ram returned to Ayodhya in the same Pushpak Vimana, after which it was never mentioned, heard of or seen anywhere. Gyanganj was a haven not just for extinct species, but also to conceal everything that humans were not equipped to understand back then, including the immortals and their astras, which the humans are still not equipped to comprehend.'

Ved Vyasa then walked out of Gyanganj and shouted, 'Ballhaar!'

The Yeti came running and bowed to Ved Vyasa. 'I appoint you the warden of the jungle of Gyanganj in the absence of Vrishkapi. Summon all the extinct animals and wait for my orders.'

Suddenly, a swift wind blew past and the incredible Pushpak Vimana emerged above, navigated by the sages. It landed right outside Gyanganj, waiting for Ved Vyasa to board.

'Be ready, Ballhaar—if the vimana returns without me, board all the animals under your protection.' Those were Ved Vyasa's final instructions for Ballhaar.

'I will follow Parashurama's voice to their location and you will follow my directions,' Ved Vyasa said to the sages

piloting the vimana. In no time, the Pushpak Vimana was
flying above the clouds over the Himalayas and rushing
southwards.

In one of the cabins at the rear end of the submarine,
Nagendra was on his knees and Shukracharya was holding
his head with both hands. There was a mystic aura engulfing
Nagendra as a magnetic wave flowed from Shukracharya's
hands to Nagendra's body. This was the same energy
that Parimal and LSD had experienced initially around
Shukracharya whenever they found themselves near him
or his cabin.

'You have half of my powers to stand against them,'
said Shukracharya, granting him the powers.

Suddenly, the submarine's progress came to a halt when
a virus hacked their entire system. No asura inside the
vessel had the slightest clue how to regain access through
the control panels. The only two experts, LSD and Parimal,
were no longer there to stop the unforeseen alien intrusion.
Before the asuras could understand anything, a deep
voice boomed inside the submarine through an unknown
frequency.

'I know you are in this vessel, Guru Shukracharya, and
I wish to have a dialogue with you.'

The spies Vibhishana had sent had solved the mystery of
Shukracharya's hideout through the asura informers.

There was pin-drop silence for a minute before
Shukracharya responded to the voice. 'It's been several
centuries, Vibhishana, but to my disappointment, I can still
recognize the voice of the traitor who wears the crown of

death and the defeat of one of my favourite protégés. What compelled you to search for me?'

'There have been a series of unprecedented events across India and some believe that you are responsible for all of them. On behalf of King Bali and myself, I request you to cease whatever your plan is,' said Vibhishana in a respectful yet cautioning tone.

Shukracharya walked towards the control room and ordered the asuras to disconnect all communication from the outer world, including the radars and navigation systems. Vibhishana had received his answer through Shukracharya's disconnected silence as he saw the submarine disappear underwater to resume its course.

Knowing that Nagendra's next destination was in one of the two southernmost states, Kripacharya and Ashwatthama had chosen Ross Island as their base. The island was placed almost perfectly between the two coasts. They informed Om of this through the phone he had given them before parting. Ved Vyasa's vimana had also now reached Ross Island, following the voice of Parashurama.

All of them stood united in the ruins of the same facility on Ross Island which Ashwatthama and Parashurama had destroyed when they rescued Om.

'It is a door, protected by snakes, that has neither a keyhole nor a key to open it. A door locked by the verse. The verse was the key that was broken and scattered so that one could never imagine breaking into it. But now, they are just one word away from re-compiling the verse and opening the door. The place where they will be found is the Padmanabhaswamy temple,' Ved Vyasa informed the immortals.

The submarine was close to Kovalam Beach in Kerala, and Nagendra hopped into a boat to get to shore, followed by Shukracharya and the other asuras accompanying him. From the beach, the map showed a distance of only 18 km by road to reach Padmanabhaswamy temple, whereas the immortals were still a few hours away.

At Ved Vyasa's request to save the child and get Mrit Sanjeevani back, Parashurama had no choice but to split the team again.

'Your mission is to get the books of Mrit Sanjeevani and destroy the vessel so that this time, Nagendra and the others cannot escape like before. Any living being inside the submarine other than the infant is your enemy and we must show no mercy,' Parashurama said, looking at Kripacharya and Vrishkapi before dropping them near the submarine with Ved Vyasa and leaving for the temple.

On their way to the temple, Parashurama was quiet as a placid lake, which discomfited Ashwatthama and Om. Breaking the silence in the Pushpak Vimana, Ashwatthama asked, 'Parashurama! Please guide us. What is our plan of action?'

Staring into oblivion, Parashurama replied calmly, 'We will bring him down to a state where he will curse himself for being an immortal and request us to grant him the boon of death.'

While Parashurama and Ashwatthama were certain that they were already too late to save the last word, Ved

Vyasa was trying to arrive in time to save a life and retrieve the books of Mrit Sanjeevani as he followed the trail of an infant's fading voice in the deep waters.

The boat carrying Ved Vyasa, Kripacharya and Vrishkapi reached 8^{0}21'25"N, 076^{0}56'12"E, right above the submarine, and stopped on Ved Vyasa's orders.

'The submarine is right below us, but it needs to be brought to the surface. The books of Mrit Sanjeevani will be lost forever and the child will die if we destroy the doors of the submarine underwater,' said a concerned Ved Vyasa, looking at Kripacharya and Vrishkapi.

'I can do this!' Vrishkapi said confidently. Both Kripacharya and Ved Vyasa looked at him doubtfully.

Vrishkapi persuaded them, 'Please, allow me to get into the water. Let me try.'

'Okay, Vrishkapi, but don't risk your life like you did the last time,' replied Ved Vyasa.

Vrishkapi dove into the water, keeping his focus intact, and continued to enlarge his size as he went deeper and deeper. The submarine's radar could not detect his presence because the vessel's comms and radar had already been disconnected on Shukracharya's orders. Vrishkapi grew to his maximum size and before the asuras had the slightest inkling, the entire submarine rattled, everyone lost their balance and tumbled to the floor. Vrishkapi then clutched the submarine like a child grabs a toy. Holding it in his palm, he swam back to the surface of the Indian Ocean, where Kripacharya and Ved Vyasa awaited him.

However, they weren't the only ones anticipating someone's arrival.

The Pushpak Vimana landed close to the Padmanabhaswamy temple. The awed locals couldn't help but capture the marvellous sight of what looked to them like an ancient, alien ship on their cell phones, too apprehensive to go near the unidentified flying object. Suddenly, at the exact moment when Parashurama, Ashwatthama and Om stepped down from the vimana, all mobiles and other technological systems, including CCTV cameras, in the area crashed. This was the impact of ancient technology on the present one. People's gaping faces peeked out of their car windows to see the three men walking out, but they could no longer record what they were witnessing. The three of them rushed into the temple, afraid of having already lost the last word.

With the ray of hope to save the last word quickly diminishing, the three men reached Vault B and found Nagendra and Shukracharya with a few asuras there. After their confrontation in Kuldhara, it was time for Om and Nagendra to confront each other again. After the three immortals presented themselves, they expected Shukracharya and Nagendra to be shocked but strangely, that didn't happen.

Nagendra looked at Om and started clapping like a madman. 'Parimal, after all, unknowingly performed his last task successfully,' said Nagendra in excitement and continued, 'Why do you think I left him alive in the submarine? Everyone knows what a father would do for his dying son right, Om? Oh . . . I wish I could've thanked that snake and told him that I was counting on him to reach out to Ved Vyasa on my behalf. Nevertheless, at least I can still thank Ved Vyasa for sending me the last piece of the puzzle after winning the war of this earth. I am so relieved you came, Om! What would I do without you?'

Om and the other two immortals standing on either side were astonished by Nagendra's statement, clueless about its implication. Shukracharya held the keyhole-shaped pupil eyeball in his hand. Parashurama had his eyes on Shukracharya, and Ashwatthama was set to handle all the other asuras while both sides waited for the other to charge first. Elsewhere, the wait was over for Kripacharya—he was ready to take on the asuras guarding the submarine.

It was Kripacharya and Vrishkapi versus the asuras, who rushed out of the vessel to stop them both. Vrishkapi had regained his normal stature and accompanied Kripacharya in fighting off the asuras with the mace Om had gifted him.

They moved farther into the submarine while protecting Ved Vyasa from any threat and scanned every cabin and corner that they passed. Vrishkapi's mace incessantly shoved away all the asuras that attempted to obstruct them. They came to a momentary halt near the cold storage and found heaps of half-eaten, decomposing corpses. Resuming their search, Kripacharya's wrath was enough to knock down the asuras guarding the cabins. Witnessing such ruthless combatants, the other asuras ran away to escape a brutal end to their lives, but none succeeded.

Crossing the long corridor, the three reached a closed cabin door. They swung the cabin door open and saw two blood-soaked corpses and another body that looked deceased but was still breathing. The infant lying smeared in the muck of blood and an emerald fluid caught Ved Vyasa's attention. Vrishkapi approached the stretcher and saw LSD lying dead—and on the floor was the lifeless Parimal.

'What happened to this man's eyes?' asked Vrishkapi, pointing towards Parimal.

'He is now finally free and has attained salvation from the curse that had started millennia ago with Aghasura. It was bound to happen someday and maybe this is the way it was meant to be. That's the law of destiny,' Ved Vyasa answered Vrishkapi.

Hearing the voices, the infant responded with a cry.

'It's a miracle how a premature baby born under such circumstances was still alive,' Mrs Batra wondered out loud.

'It was protected by the powers that the representative of Goddess Bhagavati had blessed LSD with. Goddess Bhagavati's power stood strong against the unusual process of an infant's delivery. The purpose behind that auspicious prayer in Shetpal had been fulfilled, just as Parimal had assured LSD,' said Prithvi.

Ved Vyasa scanned the baby and then quickly clamped the umbilical cord, cradled the baby in his arms and detached him from his mother. After wiping his body clean of all the blood and fluid, he securely wrapped the baby in his stole. The baby was alive and was now in safe hands.

Soon, they reached the door of Shukracharya's cabin and in a single blow, Vrishkapi's mace smashed down the metal door. Kripacharya began searching the room hastily and found the books on a platform in a corner. 'Wasn't it too easy for us to find the books of Mrit Sanjeevani? This could be a trap!' Vrishkapi alerted them and scanned the room for any hidden threats.

'Relax, Vrishkapi! There is no one here,' Ved Vyasa assured him and continued, 'The books were important to them only as long as the words had not been extracted from all the locations. Now that they have the words as well as immortality, the books are insignificant to them.' The three walked out of the submarine and Kripacharya summoned a fireball, propelling it towards the vessel and setting it ablaze. With the books of Mrit Sanjeevani and the infant now in their possession, as they walked away from the burning submarine, Vrishkapi innocently asked, 'Have we won the war?' 'Maybe! Though I wonder where the last word is hidden,' said Ved Vyasa, listening to the conversation between Parashurama and Shukracharya happening in the Padmanabhaswamy temple.

Ved Vyasa could hear Parashurama roaring in rage, 'Guru Shukracharya! I give you one last chance to stop this. Surrender all the stolen words and return alone. For all that Nagendra has done, we will take him into our custody and end it without barbarity.'

Parashurama and the team were certain that Shukracharya would never accept their proposal, but the surprises were not yet over.

'I am ready to surrender all the words,' Shukracharya replied and Nagendra began chanting all the stolen words in the sequence they were stolen.

'अविनासी अनादि अनंता | सकल जगत तिहूं-लो नियंता | |
यस्य प्राप्नोती अष्ट संग्रह| स: भविष्यति . . .'

Nagendra said all the words but the last one.

'That's not all. The last word is missing in your verse. Say the last word,' Parashurama's voice boomed, his rage evident in his voice.

Nagendra could read the anxiety on their faces and smirked with a hint of victory shadowing his smug expression. 'You think Padmanabhaswamy holds the last word that we are here to hunt?'

Om and Ashwatthama exchanged a confused look, wondering if they were wrong, and furiously clutched their weapons.

'When Dhanvantari wrote the books of Mrit Sanjeevani, he divided the verse into nine pieces and scattered them. Eight of those nine words were hidden in the eight places that we destroyed and collected, but the ninth word was never hidden in any place. Instead, it was situated where none of you would expect. The bearer of the ninth word is him.' Saying that, Nagendra smugly extended his arm and pointed towards Om.

'It's you who holds the last word, and that is why your presence here was important. Opening this door without your physical presence is impossible. You didn't exactly solve a riddle and reach here; you have been *brought* here.' In the next instant, Nagendra ran towards the Kallara door with the pupil in his hand and started repeating the verse.

Parashurama, Ashwatthama and Om immediately charged at Nagendra but were hindered by the asuras that had come with Shukracharya and Nagendra, who were now attacking them. Before any of them could get to the door, Nagendra fixed the keyhole pupil into one of the snake's eye sockets carved on the door and chanted the complete verse, adding the last word. The last word of the verse was the first name given to Om by Dhanvantari, Mrityunjay.

'अविनासी अनादि अनंता | सकल जगत तिहूं-लो नियंता | |

यस्य प्राप्रोती अष्ट संग्रह| स: भविष्यति मृत्युंजय | |'

This time, Shukracharya pronounced the complete verse loud and clear.

'What meaning do these words carry once put together?' interrupted Mrs Batra.

Prithvi recited the shloka and then described its meaning.

'अविनासी अनादि अनंता | सकल जगत तिहूं-लो नियंता | |

यस्य प्राप्रोती अष्ट संग्रह| स: भविष्यति मृत्युंजय | |

Indestructible, eternal, infinite, the conqueror of death,

The one who attains these words from the creator of the three worlds shall be invincible and immortal.'

In the ferocious struggle to reach Nagendra and stop him, Parashurama and Ashwatthama started slaughtering the asuras and the bloodshed began. However, despite their incessant efforts, the moment the verse was completed, the carved snake on the door consumed the pupil and the door began to open. There was smoke behind the door, so thick that no human could last long enough to draw a breath. It looked like a black hole. The light that came out of the partially opened door was so dark that it only invited pain and death. The entire vicinity of the temple began to tremble, but everything came to a halt the moment everybody saw someone's fingers holding the edge of the door from the inside and pulling it inwards to open it completely and come out.

Before anyone could figure out whose hand it was, they noticed another set of fingers holding the other edge of the door. Om looked at both the immortals and witnessed an increasing fear in Ashwatthama's eyes and anguish painted on Parashurama's face. Shukracharya silently distanced himself from the door as if welcoming the guests and Nagendra bowed his head in front of the opened door.

The two pairs of hands which held the door revealed their faces. The first to walk out was a cursed Parashurama, drenched in rage with blood-red eyes, and then Ashwatthama followed with a body wounded by leprosy. Nagendra stood beside the lookalike cursed counterparts who possessed the same powers as the real Ashwatthama and Parashurama. Ashwatthama and Parashurama themselves stood in front of Ashwatthama and Parashurama and beside both the sides stood a Devdhwaja with the names of Nagendra and Om.

Chapter 15

The Inauspicious Reunion

'How could that be?' asked an astonished Mrs Batra.

'Everybody has some sort of negativity coursing through them; no one is entirely pure. Parashurama, Ashwatthama and Om were no different in that respect, but what brought all three of them to their purest form was the Prithak Vyaktitwa Yagya, conducted on them in different times. The yagya that separated them from their negative selves made them the purest souls, but no one had the answer for where the immortal negative parts of their personalities, with equal powers, had gone . . . till that moment when they showed up.

'The toughest of all wars is the war we fight within.' Often, it's this very battle that goes unheeded. It is said that a person can win the world if they have the will to control and beat themselves. It was time to put that saying to the test. Shukracharya and the remaining few asuras witnessed the historic episode where the three immortals stood against their own enantiomorphs.

Guru Shukracharya, who stood aside, looked at the three immortals and said, 'Every asura and their allies, defeated and killed by the Dashavatars and other demigods, were barred from entering the earth in any form of life. They were trapped behind this door to maintain earth's balance so that the gods would not be compelled to return to the mortal realm in human form for thousands of years. So they created this door, trapped the most powerful asuras behind it, and appointed the seven immortals to keep a watch and maintain the balance of good and evil in the world. As all the pure souls and extinct animals are kept in the extreme north called Gyanganj for the next cycle of yugas, all the asuras were kept in the extreme south, trapped in the Padmanabhaswamy temple behind this door. They were to only return at set times in the next chakras of yugas after the end of Kali yuga and repeat it all over again, and that is when all these asuras were supposed to come one by one. Now that you have failed your gods, and the gate has been opened, every moment an asura will enter this world, and with every asura, the balance will be disturbed and the influence of evil in every living being will strengthen to create chaos and disruption, so that Kali yuga can reach its end much before time.'

The immortals' worst nightmare, one that was too dreadful to even imagine, had now become a reality right in front of their eyes. They had come prepared to fight the demons, but were now perplexed by the new question: how were they going to clash with their own selves?

Parashurama, Ashwatthama and Om had to reach the door to close it before the asura force grew stronger. But obstructing their way stood their own negative selves.

Parashurama had no other option but to charge and take the first shot and so he instructed, 'Our priority is not to engage with our counter-selves but to dodge them and close the door. With every minute lost, they will grow more powerful, and we are already outnumbered.'

The battle between good and evil, which every human of Kali yuga secretly fights within themselves, began.

The historic temple, which was once home to a glorious legacy, was now being subjected to destruction and a bloodbath. The battle had now spilt outside the premises, surpassing the narrow pathways adjacent to Vault B and into the open ground.

Parashurama ordered Ashwatthama to summon every astra that could surpass everything coming their way and kill the asuras right at the door. Ashwatthama closed his eyes and manifested all his weapons. The quiver appeared gradually like a tattooed pattern on his back. One after another emerged the bunch of astras he had possessed, exemplifying Ashwatthama's omnipotence. Meanwhile, Parashurama summoned his invincible axe, and Ashwatthama chose the strongest bow which had victory in its name, the Vijaya Dhanush.

The Vijaya Dhanush's potential could be gauged from its trait that every time an arrow was released from this bow, its twang led to a long-lasting aftershock that almost resembled the rumbling of thunderclouds. Painted with the darkest blue, the bow could neither be lifted by the average human nor could it be broken by any kind of astra or weapon. The energy of an arrow released by the Vijaya Dhanush was amplified multiple times the moment it was shot. The warrior who gripped the Vijaya Dhanush was never defeated. However, all these qualities of the mighty bow were soon to be negated when Ashwatthama saw his clone summoning the same weapon, while the inimical Parashurama also held the same axe, exuding the same power, as the real one.

Thus began an unimaginable combat. Two opponents of similar prowess were fighting their cursed counterparts with the same intensity with which they were being attacked. Several bruises and cuts began covering their bodies. The battle was burgeoning.

The war of astras commenced with the Agneyastra, the fiery weapon summoned and released by Ashwatthama to burn the asuras. His evil twin responded with the Varunastra, the water weapon, neutralizing the burning fire with a heavy shower of water. In no time, the surroundings were clouded by the fumes of damaged flora and fauna and broken concrete, and the armies were drenched by the impact of the Varunastra.

Parashurama summoned the Vaishnavastra, a weapon that could only be countered by another Vaishnavastra but to his surprise, the opposing Parashurama also summoned the same and gave a befitting response. Though they were two different bodies, the vengeance in their eyes was equally fiery, as if they were not just trying to get rid of the other but also their past, which kept them attached.

Simultaneously, Nagendra blocked Om in every possible manner. He appeared ferocious and unstoppable. Although now Om was aware of who he was, this time, he was struggling with a different challenge. Somewhere, his past murder by Nagendra had left a permanent psychological mark on him.

Amid all this, a cluster of conceited and destructive asuras with hairy bodies, big skulls and one eye on the left temporal ridge of their forehead walked out of the door along with countless disfigured creatures of various shapes and sizes. The immortals were now completely outnumbered as the army of asuras grew larger while the door remained open and asuras continued coming in.

Yet, their unfathomable powers seemed insufficient when it came to countering their own selves and the other asuras. Shukracharya's dream would soon transform into reality. His overjoyed voice resounded above the sharp clash of the weapons.

'The wait is over! Victory is ours. The door is open, and now there's no looking back for us. We are finally free to walk the earth and rule it. Our patience and hard work have finally reaped what we had aspired for since the start of Satya yuga,' announced Shukracharya, loudly and confidently. That pumped each and every asura to fight for victory.

'But why did the immortals not attack Shukracharya and stop him from saying the verse?' asked a perplexed

Mrs Batra. Prithvi could read Mrs Batra's anxious body language so he answered, 'Because the immortals still kept their righteousness intact. Shukracharya was given the title of a guru and harming or attacking a guru is against the ancient rules of the war, the rules that the immortals still followed. Only a scholar titled Guru can challenge a Guru.'

Parashurama could anticipate that they might lose their last chance if they didn't strategize their moves. 'Ashwatthama, demarcate an area covering 5 km from where we stand,' he commanded. 'We must restrict them within this periphery. Looking at their armies, I am afraid that if they cross this line, they will spread uncontrollably across the globe like wildfire and it will be impossible for us to stop them.'

'Take charge of separate zones and stop the asuras and their troops. They will try to break the periphery but we must not let that happen,' Parashurama added before the immortals spread across north, east and west, ready to defy the demons coming from the door on their south.

Parashurama, Ashwatthama and Om, who were fighting relentlessly, could not believe that they were on the brink of defeat. There were more than a hundred asuras against each one of them. Suddenly, a rumble tore across the sky and caught everyone's attention. The Pushpak Vimana hovered right above them at a safe height, like a chopper still in the sky. Vrishkapi and Kripacharya jumped out of the flying vessel. Vrishkapi enlarged his bulky frame and grew immense, while Kripacharya's arrow spread carnage, killing asuras at lightning speed. Their presence was potent enough to re-energize the outnumbered immortals. Nagendra, on the other hand, was dumbfounded by how enormous Vrishkapi was.

'We've recovered the books of Mrit Sanjeevani,' Kripacharya informed Parashurama in between his attacks. 'Ved Vyasa is safe in Ross Island with the books and the infant.' The three of them felt stronger and more reassured upon receiving the news.

Reunited, the five warriors now stood shoulder to shoulder in the ultimate battle, but the problem was the opened door, which was still emitting asuras from the smoke.

Soon, the asura armies began approaching the warriors. Vrishkapi swung his mace rapidly, striking down every asura charging at him. Having Vrishkapi on their side, the balance of the war seemed to be tilting towards the immortals and the asuras seemed no match for the united powers of the immortals.

Ashwatthama and Parashurama were desperate to close the door at all costs. But their counterparts kept them on their toes with their attacks.

Looking at the multiplying army, Vrishkapi intensified his attacks with the mace as he killed more and more opponents, but Om interrupted him.

'Vrishkapi, don't waste your time killing these demons. Try to reach the door as quickly as possible because that's the only way we can overpower them.'

Vrishkapi's massive frame then sprung towards the door and his muscular arm swiftly swept away all the asuras on

his way. Just when Vrishkapi had almost closed it, he felt
a sudden jolt that threw him far away from the door. His
crash sent tremors through the ground as a thick cloud of
dust engulfed Vrishkapi. The disheartened asuras hooted at
Vrishkapi's fall, looking at the door that showed a massive
figure coming out of the fumes. As the dust began to
settle, Vrishkapi also saw a colossal silhouette behind the
door and he knew that this giant was the one that had
thrown him. Hiranyaksha and Hiranyakashipu, who had
been killed by the Varaha and Narsimha avatars of Lord
Vishnu, respectively, came out of the door, followed by
their unending armies. Hiranyaksha and Hiranyakashipu
had their eyes fixed on Vrishkapi. Now, it was the giant
Vrishkapi against two equally massive giants.

When the asuras tried to surround Kripacharya, he
summoned the astra Asi, a divine sword that was meant
to send evil-doers straight to their deathbeds. The astra
emerged at his back with a shiny ray, ready to be stained
with blood. Asi caused considerable destruction in the
opposing army but no matter how aggressively Kripacharya
fought, the enemies just continued to pour in thousands
through the door. Vrishkapi and Kripacharya could now
feel what the other warriors had felt before. Though many
asuras had been killed, the remaining demons and the
identical Parashurama and Ashwatthama were enough to
overpower the warriors. They were surrounded again and
hope was diminishing.

Everything seemed futile as the divine forces were
suppressed under the triumphant hoots of the opponents.

But before they could truly celebrate, an equally loud and peculiar growling and screeching filled the air. Their cheers were drowned as the demons and the immortals stood astounded. Everyone was dumbstruck, unaware of what was happening and who was coming.

The Pushpak Vimana once again hovered over the battleground, but this time it brought other passengers. There was Ballhaar, leading an army of animals along with the Great Auk, the Sabretooth, the Black Rhinoceros, the Mammoth and numerous extinct venomous snakes and attacking birds, who rushed towards the centre of the battleground. And the most mystical of the lot was Nibhisha, whose presence comforted Om and left everyone spellbound as she exuded her majestic frame, appearing ferocious and fatal.

Parashurama and Kripacharya exchanged a knowing look as they recollected what they had seen in Om's memories at the cliff. That captivating creature was none other than Nibhisha herself.

Ballhaar and his army rained down torrential chaos as they began annihilating the asura armies. The animals who came in herds headed in different directions within the periphery and identified different targets, which seemed like a fool-proof plan made by Ballhaar and his team. Some targeted Hiranyaksha's armies while others attacked Hiranyakashipu. The Sabretooth, as commanded by Ballhaar, led the army of the other dangerous carnivorous animals of Gyanganj. The animal force had now taken the scale of the combat higher, creating complete chaos in the war zone.

Ballhaar charged at Hiranyaksha and they fought like
predators in the wild. The Sabretooth, on a rampage, tore
down the petty asuras and in that trail, he managed to carve
several gashes on Nagendra, too, while he was struggling to
get rid of Nibhisha. Though the Great Auk was flightless,
its beak was the point of danger as it stabbed the armies and
clutched them before propelling them in various directions.
With every step, the Mammoth, with its huge tusks, tossed
the asuras and squashed many under its huge feet.

Everyone on the asura side was stunned by this sudden
shift in the field. Shukracharya commanded the cursed
Ashwatthama to summon the Twashtra-astra to create
delusions and deprive the targets of their senses. The cursed
Ashwatthama closed his eyes, summoned the Twashtra-
astra and fired it on the Gyanganj army. The army of
Gyanganj instantly turned against each other and also
charged at the immortals. However, Nibhisha was the only
one unfazed. The animals took on the immortals as Ballhaar
attacked Kripacharya. A moment of relief had turned into
a nightmare! Nibhisha reached out to Om and freed him
from the attacks. Om then summoned the Mohini Astra,
which shattered the illusion and revived everybody's senses.
Ballhaar and the army of Gyanganj were revitalized.

Nibhisha had won the psychological warfare for Om.
Though Nagendra had powers identical to Om, he was now
comparatively weaker because Nibhisha was on Om's side.
Nibhisha left no room for attacks and charged at Nagendra
as if he was her biggest enemy. This allowed Om to shift
his attention to others. Nibhisha continued to overpower

Nagendra and injure him incessantly, even though his bruises kept healing simultaneously. Nagendra tried to get a hold of her but was unable to do so as every part of her was heavy with vigour. This time, it was Nagendra's turn to pay the price for every time he had made Nibhisha suffer.

Hiranyakashipu grabbed Vrishkapi as he attempted to shut the door again. The combat intensified as Hiranyakashipu wreaked havoc by pushing Vrishkapi away yet again. Despite his huge size, Vrishkapi was failing against the demon. Ballhaar ordered the giant birds to keep Hiranyaksha engaged so that he could go to Vrishkapi's aid. Hiranyakashipu then closed his eyes to summon an astra but his concentration was broken by a sudden jolt. Ballhaar had placed himself against Hiranyakashipu and began to rain down blows. The fight now had Hiranyakashipu fighting Ballhaar on one side and Vrishkapi on the other. The pair assaulted an enraged Hiranyakashipu, who countered with all his power, attacking Ballhaar. The blow was so powerful that Ballhaar's shoulder blades cracked. Vrishkapi tried to protect his friend but Ballhaar signalled to him to go towards the door and shut it with all the strength he had while he kept the demons engaged. The asuras kept coming out of the door like a flood from a broken dam.

'Enough of you, Nibhisha!' shouted Nagendra as he landed a frustrated and powerful punch on her face. 'Have you forgotten how I punished you and made you suffer for your disloyalty?' continued Nagendra. The trauma of Nagendra's treatment shook Nibhisha's confidence and this time she felt inferior. Nibhisha let out a low grumble and looked towards Om, who was now at a distance, fighting alongside Kripacharya.

Ballhaar was deeply injured but the giant kept trying to rise again. His bleeding body was starting to give up slowly, making it more difficult for him to continue and fulfil his duties.

Ballhaar looked at Vrishkapi, seeking help, but found him battling and struggling to reach the door. He saw Kripacharya cornered by asuras while he kept charging at them with his weapons. Ballhaar darted towards them and broke the swarm, growling aggressively, stomping and pushing them. His roar echoed across the entire temple and even outside. Roaring with all his might once again, he smashed every asura that came his way or near Kripacharya. Kripacharya took that momentary relief and turned towards the other demons that were lethal and still scattered across the premises. By now, Ballhaar was losing his grip as he was exhausted and wounded. His body had wounds all over and he was bleeding extensively. Patches of blood absorbed by his white fur conveyed how injured he was. Ballhaar still had more zeal and valour left in him. He took a few breaths and stood strong again to attack. Just when he raised his arm again, an axe came flying from the back straight towards him and Ballhaar's head rolled on the ground.

'Ballhaaaarr!' Kripacharya's loud cry made heads turn. For a second, everything came to a standstill. It was the cursed Parashurama behind the backslash. The asuras blew the bugle of victory, an old tradition whenever a warrior

falls on the battleground. Kripacharya remembered the
time when the Pandavas' bugles suppressed Yudhishthira's
answer to Dronacharya in Kurukshetra. Om, Vrishkapi,
Parashurama, Ashwatthama and Nibhisha mourned silently.
Vrishkapi, who was running at the speed of air, came to an
abrupt halt and sobbed internally, recalling his promise to
Ballhaar. *I will protect you, my friend. Call out to me whenever
you need me.*

Nagendra took advantage of the moment and took
out his *kharga*, a sword that could slaughter magical beings
and cut through enchantments, killing its opponents
mercilessly. He swung it at Nibhisha, slicing her in various
places.

Hearing Nibhisha's painful screams, Om turned
midway and rushed towards Nagendra to save his friend.
Once again, the fight resumed between Nagendra, Om and
Nibhisha. This time, however, Om was mightier, more
resilient and determined, whereas having Om by her side
again, Nibhisha was more dynamic and stronger than before.
Together, they were confident about defeating Nagendra.
Nibhisha's serpent tail grabbed one of Nagendra's hands
and her elephant trunk grabbed Nagendra's leg, upsetting
his balance. Nagendra collapsed like a house of cards as
Nibhisha transformed into a complete elephant and stomped
on Nagendra's chest. She expected him to cry out in pain
but nothing of the sort happened because Nagendra's
healing abilities revived him quickly!

Om and Nibhisha were certain that they would disarm
Nagendra and cage him this time but before Om could

attack him, Hiranyakashipu pulled him from behind and threw him far from Nagendra and Nibhisha.

Om stood back on his feet and found Hiranyakashipu standing between Nagendra and himself. Hiranyakashipu needed an opponent to destroy after Ballhaar's death and he found Om. Om gestured to Nibhisha to hold Nagendra down for a little longer till he got rid of Hiranyakashipu. Nibhisha nodded and Om left.

Nagendra looked at Om and Nibhisha's exchange and intentionally kept himself under Nibhisha's leg till Om turned and left. In the blink of an eye, he then swung his kharga to slice through her trunk while he was still on the ground. Nibhisha could not bear the pain and went hysterical as she rolled on the ground, her deafening cries echoing throughout the field. Everybody saw Nibhisha wailing in pain and then instantly, her cries transformed into the roar of the lion. With a roar that reverberated for quite a distance, the lion approached Nagendra while Om went to Vrishkapi's aid.

Before Nagendra could think of a counterattack, the lion's jaw had clamped on Nagendra's waist. Nagendra struggled to loosen the lion's grip on him but his teeth gnawed at his sides, ripping his waist apart. Nagendra quickly grabbed a javelin from one of the asuras and stabbed the lion's waist. For a while, the lion's jaw remained tight on Nagendra, but the brutality became unbearable when Nagendra pierced the lion's eye with a hidden khukri tucked at his back. The pain was so intense that it made Nibhisha, the lion, finally let him go. Nagendra gripped the javelin tighter and began stabbing the lion's body as that part of Nibhisha slowly faded away. In no time, two out of eight parts of Nibhisha were lost to Nagendra, leaving her with only six that she could transform into.

Whining in agony, Nibhisha turned into a long serpent and crawled towards Nagendra. She expanded her size and coiled herself from beneath up to his chest, tightening her grip and restricting his body from moving. Nibhisha opened her snake mouth wide and devoured Nagendra's entire body. Nagendra was mystified by her rapid transformations. She thought she could hold Nagendra for longer this time, but little did she realize that the tip of the khukri had already penetrated a spot inside her snake body. Without moving much, Nagendra had managed to dig the knife so deep that it split the snake into two and he came out drenched in Nibhisha's blood. Anguished by Nagendra's attack, Nibhisha didn't mourn the loss of her third body and immediately turned into a tiger. This time, the tiger, quick in its moves, scratched and bit Nagendra at an unmatched speed. Finally, she pounced on his neck and clamped down on it so tightly that Nagendra struggled to break the shackles while panting for breath. As the tiger attacked from the front, he reached for the tiger's face and with his bare hands, clawed at it as violently as a tiger's paw. This left Nibhisha baffled and in a heartbeat, Nagendra ripped its jaw into two halves.

As Nibhisha collapsed, Nagendra rose mightier than before. Nibhisha was now on the verge of mutilation and irreparable loss, yet she chose to fight till her last breath, for her friend and for her past, to stop Nagendra. Unyielding and determined, Nibhisha stood her ground now as a gigantic female dog. Despite knowing that she was no match, she approached Nagendra, growled and barked so loudly that it would make any man tremble in fear, but Nagendra was unaffected and was far more vigilant than she had expected. Before she could move another muscle, Nagendra darted his khukri and his kharga to penetrate the layers beneath, leaving her mouth wide open. Maintaining his grip on the handle of the kharga, he carved an arch and ripped her face into two so fast that she didn't even get to scream or sob this time.

Defeated and drowning in excruciating pain, Nibhisha transformed into an ox and ran murderously towards Om like a beast, knocking and dashing aside every asura and ally on her way with her hump and horns. The asuras hammered blows and cuts on her and her quivering body fell right at Om's feet before dying.

'No! Nibhisha!' Om's voice had never been heard so loudly before.

For once, the warriors thought they had lost Nibhisha too. Nagendra's victorious smile knew no bounds as he saw Nibhisha lose her qualities one after another. This time, Nibhisha turned into a woman. There was a beautiful woman on the battlefield and every asura alive wished to have a piece of her skin to taste. 'If not Kali yuga, what is it then?' thought every noble soul present in the war zone. But Nibhisha in the human form was about to tell them all that Kali yuga still had hope left. She borrowed weapons from Om and Ashwatthama and charged like a goddess at the asuras. She prepared her own battlefield, shedding the load of all the other warriors. The asuras identified her as a perishable target and easy to kill as compared to the immortals she was fighting for. This is what cowards do. 'I shall not surrender. If defeated and killed on the field of battle, we shall surely earn eternal glory and salvation.' Nibhisha's fighting and words gave confidence to all the immortals and animals of Gyanganj.

On the other hand, another battle between Om and Nagendra broke out, overloaded with wrath and vengeance. The evil Parashurama summoned the Brahmastra to end his enemy once and for all. The Brahmastra could have killed, if not Om, then many other animals from Gyanganj around Om, including Vrishkapi. It was a confirmed victory for Shukracharya. But the moment the Brahmastra was shot at Om, Nibhisha appeared as his shield and consumed the astra to save all the lives around Om. She absorbed it all within herself, just as Uttaraa did when Ashwatthama used the Brahmashirsha at the end of the war of Kurukshetra, for which he was cursed by Krishna. Om felt helpless as he knew he could not save her. Soon, he witnessed even her female part perish, consuming the impact of the weapon and smiling for the sake of the safety of all her new friends.

Nibhisha's graceful woman's avatar gazed innocently at Om, flashing him a consoling smile as if to say, *It's okay, my friend.*

The disheartened Om couldn't help but stand and witness the death of yet another part of Nibhisha's magnificence. His mind recollected their first encounter, how she stood by him through thick and thin, and how she waited for him for yugas. She was the true definition of loyalty, love, compassion and commitment.

The Brahmastra disappeared after crushing Nibhisha's human form to death; she was gone. What was left was just a leg. A leg of a horse! Nibhisha finally emerged as a pristine white horse. This was her last visible body and all that remained inside was a pumping octopus heart.

The unending sea of the asura army continued gushing out from the Kallara door. Vrishkapi bashed Hiranyakashipu multiple times but Hiranyaksha had joined his brother again. The two mighty asuras threw hard punches at Vrishkapi, who didn't have time to even react to the blows.

Meanwhile, Ashwatthama was growing increasingly exhausted and weak against his evil self, who could sense his victory over the noble Ashwatthama and immediately called out to his comrades for aid. A cluster of asuras swarmed the holy Ashwatthama and held him firmly, not giving him any room to escape while he struggled. They prepared many layers of circles around Ashwatthama. Ashwatthama, a valiant warrior and proficient archer, now looked like nothing more than a trapped bird caged by the fright of his own self. The fear of being overpowered again by his negative aspects handicapped him and he could not even attempt to free himself.

The vicious Ashwatthama walked confidently like a free soul as he maintained his gaze on the holy one, stepping closer to his destiny, while the immortal Ashwatthama looked pale and crippled as he grunted in pain. His ear-piercing wails echoed through the field and all heads turned towards him. The asuras who held him captive cheered as the sinister Ashwatthama neared his other half. Every part of his body was twitching as he looked towards Kripacharya and Om, who desperately wanted to rush to his aid and began to free themselves from their own combatants, but just then, Shukracharya's booming voice rang through the air.

'O asuras! This is our moment! Do not let any of his allies reach him. Whatever it takes, keep them away from Ashwatthama.' It was a moment where the asuras had emerged almost victorious and a formation similar to the chakravyuh, which looked unbreakable, was formed. Ashwatthama was stuck alone.

The evil Ashwatthama now stood head-to-head with his vulnerable version and stared right into his eyes before embracing him. As he had done when they were pronounced apart right after the Prithak Vyaktitwa Yagya, he looked the righteous Ashwatthama deep in his eyes, breaking the last ounce of hope left in him. That was the look that had terrified Ashwatthama for the first, but not the last, time in his never-ending life. The cursed Ashwatthama hugged him tight and thus occurred the inauspicious reunion. A thick fog engulfed the two as the dreadful Ashwatthama absorbed the pious one. Ashwatthama's once-clear body was now blotched with leprosy. His cursed state had revived the immoral immortal's existence. After a cumbersome tussle within, Ashwatthama's evil consumed his righteousness as his victorious laughter synchronized with the asuras around them.

The bugle of yet another victory was blown by the asuras inside the chakravyuh. It shattered Kripacharya's morale as he relived losing his nephew all over again. The dynamic Ashwatthama had lost to the demonic Ashwatthama. This was the victory of the cursed upon the blessed.

'अश्वत्थामा हतो हत,' Kripacharya said in a low voice, looking at Parashurama, depressed to the core—which meant, we have lost Ashwatthama.

Chapter 16

The Living Nightmare

'Upon hearing the asuras' triumphant bugle on the reunion of the two Ashwatthamas, Parashurama was crestfallen. He experienced the pain that only Ashwatthama's father Dronacharya had earlier felt at the news of his son's death before his own in the battle of Kurukshetra. Ballhaar, Nibhisha and Ashwatthama gone was a demoralizing expense for the immortals, who were now outnumbered. The land was littered with dead bodies and the soil was drenched crimson with blood. The immortal allies were no longer enough to fight the multiplying strength of the demons, who were winning all the combats one after another, getting closer to grabbing the victory flag and reinstating their supremacy on earth. A war that had begun in Satya yuga was finally about to reach its closure in Kali yuga,' Prithvi said as Mrs Batra pieced together how the journey had begun and how it was advancing towards its end.

Parashurama was failing to defeat his cursed mirror image. The asuras had gained another powerful warrior after the pious Ashwatthama had been conquered. Ballhaar was dead and Nibhisha had been mutilated. Vrishkapi still couldn't shut the Kallara door and Om was struggling to bring Nagendra down. The developments of the war were hinting towards the immortals' defeat.

Kripacharya was burdened with guilt at being unable to save Ashwatthama and continued fighting the fire blades coming his way and pushing them aside. While Kripacharya was engaged in defending himself and attacking the uncountable asuras, with a depressing demeanour and a vibrating growl, Ashwatthama walked towards Kripacharya from the other end.

Ashwatthama looked enraged and ready to devour Kripachary?. His attack was so brutal that Kripacharya was thrown away like a cannonball. Seeing this as a golden opportunity to wreak havoc on the Gyanganj army, the cursed Parashurama summoned the Naagastra and within moments, thousands of snakes were crawling across the battleground, spewing venom and raising the fatalities among the animals of Gyanganj to a much higher level.

Parashurama stood afar, regaining his composure after the cursed Parashurama's Naagastra attack and contemplating how he could neutralize this army of snakes. The one astra that could instantly restrain these snakes was a Sauparnastra that would release thousands of snake-eating birds, hence it was a good counter to the Naagastra. Parashurama summoned the Sauparnastra, feeling positive that this weapon was a perfect choice. The Sauparnastra released a massive flock of thousands of snake-eating birds that filled the visible sky.

The war was growing more lethal. The demonic Ashwatthama was taking advantage of Kripacharya's softened heart for the Ashwatthama he had lost moments ago. Kripacharya was still struggling to balance his weak emotions and his strong weapons, and Ashwatthama was charging at him with no mercy. In the blink of an eye, Kripacharya's chest began bleeding profusely due to the long, deep cut Ashwatthama had slashed. Till that moment, Kripacharya was hopefully searching for the noble Ashwatthama behind the cursed face, but the malicious attack gave him the answer that all the good had been completely conquered. So Kripacharya summoned his bow again and charged at Ashwatthama. Kripacharya rained down all that he had, which got Ashwatthama on his knees. With the force Kripacharya attacked Ashwatthama, the latter's defeat seemed inevitable.

On the other side of the battleground, Parashurama battled Parashurama with more vigour. The ill-spirited Parashurama summoned the Shishira astra, a missile of the moon god that could freeze everything. The astra had spread its wings over the battleground the moment it was invoked. Even the animals of Gyanganj, who were immune to extreme freezing temperatures, were affected by the astra. It also froze Kripacharya, who was aggressively marching towards Ashwatthama to conquer him. Seeing the impact of the Shishira astra, the mighty Parashurama invoked the

Suryastra, which released blinding lights and the warmth of the sun, something that could cease the effect of the Shishira astra. Sensing his powers diminishing and finding himself weakening against the divine powers of Kripacharya, the evil Ashwatthama took advantage of the dazzling lights of the Suryastra and escaped the periphery, crawling with his leprosy-cursed body. Since he was too caught up in one-on-one combat with his counter-self, Parashurama could do nothing but simply watch Ashwatthama flee. By the time Kripacharya was free from the blinding light of Suryastra, Ashwatthama was gone.

On another front, Shukracharya was basking in his victory of keeping the door open and not letting any immortal reach it, while he awaited the arrival of the biggest army. Exhausted and aghast by the flashes of their defeat blinding them again, the immortals failed to understand where they were going wrong. The more they killed, the more came out from the open door. The army of asuras seemed endless.

The battle at Padmanabhaswamy temple was slowly turning into the ultimate victory for Nagendra and his team and appeared to be a complete disaster for the immortals as they were growing weaker in strength and fewer in number with every passing minute.

The demons were dominating the battlefield and had complete control over it. Nagendra battled Om with Nibhisha by his side. The evil Parashurama was one step ahead of Parashurama, who could sense the asuras overpowering them. Kripacharya hopelessly looked around for Ashwatthama but later moved to support Vrishkapi, as Vrishkapi was struggling alone against the mighty demons Hiranyakashipu and Hiranyaksha. Suddenly, everything came to a halt.

The asuras and the immortals paused as every being turned towards the Kallara door, where the void behind it was booming with marching sounds. In the moment of utter silence on the ground, everyone fighting for the immortals huddled close to figure out the reason behind the sudden change in the temperament of the raging battlefield. All eyes were fixed on the door, which was now vibrating, with the heart-thumping marching sounds growing louder as they inched closer towards the battleground.

And then the demons broke into a loud cheer which echoed till the seventh sky.

The biggest army of the asuras had finally arrived. The immortals, who were far from accessing the door all along, were now witnessing crowned heads being followed by thousands of other heads. Their arrival was welcomed by a sea of cheers echoing in the asura armies, as if they knew that victory was now inevitable.

'What else was left? Who else was coming? Weren't the challenges that the immortals had to face already enough?' Mrs Batra was intrigued.

'Neither the battle nor the purpose of opening the door had been fulfilled yet,' said Prithvi.

'The attacks were just an example of the animosity that these prisoners of time had planned against the immortals and the earth they had vowed to protect.'

First emerged an enormous figure bigger than
Hiranyaksha and Hiranyakashipu. With him walked a
supreme man in a crown who was commanding the army.
The asura with the crown stepped out of the Kallara door
and greeted Shukracharya with folded hands. A new troop
of asuras followed him as he went ahead to assume full
control of the chaotic unorganized war.

The man exuded a royal charisma and his valour was
evident in his stride. He was clad in a multi-layered outfit,
accessorized with precious jewels along with a necklace
made of nine of the rarest and most exquisite pearls beaded
together. His might glorified his face and had everyone
spellbound. While many asuras rejoiced in the presence
of his imposing personality, some remained starstruck and
others were simply intimidated as they were aware of the
extent of his cruelty.

The asura armies, which had been giving a tough time
to the immortals so far, bowed down with folded hands,
making way for the regal man. He scanned the place and
commanded his subordinate asuras, who then ordered
their troops to charge at the immortals and the animals of
Gyanganj once again with double the strength and brutality.
The way he had cemented triumph for the asuras, infused
within them a spirit of superiority and elevated their morale
by simply walking into the war was unfathomable. All the
asuras started screaming with motivation and zeal to defeat
the immortals right then and there.

Thus came the most difficult phase of the battle for the
immortals, as until then, the demons had been attacking

separately. But after receiving orders from their new superior, their strategies had changed and became more organized, more aggressive and more diligent towards destroying their opponents. The endangered species of Gyanganj were the most severely inflicted. The demons slaughtered them mercilessly, causing utter bloodshed. The immortals, who were still engaged with their mirror images, and other beasts could not come to their allies' aid as they were forced to remain mere spectators.

The behemoth walking beside the commander continued thrashing everything that came his way.

Kripacharya, however, managed to reach Parashurama and said, 'Ever since this crowned asura has entered, all the asuras have suddenly become organized. I'm afraid that if they continue the battle with the same vigour, our diminishing chances of containing them and sending them back behind the door will also disappear. There's only one way out.'

'What's your plan, Kripacharya?' asked Parashurama.

'If we kill their commander, we can stop the whole army at once as they would be consumed by their own mayhem,' said Kripacharya and then requested Parashurama, 'O mighty Parashurama, take charge and behead their new chief! His death at your hands is the only hope of survival for earth and victory for us, as it will break the asuras to the core. The rest of us must pave your way to approach him.'

Unaware of what they were progressing towards, the allies surrounded Parashurama and carved a path aggressively and speedily through the crowd of asuras.

Everyone protected Parashurama as he clenched his axe for the final blow in the centre. The next second, Parashurama jumped high in the air and swung his axe at their supreme commander and beheaded the demon in one go.

The battle came to an abrupt halt once again as a piercing silence engulfed the premise. The chief's crowned head rolled off his shoulders and on to the ground. Everybody looked at the headless body standing tall as Parashurama panted lightly. With his hand still gripping his axe, he walked towards Kripacharya as the immortals and allies waited for the headless body to collapse. They expected the asuras to break into mournful chaos, but to their dismay, the silence was shattered by cheers of celebration once again.

'A cheer and celebration on the beheading of their own chief!' thought Parashurama and turned around to find the reason for such rejoicing. What he saw explained the asuras' happy hooting. The headless body was regaining its head!

This shocked all the allies. A perplexed Parashurama didn't think before bringing his axe down again, but this time, the head didn't budge.

'Who was he?' asked an anxious Mrs Batra.

Prithvi looked at her and replied, 'It took a while for everyone to realize that the man ordering the biggest giant and other asura armies on the battlefield was none other than the scholar well-versed with Shastra Vidya and the Vedas. He was an extremely courageous warrior, the king of kings, the mightiest of all. He was the renowned demon king with many names. He was none other than Ravana himself!

'The giant who was larger than Vrishkapi and walked beside Ravana was his brother, Kumbhakarna. Behind him followed Ravana's son, Meghnaad, and their armies from Treta yuga.'

This was the only time when the devotee Nagendra, who had once named himself Nanshad, had the opportunity to see and stand in front of his deity, Dashanan. Nagendra was overjoyed by his presence and greeted him with folded hands, ready to make the day historic by defeating the immortals.

After a short pause among the powerful warriors, the petty asuras continued their fight with the extinct fauna. Ravana ordered his brother, son and their troops to destroy everything coming their way like an earthquake rattles the world and a flood washes everything away.

By then, the immortals had begun to comprehend that despite being backed up by the Gyanganj residents and the vigorous Vrishkapi, it was impossible to contain the asura armies inside the set boundaries of Padmanabhaswamy's premises. They knew now that no force could stop the asuras from infecting the world and overthrowing God's will to hold the reins of earth in the immortals' hands.

The asuras began destroying everything bit by bit. Om could anticipate what this was leading up to and was aware that he needed to buy some time for himself and other warriors. Therefore, he summoned the Sammohana-astra to muddle the demon troops. The Sammohana-astra changed the battle scenario as all the asuras dropped unconscious. The immortals and all the remaining army of Gyanganj got to take a breath.

The mighty Ravana chanted a verse and invoked the Prajnastra, which was believed to bring back consciousness to those who were unconscious on the battlefield. Pointing it towards the sky, he shot the arrow and soon, all the asuras were back, conscious and on their feet. The effect of the Sammohanastra slowly disappeared. Vrishkapi picked up his mace and charged at Kumbhakarna. Feeling the sudden blow, Kumbhakarna lost his balance temporarily and was taken aback. An infuriated Kumbhakarna summoned a mace to match Vrishkapi's and attacked him with it.

Ravana had had his eyes on Om ever since he had seen him summon the Sammohanastra. Walking a few steps ahead, Ravana summoned the trident, the chakra, the mace and a few javelins and spears with a bone-chilling chant. Looking at the ferocity of his assaults, one could see his long-suppressed anguish and hatred at being confined.

Kripacharya could see Ravana proceeding towards Om, knowing that Ravana would be charging at him. He was aware that with the kind of power Ravana possessed, his attacks would be fatal. Kripacharya had to fight on many sides to match Ravana's weapons but Ravana stood infallible and nothing seemed to faze him.

Thus, Kripacharya closed his eyes and summoned the Indrastra, the weapon that could shower arrows and was an apt choice to neutralize thousands of armies. But before he could release the astra, Meghnaad challenged him by shooting a bunch of arrows at Kripacharya. Meghnaad, having the power to turn invisible, planned for his next hunt.

While Kripacharya tended to his combat with Meghnaad, Om was cornered by Nagendra and Ravana walked towards him. Dodging his negative self, Parashurama came to the aid of Om. He summoned Maghavan and shot it at Ravana. Maghavan was one of Indra's weapons that could invoke hundreds and thousands of flaming weapon showers capable of baffling armies. That gave Om a few minutes to hold his ground again.

While Om fought Nagendra, the immortals were hammered with double blows as almost all of them were facing two powerful asuras at the same time. Vrishkapi battled ferociously against the two brothers Hiranyaksha and Hiranyakashipu, Kripacharya was thrashed minute after minute by the invisible Meghnaad while battling Kumbhakarna, Parashurama was facing his evil self and now stood against the king of kings.

The asura armies were still dominating the war and there was no new ray of hope, no other aid that would arrive for them. Exhausted and impaired, with fading hope, the immortals could only sense victory hovering over the asuras as not even their own spirits could reassure them any more. The armoured immortals had been decimated by the asuras' attacks and had no way left to overpower them. The earth felt overburdened by the looming defeat of the immortals and the victory of the asuras, which was approaching rapidly.

While Parashurama was preoccupied with releasing himself from the grip of Kumbhakarna and the swarm of asuras, the cursed Parashurama wanted to take complete control over Parashurama and hence rushed towards him. Parashurama was held in place with his limbs pinned down by the asuras as he helplessly saw the cursed Parashurama advancing towards him. It was now time for Parashurama to lose himself to his negative self. Everything was repeating itself as it happened with Ashwatthama. The cursed Parashurama, with his blood-red eyes full of rage, looked into the eyes of his mirror image before consuming him. All the other immortals and Vrishkapi could see Parashurama but they themselves were facing more than one challenge. Parashurama was trying hard to free himself of Kumbhakarna and other asuras but the numbers were too large for him to fight. No immortal could break the number of circles as another chakravyuh of asuras encircled Parashurama and they helplessly watched their commander, who was about to be lost in the process of absorption, just like Ashwatthama. The asuras were ready again with their next bugle of victory over Parashurama and the cheering started as the cursed Parashurama opened his arms to tightly hug Parashurama and consume him fully. But just before he could touch Parashurama, a pair of hands emerged from the cracks of the ground and grabbed the cursed one!

The cursed Parashurama fell to the ground and the cheering stopped. Before either side could understand what had happened, suddenly, the battlefield began cracking up in various places as thousands of hands sprouted from those gaps.

'Whose hands were those?' questioned Mrs Batra.

Prithvi's gaze scanned her body language and sensed her visibly agitated demeanour. 'It was King Bali, who had emerged from Sutala with his army of asuras.'

Along with King Bali entered Vibhishana, who had sailed through the Sri Lankan waters to reach Padmanabhaswamy with his army, which was as large as that of his elder brother Ravana.

All the asuras and their generals' attention was divided in two directions—one was towards Vibhishana and his army charging at the asuras on the ground amid the set parameters, and the other was towards King Bali and his army, which was appearing gradually from underground to ambush the asuras.

Nagendra looked at Shukracharya with a befuddled expression that said, 'How's King Bali walking on land?'

'It's the month of भाद्रपद (August), the month of Onam,' answered Shukracharya.

'What's the connection between this month and King Bali?' asked Mrs Batra.

'Lord Vishnu had allowed King Bali to walk on earth only during the time of Onam,' Prithvi explained.

Watching Vibhishana and King Bali joining the war had subjected the warriors to a myriad of emotions.

'O brother, I didn't anticipate your arrival,' Ravana said to Vibhishana in a taunting tone

'I didn't want to be here, but I was left with no choice,' Vibhishana replied.

'Vibhishana, let's talk and rid ourselves of these differences among us once and for all,' Shukracharya requested.

'Talk? I had approached you for a peace talk but your response in the submarine has taken away your final chance. I regret to inform you that the time to talk has run out.' Vibhishana's voice was heavy with anger.

'You are still against us? Why?' questioned Ravana.

'Because I still carry the burden of your deeds and I don't want to add any new weight to it,' Vibhishana retorted.

Disappointed by his brother's response, Ravana said, 'You were misguided then and you are misguided now. What we did was righteous. It's not a good sight to see my own brother stand against me, and so you must fall.' Ravana was livid. Unwilling to fuel the fire, Vibhishana simply turned to join the immortals along with King Bali. Ravana ordered all his generals to take on their enemies.

The invisible Meghnaad had jolted multiple attacks on Kripacharya. King Bali wrestled with his two elusive asura ancestors, Hiranyaksha and Hiranyakashipu, and engaged them in hand-to-hand combat. King Bali was still grasping the situation and seemed to struggle in front of his asura ancestors.

Inside the chakravyuh, the cursed Parashurama got back on his feet, burning in anger, and summoned Sharanga, the bow of Lord Vishnu himself, also called Vaishnav Dhanush.

To counter that, Parashurama summoned the Govardhana, another powerful bow of Vishnu.

Nagendra dominated Om with the best of his astras, like Vasavi Shakti, the second most powerful weapon of Indra. It could be used only once to destroy the opponent.

This was the same astra that Karna used on Ghatotkacha to kill him.

Ravana went for his brother Vibhishana on the battlefield. Kumbhakarna saw his brothers ready to confront each other and wanted to join in, but Vrishkapi held him by his bottom and thrashed him to the ground. This made Kumbhakarna furious and he started raining blows on the tired Vrishkapi.

Om screamed out loud to all the immortals, 'The only mortal fighting for us is Vrishkapi. He will die if not helped. His survival is important for the faith of mortals in us and for ours in them.' Everybody heard Om but nobody could come to the rescue except Vibhishana, who was fighting the most powerful asura present in the war zone—Ravana. He did not bother about himself, turned back towards Vrishkapi and closed his eyes to summon an astra. Looking at Vibhishana turning his back, Ravana taunted, 'This is the best you can do, Vibhishana. You turn your back towards your own. What you just did proves that the character of a man never changes.' Ravana showered arrows on Vibhishana's back in anger, but when Vibhishana opened his eyes, his bow had Praswapastra, the arrow that can cause the afflicted to fall asleep on the battlefield. The arrow was for his own brother Kumbhakarna, while Vibhishana's injuries continued to multiply, inflicted by his own brother Ravana. Vibhishana released the astra on Kumbhakarna and in a moment, he fell to the ground like a mountain. Without wasting any time, the panting Vrishkapi lifted him with all his might and threw him back inside the door. That was a setback to the asuras and to Ravana in particular. What added to the insult was the fact that Vibhishana was the turning point of the war again, just as he had been in the war with Lord Ram in Treta yuga.

Vibhishana continued to take devastating blows on his back as he decided to help Kripacharya next instead of himself. Vibhishana fought with his magical powers as his actions were fuelled by betrayal. Kripacharya had been beaten and attacked from all sides and was no match for Meghnaad only because he was invisible.

With all the pain and scars inflicted on him from his back by the mighty Ravana, Vibhishana closed his eyes again, this time to summon Sabdaveda astra, which prevents an opponent from turning invisible, and shot it at his nephew Meghnaad, which revealed his position. Meghnaad was now visible and in Kripacharya's sights. Before Meghnaad could have registered it, Vrishkapi came flying with his mace while Meghnaad had his eye fixed on Kripacharya. A single blow of Vrishkapi's mace blew him into the air, unconscious. In no time, Meghnaad was also sucked back inside the door. The injured Vibhishana was now taking arrows and other attacks by Ravana on his chest as he turned towards him and fell to his knees. It seemed that Ravana needed just one last shot to bring Vibhishana down.

'I shall now send you where I was for thousands of years,' said the mighty Ravana and shot an arrow, this time targeting his forehead. But just before the arrow could pierce its target, Kripacharya destroyed the arrow using one of his shots and Vrishkapi landed straight in front of Vibhishana, securing him. Kripacharya now joined Vrishkapi against Ravana. Vibhishana had selflessly helped Kripacharya and Vrishkapi. It was time for both of them to return the favour by defending him.

Vibhishana took a few minutes to stand strong again and took out all the arrows and weapons piercing his body. Vibhishana saw King Bali struggling; he requested Vrishkapi to help King Bali against his ancestors and said, 'We can stop Ravana for some time. Help King Bali against his predecessors.'

Vrishkapi immediately flew in and shoved Hiranyaksha with his powerful arms, making him lose his grip on King Bali. This allowed King Bali and his asuras to take complete control over Hiranyakashipu and his allies. It was now Hiranyaksha versus Vrishkapi and King Bali versus Hiranyakashipu.

Parashurama looked at the cursed Parashurama and saw his wild and wicked face ready to take the plunge. Parashurama didn't want to lose even a single moment as an opportunity to overpower him and the same was the plan of the cursed one. Therefore, to suppress their respective opponents, both invoked their astras in their powerful bows. One summoned the illusive Aindra astra and the other summoned the Lavastra. While Aindra astra fogged everyone's view, the Lavastra caused the ground to ooze out molten lava in several places. This burnt a few small animals of Gyanganj and the air reeked with the pungent smell of toxic chemicals, also burning up several asuras on the ground, thus leading to some collateral damage. As the

counter of Lavastra, Parashurama summoned the Varunastra,
a water weapon. The atmosphere was filled with gases that
were a result of the reaction between hot lava and water.

On the other side of this, Om decided to summon the
Narayanastra, an astra whose powers would increase the
more it was resisted. The moment the Narayanastra was
released, it unleashed a volley of missiles and the only way to
stop it was complete submission, something Nagendra was
refusing to do. The greater was the impact of Narayanastra
the more Nagendra tried to counter it.

As Om continued his battle, he tapped into his true
potential, sat on the only remaining part of Nibhisha, the
pristine white horse she had transformed into, and rode
it. A luminously blazing sword appeared out of nowhere
which lit almost the whole sky. Om grabbed it and felt his
new powers surging. He felt a boost of confidence in his
abilities. He had lost many who were dear to him since
Satya yuga and now, after witnessing Ashwatthama's loss,
his anguish had deepened, resulting in the cold-blooded
massacre of the despicable asuras. With his luminous
magical sword in hand, Om was unstoppable as he moved
swiftly past the enemies, making several of them drop
dead in a single motion, which significantly lessened the
burden of the asuras on the land. Om finally reached
Hiranyaksha, who was fighting Vrishkapi, and slayed
him. Hiranyaksha was also sucked back in like Meghnaad
and Kumbhakarna. The blades of Om's sword took down
many other asuras one after the other. Every immortal
was in awe of the surge in Om's powers. Nobody, not

even Om himself, knew what kind of sword he held and how he had summoned it.

Hiranyakashipu was now facing both Vrishkapi and King Bali. Before Hiranyakashipu could plan his attack, King Bali and Vrishkapi lifted him off the ground and brought him down with all the power they had. The impact crushed many of his bones, leaving Hiranyakashipu groaning in immense pain. Vrishkapi hammered his mace on Hiranyakashipu's chest and shattered his rib cage. Hiranyakashipu could barely move as he hunched over, screaming in agony. King Bali then picked up Hiranyakashipu and flung him back inside the door.

Om then headed towards Parashurama and found that the evil Parashurama was trying to devour him. He reached the cursed Parashurama and pulled him away. The fight now had Om and Parashurama on one side and the demonic Parashurama on the other.

The pair then bombarded the demonic Parashurama with a combination of their divine weapons, restricting him from attacking back. This time, the cursed Parashurama failed to fight back and was terribly wounded. They continued with their ceaseless assault, pushing him towards the frame of the Kallara door with all their might. While Parashurama continued pushing him back with his arrows, Om summoned the Anjalika-astra, which had the power to behead the target straight away. As anticipated, the astra found its way to the cursed Parashurama and executed him then and there. The cursed Parashurama was defeated and was sucked back into the door, to the same place where he had remained for aeons.

The war, which was once in favour of the asuras, was now tilted towards the triumph of the immortals.

Ravana saw the asuras falling back one after another while still facing Kripacharya, Vibhishana and now King Bali too. Nagendra, on the other side, also watched this brutality, still trying to counter the Narayanastra, which kept him fully occupied until Shukracharya guided him that the only way to get rid of the Narayanastra was to surrender completely. Nagendra did as guided and the celestial Narayanastra disappeared. Nagendra was free again to face the immortals, but it was too late.

Meghnaad's death, Kumbhakarna's defeat, King Bali's ancestors fallen and Ravana battling alone were adding to Nagendra's distress. He sprinted towards Om to even the score once and forever. He shot a series of arrows at Om but they either failed to touch him or simply brushed past him before landing flat. Nagendra was clueless about how that happened and what changed Om's power to the extent that his arrows could not even touch him. They were no longer equals in the combat because Nibhisha was quick with her lightning speed movements and her mind was in sync with Om. Om was now at the peak of internalizing the power of his existence and accepting the vigour he possessed. He was the one who had defeated Parashurama's cunning identity, helped King Bali overcome Hiranyaksha and Hiranyakashipu, fought the asuras of different calibres, and yet, remained undeterred and focused towards his goal. All this confidence was building his power, making him appear the mightiest warrior on the battleground.

In contrast, every astra Ravana tried to invoke was being felled by King Bali, Kripacharya and Vibhishana. Stuck in a loop of failures, Ravana was growing frustrated and thus summoned the Dharmapasha, the powerful noose of death.

However, the immortals were ready with a bigger plan.

Chapter 17

It's Not Over Yet!

Just when the enraged Ravana was about to release the Dharmapasha, Kripacharya thrashed him. King Bali and Vibhishana ambushed Ravana and hurled continuous punches at him. Ravana's agitation doubled and his wrath was equivalent to the blinding flare of the blazing sun. But just when he tried to counter, the fear of an irrevocable fate gripped Ravana when Parashurama joined King Bali, Vibhishana and Kripacharya. The king of demons and one of the mightiest asuras was drenched in his own blood, which was a result of countless attacks that he could not dodge. It was a dreadful, almost pitiful sight. Ravana was alone and perturbed. Watching his brother Vibhishana also supporting the immortals and all of them invoking a lethal combination of astras left Ravana horrified. While Ravana looked at them, the immortals conjured up the powers of Naagastra, Naagpasha and Dharmapasha—the very astras that Ravana had summoned. They merged the powers of the three divine weapons and released them. The sacred formula caged Ravana, compelling him to count the last few breaths left in him.

Sensing victory in the air, all four immortals united to unleash a cascade of arrows on Ravana until he was pushed back inside the door by the weight and impact of the million arrows piercing his body. The king of demons fell into the deep, dark ditch behind the Kallara door, shattering the confidence and destroying the dream of the remaining asura army.

From a distance, Om watched it all happen and saw how the asuras began to falter. Yet, there was something more to be done.

Once Ravana was gone, all the asura armies began to wilt and the door began closing slowly, which made the asuras scramble back to it because otherwise, they wouldn't be able to escape. As Vrishkapi was throwing the remaining asuras back into the door, Vault B shut itself. The keyhole-shaped pupil extracted from the infant popped out of the eye socket of the snake carved on the Kallara door, just the way it had once popped out of Aghasur's eye socket in Dwapara yuga after Lord Krishna had killed him. Once it touched the ground, it melted away and the earth's surface soaked it up, wiping away its existence forever.

Vrishkapi shrunk down to his normal size once he was done sweeping off all the asuras. Om descended from his horse, still gripping his mighty sword. All the immortals now turned to Nagendra, who had encapsulated the words from the books of Mrit Sanjeevani inside his own body.

As Om saw Nagendra surrounded by the immortals, Om remembered Parashurama's words on their way to Padmanabhaswamy temple: *We will bring him down to a state where he will curse himself for being an immortal and request us to grant him the boon of death.*

The memory of Ellora transforming back into a mere mountain was evident in Parashurama's angered eyes. Parashurama then gathered all his strength in his mighty axe and directed it towards Nagendra from a distance. This ultimate astra pierced Nagendra's body and he collapsed on the ground without any further retaliation as he was deeply bruised by the impact. Call it a boon or a curse, but he was an immortal too as the rest of them standing against him and so he started healing. Vrishkapi was burning in anger at Ashwatthama's loss and the events of Roopkund, which had almost killed him. He attacked Nagendra with his mace, crushing many of his bones. Kripacharya, too, joined in mourning for the loss of Ashwatthama and Ballhaar. Nagendra was still smiling shamelessly while his bones resurrected him back on his feet. Lost yet not defeated, Shukracharya proudly said, 'By now, you all know that he also is an immortal. It has become a war that you can never win as you can never kill him.' Everyone knew that Shukracharya was right. The immortals looked to Parashurama, hoping for the solution to Nagendra's end, but the answer came from the sky as the Pushpak Vimana landed on the ground and Ved Vyasa stepped out of it.

Ved Vyasa looked at Nagendra and Shukracharya and said, 'The solution to this problem has already been given by Nagendra himself.' Everybody, including Nagendra and Shukracharya, looked at each other, confused. Ved Vyasa reminded Nagendra of the statement he once made to Shukracharya about Parashurama: 'He can't be killed but he can be held captive to bar his participation any further.' I hope both of you remember that statement! What you forgot then was that I hear everything and I heard that too.' Everybody had the answer and the solution. Nagendra was now fuming in agony and Shukracharya seemed helpless. Addressing all the immortals, Ved Vyasa continued, 'The words of the verse he has stolen and the power they hold are deeply embedded inside his body. To forbid him from ruling the world with his evil mind, you need to cut his body into pieces.'

Ved Vyasa turned towards Om and said, 'Om, if you wish to bring an end to this madness which has haunted you for yugas, you need to summon all your strength in the sword you hold to bring closure to it all.'

Om stepped closer to Nagendra, who was now held captive by Parashurama and Kripacharya. All the immortals and Vrishkapi, along with the remaining animals of Gyanganj and Nibhisha in the form of a beautiful white horse, stood strong beside Om.

Ved Vyasa's words hit the right chord and Om concentrated on summoning all his powers, which were far more intense than any astra. The blade of his sword shone brilliantly as the fiery blaze reached the clouds, illuminating the entire area. His power, emotions and actions, everything aligned, Om brought down the sword to slice Nagendra into nine pieces.

Ved Vyasa turned towards Shukracharya, joined his hands and said, 'Gurus are to guide and we have no place in the war zone, Shukracharya. I request you to accept your defeat gracefully and leave.' Seeing Nagendra cut into pieces, Shukracharya looked at Om in fury, saying, 'It's not over yet!' and vanished.

However, despite being chopped up, Nagendra was still alive as the nine parts vibrated with life, struggling to reunite, but the immortals held them apart. Ved Vyasa came closer to Nagendra's head, looked into his desperate eyes, struggling to get his body back, and said, 'I heard you wanted a fresher's party as you became an immortal. Consider this your farewell from the clan of immortals.' Ved Vyasa then took a metal box from the Pushpak Vimana and locked his head inside it.

When King Bali was about to leave, Parashurama stopped him with a question. 'You were adamant about not supporting either side and wanted to remain neutral. What made you change your mind?'

'If my ancestors Hiranyakashipu and Hiranyaksha had not appeared, I would not have interfered,' answered King Bali.

'We are immortals and so is Nagendra. I entrust all immortals here with the responsibility of taking his body parts to different locations, far away from the reach of any human or demon,' said Parashurama.

'Vibhishana, Kripacharya, King Bali and I will take care of two pieces each and Om will be given one of Nagendra's body parts,' Parashurama said, distributing the parts among everyone.

Everyone took the parts with their blood-stained hands. Without any further delay, Kripacharya walked off the temple premises and disappeared from the battleground.

King Bali returned underground to Sutala with two pieces of Nagendra's body. Vibhishana held on to the parts he had in his custody, and returned to his ship with his remaining army of demons.

Before boarding the Pushpak with the books in their protection, Ved Vyasa took the infant in his hands and carefully handed him over to Om. Om cradled the baby in his arms with a confused expression, expecting an explanation.

Vrishkapi hugged Om goodbye and said, 'I will be grateful to you all my life. You saved my life more than once. You trusted and taught me so much. I will keep this mace safe forever and whenever I hold it, I will respectfully treat it as a token of respect, gratitude and the bond we have made.'

'Your little speech tells me that you have grown up in this war,' replied Om with an affectionate smile.

Parashurama requested Ved Vyasa to take care of Gyanganj until he returned.

Vrishkapi, along with Ved Vyasa and all the remaining animals of Gyanganj, boarded the Pushpak Vimana to go back to Kailash.

'I am proud of you. Take care of yourself, Om,' said Ved Vyasa with respect and affection before the Pushpak took off for Gyanganj.

As they left, Parashurama said to Om, who was still holding the infant in his arms, 'I need to find Ashwatthama and take him back to where he belongs. Your time in this mortal realm is not yet over. Take care of this child till he is an adult.' And with that, Parashurama started walking in opposite direction.

Om retaliated, 'Earlier, you wouldn't let me leave Gyanganj, and now you are not allowing me in. Why can't I go back with all of them?'

Parashurama turned and spoke to Om for the last time. 'तुम बीते हुए कल की भी आवश्यकता थे और आने वाले कल की भी आवश्यकता हो। तुम कल्कि हो। तुम दशावतार को संपन्न करने आए हो, अंतिम अवतार बन कर।

(You were the need of yesterday and you will be the need of tomorrow. You are Kalki, the last incarnation of Lord Vishnu that completes the Dashavatar).'

Om stood perplexed and his expressions demanded an elaboration of Parashurama's statement.

Parashurama explained, 'A prophecy in Shrimad Bhagwat Mahapurana states

'शम्भल ग्राम मुख्यस्य ब्राह्मणस्य महात्मनः।
भवने विष्णुयशसः कल्किः प्रादुर्भविष्यति॥

(At the village of Shambhala, principally of great soul Brahmins.

In future at the home of Vishnu, worthy Kalki will be born).'

Prithvi explained to Mrs Batra, 'His name, Kalki, is derived from *kal*, which means "time" in Sanskrit, as he is timeless. It also stands for "yesterday" and for "tomorrow" in Hindi.'

Parashurama continued explaining to Om: 'Your advent has been foretold for thousands of years in several holy scriptures. These books also share details about the Kalki avatar, that was written by Sage Shuka 5000 years ago on hundreds of palm leaves. As mentioned in the ancient Hindu scriptures of Vishnu Purana and Kalki Purana, the prophecy highlighted that Kalki would be born as a child to Vishnuyasha, a Brahmin in the city of Shambhala. Shambhala is also derived from Sanskrit and means a place where peace dwells. The place's existence can be dated back to thousands of years.

'Kalki Purana has mentioned in a few instances that the Kalki Mahavatar would be seen on the outskirts of River Tamirabarani. The Bhagavatam mentioned that Kalki would be born in Dravida Desham, where the river Tamirabarani would flow. As Devdhwaja, that was exactly your birthplace—at the house of a Brahmin named Vishnuyasha, which happens to be the name of Kalki's father in the prophecies.

'The purpose of Kalki's descent to earth is to eradicate evil, purify people's consciousness and restore balance in the world, which was overburdened by all negative elements in Kali yuga. It would also set the course for the beginning of Satya yuga once again in the infinite cycle of existence, as per Vaishnava cosmology.

'Any scripture you read will tell you that Kalki is the avatar of rejuvenation. The white horse that Kalki rides would be Devdutta holding his sword Nadaka in one hand. This white horse will actually be the manifestation of Garuda, the divine vehicle of Lord Vishnu himself. Devdhwaja! The white horse you see in front of you is the last visible and external body part of Nibhisha. That is Devdutta, the one mentioned in these texts.

'You were always in search of your true identity. This is who you are and today, not only do you receive your true identity, but Nibhisha, too, receives hers. You were surprised when this divine sword appeared in your hands exactly when you needed something that lethal, just as the mace appeared in your hands when you had to rescue me. Everyone present here today has witnessed you riding Devdutta, not Nibhisha. They have seen you holding the Nandaka, which is not just a fiery sword—it is the most powerful sword of Vishnu. The mace that appeared in your hands and which you gifted to Vrishkapi is the divine mace of Vishnu called Kaumodaki Gada, which would destroy whole armies, which is why Vrishkapi could fight asuras like Kumbhakarna and Hiranyaksha—because the mace gave him the power. Lord Krishna slew the demon Dantavakra with it.'

'How do you realize it and I don't?' asked Om and Parashurama replied, 'Every man takes two births in his life. The first is when he is born physically and the second occurs when he realizes the purpose of his existence. You were born on the outskirts of Tamirabarani and your destiny brings you back to Tamil Nadu for the war that helps you learn who you are. Today, on this land, you are born again as the prophecy claimed. The prophecy in Kalki Purana had also given the astronomical positions of stars and planets at the time of your birth. Today, the stars and planets are in the exact same position as they were drawn in the text and as they were on the date of your birth in the ancient world, when the pole star was right on top of Mount Kailash,' Parashurama said, pointing towards the pole star to their north.

'According to the Kalki Purana, Bhagavatam and Vishnu Purana, the Kalki Mahavatar is a Kshatriya (royal race) as well as a Brahmin (rishi), who would renounce the world and lead the life of a high priest. That is why you were inclined towards knowledge and the sword simultaneously, as in Satya yuga, you were born in a matriarchal society where your father was a Brahmin and your mother led the civilization.

'It's time for you to go and perform your duties and for me to perform mine. I have to find Ashwatthama.'

This revelation triggered tumultuous waves of emotions in Om. His faith in Parashurama's words was his only hope. He relived his days in Satya yuga, mulling over how the pages of his life unfolded. He was too overwhelmed to embrace the new revelations, so he asked Parashurama, 'Where do I go now? What do I do?'

'For the next twenty years, take care of this infant that you hold in your hands. Ved Vyasa has cremated his parents and so he wishes this child to be safe and brought up well, as it was Parimal's last wish. This child is a mortal and so cannot be brought to Gyanganj. You are his guardian from now on and he is your responsibility while you fulfil your duties as Kalki, to take care of humanity. From now on, this child will be called Prithvi,' replied Parashurama.

'So, that means . . .' Mrs Batra said in astonishment, but Prithvi answered her before she could finish her question.

'Yes. I am the infant named Prithvi by Parashurama. My name means earth in Hindi and I was given this name so that Om could continue what Lord Vishnu does as the protector of the earth, till the emergence of Kalki for the world.'

Mrs Batra's eyes went wide with the shocking realization that the one narrating this series of incidents was the same infant who survived among asuras, the same baby who was born in the puddle of his own parents' blood.

Reminiscing about his extended past left Prithvi in tears, which he managed to hold back while Mrs Batra looked at him sympathetically. A heavy silence settled between Prithvi and Mrs Batra.

'Can I have a glass of water?' Prithvi's humble request interrupted the silence.

'Yes, sure. Give me a moment,' Mrs Batra replied, slowly walking towards the kitchen, processing everything she had heard from Prithvi so far.

She came back with a transparent glass bottle filled with water and an empty glass. She poured some water into the glass and handed it to Prithvi. He took a few sips before Mrs Batra asked, 'So, you're the son of LSD and Parimal, named by Parashurama and raised by the tenth avatar, Kalki himself?'

'Yes,' Prithvi replied, gulping the water down.

'And you are in search of your foster father Kalki? Where is he now?'

Parashurama also said to Om, 'The Kalki Purana prophecy states that Kalki will marry Padma, the daughter of Vrihadrath and Kaumudi of Sinhala Dwipa, which is now known as Sri Lanka. Padma is believed to be the reincarnation of Goddess Lakshmi. You shall go to Sinhala Dwipa, marry your beloved Padma and begin your married life. Stay in Sinhala Dwipa for some time and then return to India. The Kalki Purana also talks about all the deeds that you as the Kalki Mahavatar will accomplish. It mentions how Kalki will confront the demon Kali directly and annihilate him when the time comes.'

'The demon Kali!' Mrs Batra repeated to confirm whether she was listening correctly.

'Yes! The demon Kali. He is the manifestation of Adharma, who, at the beginning of Kali yuga, was confined to only five places where he could reside—where there was gambling, alcoholism, prostitution, animal slaughter and gold. The demon Kali is the reason behind the last incarnation of Lord Vishnu. The Kalki avatar is meant to end Kali yuga.'

Just before he left, Parashurama said, 'Dear Om! Your present name carries the name of Lord Shiva and your incarnation is rooted in Lord Vishnu. Everything that you do in the times to come is destined to happen and has already been written in the Kalki Purana. Consider the Kalki Purana as the manual of your future deeds if you ever want guidance. The time for you to emerge as Kalki has not yet arrived and until it does, you must live undetected as Om and remain hidden as you were before Nagendra found you and brought you to Ross Island. This episode of your eternal life started on this island and now will end on the island of Sri Lanka. Islands are good at keeping secrets. It's time for me to leave in search of Ashwatthama.'

'I have already lost my friend Ashwatthama. Will I ever see you again?' Om's voice was heavy with sorrow. As he saw Parashurama leaving, the anxiety of losing his people gripped him.

Parashurama turned towards Om, hugged him with a smile and said, 'Yes, dear Om! We are destined to meet again. The Vishnu Purana states that all the seven immortals are alive just to help Vishnu's tenth and final Avatar, Kalki, destroy sinners, restore dharma or righteousness to end Kali yuga and open the portal for the new epoch of Satya yuga in this cycle of existence. Till then, you must wait for us to return and we must wait for Kalki to emerge.'

Mrs Batra interrupted again. 'I understand that you know this side of the story because Om told it to you while he raised you for all these years. But the question that arises now is, how do you know the other side of the story? I mean, how could you describe each and every event of their lives in such detail when you've never even met Nagendra, LSD and Parimal?'

Prithvi paused before answering, 'Mrs Batra! Do you remember our first conversation? I told you that I remember everything as clearly as if it happened in front of my eyes. You're right to say that I heard Om's side of the story because he's the one who narrated it to me. But when it comes to the other side, I've been a witness to every event in Nagendra's life as it happened, since he came to Dhanvantari's hut with the dead body of Devdhwaja, including my deaths as Devdrath and LSD and my birth as Prithvi.'

Hearing that, all the colour drained from Mrs Batra's face. The horrifying revelation that Prithvi was none other than Devdrath himself and was known as LSD in his last body shook Mrs Batra to her core. She took a few steps backwards to create a safe distance from Prithvi after she realized she was standing right in front of her husband's killer, but a carefree Prithvi continued.

'The infant continued crying after my death. I had no choice but to enter the body of my own son as there was no other newborn being that could host my soul. I was left with no other choice but to have my child for myself. Even after acquiring the child's body, the infant continued to wail because now it was a wife crying for her husband who was dying right in front of her eyes. Neither could I help him nor could I tell him that I was still alive and with him.

'Poor Parimal. He wished salvation for me but instead got his salvation, which I desired for myself more than anything else. Yet again, I was left bound in Nagendra's words.'

Swallowing nervously, Mrs Batra braced herself and dared to ask in a quivering voice, 'Why are you here and why did you tell me all this?'

Prithvi picked up the water bottle and poured it empty on the floor. He then got up from his seat and walked up to Mrs Batra, cornering her, and said, 'Because, Mrs Batra, just like Om, everyone deserves to know the purpose of their lives and why they died . . . even you.' Before Mrs Batra could have deciphered the puzzle, in the blink of an eye, Prithvi slit Mrs Batra's throat and placed the mouth of the transparent empty bottle at the cut on her neck to collect the blood that flowed like water from a tap. Mrs Batra was unable to scream in pain as she choked on her own blood and her senses began to dim before she fell to her knees, gasping for breath.

As the bottle collected Om's blood, which was running through her veins, Prithvi continued talking to her coldly as if nothing had happened. 'In order to gather Nagendra's body parts to bring him back, I need to keep living. After all, he is still alive, and I am still deprived of my salvation.' Prithvi looked into Mrs Batra's eyes for the last time and she saw the sheer monstrosity in his eyes as a sense of achievement accompanied by a cunning celebration.

Devdrath's soul in Prithvi's body now possessed Om's blood from Mrs Batra's body in a transparent bottle. What he needed next was the process of Mrit Sanjeevani, which the book had taught Shukracharya. The moment Mrs Batra breathed her last, a familiar voice echoed in the room.

'We have a long way to go and much to seek, achieve, collect and restore. Let's go!' The familiar voice was of Shukracharya guiding Prithvi the way he had once mentored Nagendra.

THE END

. . . But as Shukracharya said to Om before disappearing: 'It's not over yet!'

Symbols

 What appears to be the tiniest can be the mightiest piece. The eyeball with the key hole pupil in the palms of the infant without which opening the door was impossible.

Satya Yuga	Dwapara Yuga
Kali Yuga	Treta Yuga

The unending cosmic loop of yugas starting with **Satya** Yuga, moving through Treta and Dwapara Yuga and ending with Kali Yuga only to start back again from Satya Yuga.

 A mysterious search across Incredible India!

 It is time for all the 7 immortals to unite.

Lost in the Timeless journey through all Yuga,
Who is Om?

Can time run out for the immortals too?
Will they win the race against time?

Acknowledgements

Rajat! You have always been very patient with me.

The grace with which you accept everybody and the strength with which you stand by your people. The calmness with which you listen to problems and the wisdom with which you handle them. The innocence you have miraculously managed to save in your soul and the warmth in your hug. The smile with which you forgive the ones who hurt you and the promise that you will never hurt anybody.

I envy you for all the above and I'm blessed to call you my brother, thanks to our fathers who made us so. I am sorry for my mistakes, and I thank you with all my heart for being there silently but always. I love you, brother!

Vidhyut Bhai and Meenal ji, you are in my heart and soul. The most innocent and selfless couple who are the pillars of my bestselling success and the fuel in my journey. There is only gratitude towards you.

Sushma Tripathy! My childhood friend. It's been a beautiful journey from being friends to working professionals. Thank you for being with me during my first few steps of life and now to the final parts of my trilogy.

I remember sitting next to you on the flight and giving you a copy of *The Hidden Hindu* and not telling you who I was. I hadn't expected that you would get so engrossed in it and finish it in two hours! Thank you Neha Purohit for being one of the best reviewer and helping us present the book better. May this journey continue for the lifetime.

Ranveer Allahbadia! Your humble astra has pierced my heart for eternity. Thank you so much for being a part of my journey selflessly. Your soul is visible through the innocence in your eyes. May you always keep smiling and reach the hearts and heights you wish to. Love and blessings. Thanks to the amazing Beerbiceps team!

Jignesh bhai and Siraj bhai! I am short of words to thank you both and team Digiworx for showing immense faith in me. I will do my best to surpass your expectations. Let's move ahead at lightning speed, together!

Bold and loving Sowjanya, I wish you all the success. Keep smiling.

A full of life, beautiful and kind soul, Shweta Rohira you are just amazing! May you keep shining and smiling. May you get all you that you dream for.

To the hardworking Penguin editing and marketing team, your efforts are very much appreciated. Chandna Arora, thanks to you personally for the final inputs.